G. H. Nall

The Fables of Phaedrus

G. H. Nall

The Fables of Phaedrus

ISBN/EAN: 9783744790055

Printed in Europe, USA, Canada, Australia, Japan

Cover: Foto ©Andreas Hilbeck / pixelio.de

More available books at **www.hansebooks.com**

THE FABLES OF PHAEDRUS

THE
FABLES OF PHAEDRUS

Edited for the Use of Schools

WITH INTRODUCTION, NOTES, AND VOCABULARY

BY THE
REV. G. H. NALL, M.A.
ASSISTANT MASTER AT WESTMINSTER SCHOOL

London
MACMILLAN AND CO.
AND NEW YORK
1895

PREFACE.

THE Text of this Edition is Alexander Riese's, expurgated for school use. The Perottine Appendix has been omitted at the desire of the Publishers, as the book is long without it. The Notes are short, but I hope sufficient; difficult phrases not explained in the Notes will be found in the Vocabulary. The Introduction is meant for older boys, and is intended rather to suggest some of the questions which arise in connection with a study of Phaedrus, than to exhaustively discuss them. References are given for those who wish to pursue any line of enquiry further.

G. H. NALL.

18 DEAN'S YARD, WESTMINSTER.
        January, 1895.

CONTENTS.

INTRODUCTION.*

NOTHING is known about the life of Phaedrus except what can be gathered from the scanty notices in his fables.

Phaedrus.

He was born in the mountainous district of Pieria, in the south of Macedonia,† whether of free or servile parentage we cannot tell, in the latter part of the 1st century B.C. At an early age, for some reason unknown to us, he was removed to a Latin speaking country, probably Italy, for he tells us that as a boy he read the line of Ennius "*Palam muttire plebeio piaculum est.*" ‡

The title of the early manuscripts describes him as "*Augusti libertus,*" the freedman of Augustus. He must, therefore, have been a slave of the Emperor, who granted him his freedom probably as a reward for his literary skill and services.

The first two books of the fables seem to have been published during the reign of Tiberius. These brought Phaedrus under the displeasure of the imperial favourite Sejanus. The precise reason is uncertain, but the words of Phaedrus, *suspitione si quis errabit sua et rapiet ad se, quod erit commune omnium,* § certainly imply that some of his fables were

---

* For an exhaustive discussion of all questions connected with Phaedrus see Hervieux, *Les Fabulistes Latins.*
† Pierio iugo. III. Epil. 17.   ‡ III. Epil. 34.   § III. Prol. 45.

vii

supposed to reflect on individuals. In the collection as we have it at present it is easy to find passages which might readily bear such an interpretation, *e.g.*, in Book I., Fable ii., the frogs asking for a king; Fable iii., the conceited daw; Fable vi., the marriage of the sun; Fable xxiv., the frog which burst; all these might be supposed to reflect on Sejanus or his clique, and Fable v. of Book II. might have aroused the imperial displeasure, as an impertinent anecdote about the Emperor's sacred person in days before court gossip had become the common property of every scribbling journalist. But, whatever the reason, Phaedrus was certainly prosecuted, probably for *maiestas* or high treason. He was condemned, but concerning his punishment we have no information.

To relieve his distress Phaedrus wrote the Third Book of the Fables, dedicated to Eutychus, who has been identified with the charioteer and freedman of Caligula, the third Roman Emperor. Book IV. is dedicated to Particulo, about whom nothing is known. He is described as so fond of Phaedrus' fables that he copied them 'on to his own pages,' whatever that may imply. (See Note on IV. Prol. 18.) Phaedrus in this prologue says that he had intended to end his work with Book III. to avoid exhausting his material and leaving nothing for his successors, but that he had deliberately changed his mind (IV. Prol. 1 fol.). The book contains frequent reference to detractors. Book V. is dedicated to Philetus, who may possibly be a Tib. Claudius Philetus, a freedman of the Emperor Claudius. In the last fable of this book, that of the Aged Hound, Phaedrus may perhaps allude to his old age.

The date of Phaedrus' death is not known, nor any further facts about his life. Few writers have dragged their personality more frequently into their writings, yet we can form but little idea of his character. He claims to be utterly indifferent to money; but this is a claim not unfrequently made by poor men. He is supremely conscious of his greatness as a writer, yet he constantly indulges in childish complaints against detractors. We may safely say that he was not a great man; how little he was we can scarcely determine.

There is no reason to doubt that Phaedrus won a certain amount of fame in the world of literature before his death. The next generation seems to have forgotten him. Seneca speaks of Aesopian stories as a work unattempted by Roman genius;* Quintilian does not mention him; Priscian in a passage dealing expressly with Aesop and the literature of fables, mentions Hesiod, Archilochus, Plautus, and Horace, as using them, but says nothing about Phaedrus. Martial, however, refers to him in a disparaging line, *an aemulatur improbi iocos Phaedri* (*Epigr.* iii., 20, 5), and imitates him in several phrases; and Avianus, in a passage given below, refers to him and Babrius.

The fables, as they have come down to us, are ninety-three in number, written in iambic verse and divided **His Writings.** into five books. Book I. contains thirty-one, Book II., eight, Book III., nineteen, Book IV., twenty-five, and Book V., ten. Besides these there is an Appendix of thirty-one 'Perottine' Fables of doubtful authorship, not printed in this edition (see below, p. xi).

Of the original fables many are certainly lost, for Avianus in speaking of them says that Phaedrus *expanded* a part of his fables into five books, *Phaedrus partem aliquam quinque in libros resolvit.* The term '*expanded*' is scarcely suitable to our collection. Phaedrus, further, in his Prologue to Book

* Aesopios logos intemptatum Romanis ingeniis opus. *Consol. ad Polyb.* xxvii.

I. (line 6) refers to fables in which trees speak, of which there is no trace in our fables. Books II. and V. are very short, even compared with the other books. Book IV. bears signs of mutilation, not only in single fables, *e.g.* xiii. and xiv., but throughout, for the insertion of poems headed 'Poeta' 'Phaedrus,' can only be satisfactorily explained by supposing that these mark divisions in the book, and were originally separated by some ten or twenty fables. Further, at the beginning of the Prologue to Book IV. Phaedrus says that he had intended to finish his work with the Third Book *ut aliis esset materiae satis*, 'that there might be enough material for other writers,' an expression which would be ridiculous if the fifty-eight fables of these three books, many of which are not fables proper at all but only stories or anecdotes, represented all that he had published.

Hence it is certain that a large portion of Phaedrus' Fables has been lost, and as our earliest MS., the *Pithoeanus*, dates from the 9th or early 10th century, the loss must have been between then and the 4th century in which Avianus lived.

The story of the MSS. is most interesting, but cannot be **The MSS.** given here.* Only five MSS. have been discovered; two, the *Codex Pithoeanus* and *Codex Remensis*, dating from the 9th or early 10th century, the latter of which is now lost; the *Codex Danielis* containing only eight fables, dating from the 11th century; and the *Codex Perottinus* and its duplicate the *Codex Vaticanus* dating from the 15th and early 16th century.

The *Codex Perottinus* is called after Niccolo Perotti (*b.* 1430, *d.* 1480) who became Archbishop of Siponto (afterwards Man-

---

*An admirable summary will be found in Prof. Robinson Ellis' Inaugural Lecture, *The Fables of Phaedrus.* Clar. Press.

fredonia) in 1458. In early life, he says, he employed his leisure in copying out, evidently from some MSS. now lost, with no regular order or sequence, fables **The "Perottine" Fables.** of Aesop, Avianus, and Phaedrus. With these fables he interspersed epigrams of his own composition and letters to his friends, and dedicated the whole work to his nephew, Pyrrho Perotti, in these terms : *" Nicolai Perotti epitome fabellarum Aesopi Ariani et Phedri ad Pyrrhum Perottum fratris filium adolescentem suavissimum incipit foeliciter."* The MS. remained unknown till 1727 ; the new fables in it, those of ' Aesop,' were first published in 1808 ; about twenty years later a second MS. of the same work was discovered in the Vatican, the *Codex Vaticanus*, and published in 1831.

The thirty-two fables of Phaedrus and thirty-six of Avianus which this MS. contains correspond with fables in our collection of those writers.   The great controversy has arisen over the so-called Fables of ' Aesop.'

' Aesop ' we know to be but a name (see p. xii), and hence many critics have maintained that these 'Aesopian' Fables of Perotti are the genuine work of Phaedrus. They are usually printed now as an Appendix to a complete edition of the fables.

The arguments may be summarized as follows.   Those who maintain that the Perottine Fables are by Phaedrus say that internal evidence, viz., the style and subject-matter, prove them to be by the same writer as the five genuine books of fables ; that our Phaedrus is undoubtedly abridged and mutilated ; and that therefore there is every reason to believe that these fables are a portion of those contained in the original and complete Phaedrus. To which their opponents reply that the Perottine Fables, though similar in style and language and metre, with very few exceptions fall below the

average goodness of Phaedrus, that the similarity of style
does not prove they are from the same hand, because an
imitator consciously endeavours to reproduce the characteristics of his model; and that there is no proof that a
completer Phaedrus than we possess existed in the days of
Perotti; Perotti by speaking of Fables of Aesop, they further-
more observe, clearly showed that he had included in his MS.
a series of fables which he believed not to be by Phaedrus or
Avianus, a series probably taken from some larger collection
of Latin iambic fables, the authorship of which was unknown,
and which went under the general name of the Fables of
Aesop.

Aesop in fact is the name of a particular class of fable
Aesop. rather than of the work of any individual
man. There is no sufficient reason however for
doubting that a man named Aesop did once live. Herodotus
first mentions him, describing him as a slave and the con-
temporary of Sappho (about 600 to 570 B.C.), but since all the
stories we have of him come from a late source, and quite an
untrustworthy one, it is clear that the Greeks of that time
knew very little about him. At what period the practice of
ascribing beast fables to Aesop became common we cannot tell.
None of the earlier writers who employ fables use his name.
But when we come to Aristophanes and later writers it is the
exception if Aesop is not mentioned in introducing a fable.
"We see in Aristophanes the mouthpiece of a tendency to
exalt Aesop into the high priest of fable, which appears
to have been gradually gathering strength and to have
reached a climax in the literary circles of Athens about the
meeting-point of the 5th and 4th centuries before the
Christian Era. In my judgment it cannot be explained
except by regarding Aesop as a real personage, imbued with
the spirit of that primeval lore of fables which all peoples

seem to have once possessed in a greater or less degree, and which the Greeks, if their place in intellectual history means anything at all, must have preserved with more than common precision. Moreover, this Aesop was able to extract from its traditional embodiment so much of the primitive naturalness and essential simplicity of fable, that to the new apologues which he formed after the old types men were so partial, that his name became associated with all. He was the children's Homer, and the willing lips of granddames and nurses pre-served his λόγοι, μῦθοι or αἶνοι, with as loving care as the ῥαψῳδοί devoted to the ἔπη of Homer." *

About 300 B.C. Demetrius Phalereus, who had fled from Athens to Alexandria and there founded the world famous Alexandrine Library,† collected all the fables he could find under the title of Λόγων Αἰσωπείων συναγωγαί (Collections of Aesopic Tales). This is the collection from which Phaedrus borrowed all his fables proper.‡

Fable seems to be part of the common mental stock of all nations, due to a tendency of the human mind to ascribe to beasts the thoughts and feelings of **Fable.** reasoning man. The use of the fable and the analogous use of the parable were familiar to the Hebrews (see the Fables of Jotham, Judges ix. 8, and Jehoash, 2 Kings xiv. 9), but it was in Greece and in India that the fable reached its highest development. To discuss, however, the origin and history of fable would be to **Phaedrus' Treatment of the Fable.** enter upon a far wider field of enquiry than can be attempted here.§ The only point that

* Rutherford, *Babrius*, p. xxxv.   †See notes on V. 1. 1.
‡ See first vol. of Jacob's ed. of Caxton's *Fables of Aesop* (Nutt.) for a very full discussion of the question.

§ For a short summary see Introd. to Jacob's *Fables of Aesop* (Macmillan); for a longer and more exhaustive discussion the first vol. of Jacob's ed. of Caxton's *Fables of Aesop* (Nutt.).

can be considered is Phaedrus' treatment of the fable. We
must note first that Phaedrus uses the term 'fable' in a very
wide sense. He includes in his miscellaneous collection not
only the beast fable proper, or apologue, the Aesopian fable,
but also stories, anecdotes, and myths of all kinds, chiefly,
but not all, of Greek origin. One, *Caesar ad Atriensem* (II. v.)
is simply an anecdote about the reigning Emperor.* For
this he apologizes in the Prologue to Book II. : "I will do
my best to follow Aesop's example," he says, "but if I introduce other matter for variety's sake you must take it in good
part." Secondly, we must note that the fable of old days
was not based on, nor did it pretend to be based on, an
accurate study of the habits and ways of the animals which
played a part in it. We must not, therefore, compare a
fable of Phaedrus with the beast stories of modern writers
such as Rudyard Kipling. In these old fables we have a
certain number of conventional characters ; the sly fox, the
greedy wolf, the lordly lion, and they are used merely as
pegs to support a story with a moral. Hence, all sorts of
absurdities occur which it does not require the astuteness of
a German to detect.† In thus treating the fable, Phaedrus
was merely treading the conventional path, but he seems to
have thought, or tried to make himself and his readers
believe, that fables may be used as a means of conveying
valuable lessons to grown-up men, for it is to men and not
children that he appeals. Such a claim could never have
been made good. It is an attempt "to make a drink for
strong men out of the sugared milk on which children thrive."
Among the Greeks of the best period fable played the same

---

* In Bk. I. there are twenty-nine fables proper out of thirty-one ; in
Bk. II., five out of eight ; in Bk. III., nine out of nineteen ; in Bk. IV.,
thirteen out of twenty-two ; in Bk. V., four out of six.

† *e.g.* Lessing, *Abhandlungen über die Fabeln.*

part in literature, in oratory, and in cultured conversation that is now taken by the apt quotation or the pithy anecdote ; it pointed a moral or rounded off an argument. At a later period it became the favourite exercise ground for the teacher of rhetoric.

But we have changed all this. The modern schoolboy writes his essay on the relative merits of football and cricket, or discusses the historical novel, or the British constitution. To invent a fable is no longer the fashion ; we know too much about the ways of birds and beasts to tolerate the crude conventional types that satisfied our ancestors. We have relegated the fable to the nursery, and even there the critical spirit of the young generation gives it an uneasy resting place.

The other claim advanced by Phaedrus is a literary claim. *Aesopus auctor quam materiam* REPPE- RIT, *hanc ego polivi versibus senariis,* "Aesop's **His Literary Claims.** rough material I have polished."* And again, *invenit ille, nostra perfecit manus,*† "Aesop invented, I perfected." In other words, he claims to have taken the rough material handed down by Aesop and other fable makers, and to have given it literary form and value. This claim he still further expands. "If Rome recognizes my genius," he says, "she will have more great writers to compare with the great ones of Greece."‡ "If Phrygian Aesop and Scythian Anacharsis could win eternal fame by their writings, why should not I try to gain glory for my country, I who am nearer akin to Greece than they, I who am of the same race as Linus, son of Apollo, and Orpheus, son of the Muse."§

These claims are expressed in an extravagant manner, but

* I. Prol. 1. † IV. xxi. S.
‡ II. Epil. 8. § III. Prol. 52.

they are based on real literary merit.   His subject-matter
Style.   is poor enough, trite, conventional, and rarely
relieved by a touch of humour or a brilliant
thought; but the form is admirable.   He is a master of the
art of terse expression; his language is pure, simple and direct.
" Whether in language or in the general style of his fables,
Phaedrus may be ranked among the best writers of Rome ;
the Latin of the fables is the pure undebased Latin of
the best period of the golden, not the silver age. . . .
The style of the fables is admitted to be excellent.   The
story is told naturally and without effort or parade of words,
contrasting very favourably with Avianus, whose aim is to
show off his command of Vergilian diction and the grand
style. . . .   In Phaedrus the narrative is uniform, equable,
and with a certain charm which lingers in the memory." *

The metre used by Phaedrus is the iambic trimeter of
Metre.   Roman comedy, called the 'impure iambic'
to distinguish it from the stricter iambic of
Greek tragedy and such Roman poets as Catullus and
Horace.   The spondee (and its equivalents the dactyl and
anapaest) are found in every foot except the last, but
Phaedrus is careful not to overweight his lines with spon-
dees, and in the variety and polish of his lines shows con-
summate skill.†

* Robinson Ellis.
† A short summary of the Metrical Laws of Phaedrus will be found in
the Introd. to L. Müller's editions.

INDEX TO THE FABLES.

xvii

PHAEDRI

AVGVSTI LIBERTI

FABVLARVM AESOPIARVM

LIBER PRIMVS.

PROLOGVS.

Aesopus auctor quam materiam repperit,
hanc ego polivi versibus senariis.
duplex libelli dos est : quod risum movet
et quod prudenti vitam consilio monet.
calumniari si quis autem voluerit,   5
quod arbores loquantur, non tantum ferae,
fictis iocari nos meminerit fabulis.

I. LVPVS ET AGNVS.

Ad rivum eundem lupus et agnus venerant
siti compulsi ; superior stabat lupus

S   A

longeque inferior agnus.   tunc fauce improba
latro incitatus iurgii causam intulit.   -
'cur,' inquit, 'turbulentam fecisti mihi   5
aquam bibenti?'   laniger contra timens :
'qui possum, quaeso, facere, quod quereris, lupe ?
a te decurrit ad meos haustus liquor.'
repulsus ille veritatis viribus :
'ante hos sex menses male,' ait, ' dixisti mihi.'   10
respondit agnus : ' equidem natus non eram.'
'pater hercle tunc tuus,' inquit, ' male dixit mihi.'
atque ita correptum lacerat iniusta nece.

 Haec propter illos scripta est homines fabula,
qui fictis causis innocentes opprimunt.   15

II. RANAE REGEM PETIERVNT.

 Athenae cum florerent aequis legibus,
procax libertas civitatem miscuit
frenumque solvit pristinum licentia.
hic conspiratis factionum partibus
arcem tyrannus occupat Pisistratus.   5
cum tristem servitutem flerent Attici
(non quia crudelis ille, sed quoniam grave est
omne insuetis onus) et coepissent queri,
Aesopus talem tum fabellam rettulit.

 Ranae vagantes liberis paludibus   10
clamore magno regem petiere a Iove,
qui dissolutos mores vi compesceret.

pater deorum risit atque illis dedit
parvum tigillum, missum quod subito vadis
motu sonoque terruit pavidum genus.　　　　15
hoc mersum limo cum lateret diutius,
forte una tacite profert e stagno caput
et explorato rege cunctas evocat.
illae timore posito certatim adnatant
superque lignum turba petulans insilit.　　　20
quod cum inquinassent omni contumelia,
alium rogantes regem misere ad Iovem,
inutilis quoniam esset, qui fuerat datus.
tum misit illis hydrum, qui dente aspero
corripere coepit singulas. frustra necem　　　25
fugitant inertes; vocem praecludit metus.
furtim igitur dant Mercurio mandata ad Iovem,
adflictis ut succurrat. tunc contra deus :
'quia noluistis vestrum ferre,' inquit, ' bonum,
malum perferte.' — ' vos quoque, o cives,' ait,　30
'hoc sustinete, maius ne veniat, malum.'

III. GRACVLVS SVPERBVS ET PAVO.

Ne gloriari libeat alienis bonis
suoque potius habitu vitam degere,
Aesopus nobis hoc exemplum prodidit.
Tumens inani graculus superbia,
pennas, pavoni quae deciderant, sustulit　　　5
seque exornavit. deinde contemnens suos

se miscuit pavonum formoso gregi.
illi impudenti pennas eripiunt avi
fugantque rostris.   male mulcatus graculus
redire maerens coepit ad proprium genus ;   10
a quo repulsus tristem sustinuit notam.
tum quidam ex illis, quos prius despexerat :
'contentus nostris si fuisses sedibus
et quod natura dederat voluisses pati,
nec illam expertus esses contumeliam   15
nec hanc repulsam tua sentiret calamitas.'

IV. CANIS PER FLVVIVM CARNEM FERENS.

Amittit merito proprium qui alienum adpetit.
Canis per flumen carnem cum ferret natans,
lympharum in speculo vidit simulacrum suum,
aliamque praedam ab alio cane ferri putans
eripere voluit : verum decepta aviditas   5
et quem tenebat ore dimisit cibum,
nec quem petebat potuit dente attingere.

V. VACCA, CAPELLA, OVIS ET LEO.

Numquam est fidelis cum potente societas :
testatur hacc fabella propositum meum.
Vacca et capella et patiens ovis iniuriae
socii fuere cum leone in saltibus.
hi cum cepissent cervum vasti corporis,   5
sic est locutus partibus factis leo :

'ego primam tollo, nominor quoniam leo;
secundam, quia sum fortis, tribuetis mihi;
tum, quia plus valeo, me sequetur tertia;
malo adficietur, si quis quartam tetigerit!'   10
sic totam praedam sola improbitas abstulit.

VI. RANAE AD SOLEM.

Vicini furis celebres vidit nuptias
Aesopus et continuo narrare incipit:
'Uxorem quondam Sol cum vellet ducere,
clamorem ranae sustulere ad sidera.
convicio permotus quaerit Iuppiter   5
causam querelae. quaedam tum stagni incola:
'nunc,' inquit, 'omnes unus exurit lacus
cogetque miseras arida sede emori.
quidnam futurum est, si crearit liberos?'

VII. VVLPES AD PERSONAM TRAGICAM.

Personam tragicam forte vulpes viderat:
'o quanta species,' inquit, 'cerebrum non habet!'
Hoc illis dictum est, quibus honorem et gloriam
fortuna tribuit, sensum communem abstulit.

VIII. LVPVS ET GRVIS.

Qui pretium meriti ab improbis desiderat,
bis peccat: primum quoniam indignos adiuvat;
impune abire deinde quia iam non potest.

Os devoratum fauce cum haereret lupi,
magno dolore victus coepit singulos   5
inlicere pretio, ut illud extraherent malum.
tandem·persuasa est iure iurando gruis,
gulaeque credens colli longitudinem
periculosam fecit medicinam lupo.
a quo cum pactum flagitaret praemium :   10
'ingrata es,' inquit, 'ore quae nostro caput
incolume abstuleris et mercedem postules.'

IX. PASSER AD LEPOREM CONSILIATOR.

Sibi non cavere et aliis consilium dare
stultum esse paucis ostendemus versibus.
Oppressum ab aquila et fletus edentem graves
leporem obiurgabat passer : 'ubi pernicitas
nota,' inquit, 'illa est?   quid ita cessarunt pedes?' 5
dum loquitur, ipsum accipiter necopinum rapit
questuque vano clamitantem interficit.
lepus semianimus : 'mortis en solacium !
qui modo securus nostra inridebas mala,
simili querela fata deploras tua.'   10

X. LVPVS ET VVLPES IVDICE SIMIO.

Quicumque turpi fraude semel innotuit,
etiam si verum dicit, amittit fidem.
hoc adtestatur brevis Aesopi fabula.
Lupus arguebat vulpem furti crimine ;

negabat illa se esse culpae proximam. 5
tunc index inter illos sedit simius.
uterque causam cum perorassent suam,
dixisse fertur simius sententiam :
'tu non videris perdidisse quod petis;
te credo subripuisse quod pulchre negas.' 10

XI. ASINVS ET LEO VENANTES.

Virtutis expers verbis iactans gloriam
ignotos fallit, notis est derisui.
Venari asello comite cum vellet leo,
contexit illum frutice et admonuit simul,
ut insueta voce terreret feras, 5
fugientes ipse exciperet. hic auritulus
clamorem subito tollit totis viribus
novoque turbat bestias miraculo.
quae dum paventes exitus notos petunt,
leonis adfliguntur horrendo impetu. 10
qui postquam caede fessus est, asinum evocat
iubetque vocem premere. tunc ille insolens :
'qualis videtur opera tibi vocis meae ?'
'insignis,' inquit, 'sic, ut, nisi nossem tuum
animum genusque, simili fugissem metu.' 15

XII. CERVVS AD FONTEM.

Laudatis utiliora, quae contempseris,
saepe inveniri haec eruit narratio.

Ad fontem cervus, cum bibisset, restitit
et in liquore vidit effigiem suam.
ibi dum ramosa mirans laudat cornua   5
crurumque nimiam tenuitatem vituperat,
venantum subito vocibus conterritus
per campum fugere coepit et cursu levi
canes elusit. silva tum excepit ferum,
in qua retentis impeditus cornibus   10
lacerari coepit morsibus saevis canum.
tunc moriens vocem hanc edidisse dicitur :
'o me infelicem ! qui nunc demum intellego,
utilia mihi quam fuerint, quae despexeram,
et, quae laudaram, quantum luctus habuerint.'   15

XIII. VVLPES ET CORVVS.

Qui se laudari gaudet verbis subdolis,
sera dat poenas turpes paenitentia.
Cum de fenestra corvus raptum caseum
comesse vellet, celsa residens arbore,
vulpes hunc vidit, deinde sic coepit loqui :   5
'o qui tuarum, corve, pinnarum est nitor !
quantum decoris corpore et vultu geris !
si vocem haberes, nulla prior ales foret.'
at ille stultus dum vult vocem ostendere,
emisit ore caseum, quem celeriter   10
dolosa vulpes avidis rapuit dentibus.
tum demum ingemuit corvi deceptus stupor.

[Hac re probatur ingenium quantum valet.]
[Virtute semper praevalet sapientia.]

XIV. EX SVTORE MEDICVS.

Malus cum sutor inopia deperditus
medicinam ignoto facere coepisset loco
et venditaret falso antidotum nomine,
verbosis adquisivit sibi famam strophis.
hic cum iaceret morbo confectus gravi   5
rex urbis, eius experiendi gratia
scyphum poposcit: fusa dein simulans aqua
antidoto illius se miscere toxicum,
ebibere iussit ipsum posito praemio.
timore mortis ille tum confessus est,   10
non artis ulla medicae se prudentia,
verum stupore vulgi factum nobilem.
rex advocata contione haec edidit:
'quantae putatis esse vos dementiae,
qui capita vestra non dubitatis credere,   15
cui calceandos nemo commisit pedes?'
Hoc pertinere vere ad illos dixerim,
quorum stultitia quaestus impudentiae est.

XV. ASINVS AD SENEM PASTOREM.

In principatu commutando saepius
nil praeter domini nomen mutant pauperes.
id esse verum parva haec fabella indicat.

Asellum in prato timidus pascebat senex.
is hostium clamore subito territus   5
suadebat asino fugere, ne possent capi.
at ille lentus : 'quaeso, num binas mihi
clitellas impositurum victorem putas ?'
senex negavit. 'ergo quid refert mea
cui serviam, clitellas dum portem meas ?'   10

XVI. OVIS, CERVVS ET LVPVS.

Fraudator homines cum vocat sponsum improbos,
non rem expedire, sed mala inferre expetit.
  Ovem rogabat cervus modium tritici
lupo sponsore. at illa praemetuens dolum :
'rapere atque abire semper adsuevit lupus,   5
tu de conspectu fugere veloci impetu :
ubi vos requiram, cum dies advenerit ?'

XVII. OVIS, CANIS ET LVPVS.

Solent mendaces luere poenas malefici.
  Calumniator ab ove cum peteret canis
quem commodasse panem se contenderet,
lupus, citatus testis, non unum modo
deberi dixit, verum adfirmavit decem.   5
ovis damnata falso testimonio
quod non debebat solvit. post paucos dies
bidens iacentem in fovea conspexit lupum.
'haec,' inquit, 'merces fraudis a superis datur.'

XIX. CANIS PARTVRIENS.

Habent insidias hominis blanditiae mali :
quas ut vitemus, versus subiecti monent.
  Canis parturiens cum rogasset alteram,
ut fetum in eius tugurio deponeret,
facile impetravit : dein reposcenti locum   5
preces admovit, tempus exorans breve,
dum firmiores catulos posset ducere.
hoc quoque consumpto flagitare validius
ubi coepit illa : ' si mihi et turbae meae
par,' inquit, ' esse potueris, cedam loco.'   10

XX. CANES FAMELICI.

Stultum consilium non modo effectu caret,
sed ad perniciem quoque mortales devocat.
  Corium depressum in fluvio viderunt canes.
id ut comesse extractum possent facilius,
aquam coepere ebibere : sed rupti prius   5
periere, quam quod petierant contingerent.

XXI. LEO SENEX, APER, TAVRVS ET ASINVS.

Quicumque amisit dignitatem pristinam,
ignavis etiam iocus est in casu gravi.
  Defectus annis et desertus viribus
leo cum iaceret spiritum extremum trahens,
aper fulmineis ad eum venit dentibus   5

et vindicavit ictu veterem iniuriam.
infestis taurus mox confodit cornibus
hostile corpus.   asinus, ut vidit ferum
impune laedi, calcibus frontem extudit.
at ille exspirans : 'fortes indigne tuli   10
mihi insultare : te, naturae dedecus,
quod ferre cogor, certe bis videor mori.'

XXII. MVSTELA ET HOMO.

Mustela ab homine prensa cum instantem necem
effugere vellet : 'parce, quaeso,' inquit, 'mihi,
quae tibi molestis muribus purgo domum.'
respondit ille : 'faceres si causa mea,
gratum esset et dedissem veniam supplici.   5
nunc quia laboras, ut fruaris reliquiis,
quas sunt rosuri, simul et ipsos devores,
noli imputare vanum beneficium mihi.'
atque ita locutus improbam leto dedit.

Hoc in se dictum debent illi agnoscere,   10
quorum privata servit utilitas sibi,
et meritum inane iactant imprudentibus.

XXIII. CANIS FIDELIS.

Repente liberalis stultis gratus est,
verum peritis inritos tendit dolos.

Nocturnus cum fur panem misisset cani,
obiecto temptans an cibo posset capi :

'heus,' inquit, 'linguam vis meam praecludere, 5
ne latrem pro re domini? 'multum falleris. ;
namque ista subita me iubet benignitas
vigilare, facias ne mea culpa lucrum.'

XXIV. RANA RVPTA ET BOS.

Inops, potentem dum vult imitari, perit.
In prato quondam rana conspexit bovem
et tacta invidia tantae magnitudinis
rugosam inflavit pellem : tum natos suos
interrogavit, an bove esset latior. 5
illi negarunt. rursus intendit cutem
maiore nisu, et simili quaesivit modo,
quis maior esset. illi dixerunt bovem.
novissime indignata dum vult validius
inflare sese, rupto iacuit corpore. 10

XXV. CANES ET CORCODILI.

Consilia qui dant prava cautis hominibus,
et perdunt operam et deridentur turpiter.
Canes currentes bibere ex Nilo flumine,
a corcodilis ne rapiantur, traditum est.
igitur cum currens bibere coepisset canis, 5
sic corcodilus : 'quamlibet lambe otio ;
noli vereri.' at ille : 'facerem me hercules,
nisi esse scirem carnis te cupidum meae.'

XXVI. VVLPES ET CICONIA.

Nulli nocendum, si quis vero laeserit,
multandum simili iure fabella admonet.
Vulpes ad cenam dicitur ciconiam
prior invitasse et illi in patina liquidam
posuisse sorbitionem, quam nullo modo   5
gustare esuriens potuerit ciconia.
quae vulpem cum revocasset, intrito cibo
plenam lagonam posuit : huic rostrum inserens
satiatur ipsa et torquet convivam fame.
quae cum lagonae collum frustra lamberet,   10
peregrinam sic locutam volucrem accepimus :
'sua quisque exempla debet aequo animo pati.'

XXVII. CANIS ET THESAVRVS ET VVLTVRIVS.

Haec res avaris esse conveniens potest
et qui humiles nati dici locupletes student.
Humana effodiens ossa thesaurum canis
invenit et, violarat quia Manes deos,
iniecta est illi divitiarum cupiditas,   5
poenas ut sanctae Religioni penderet.
itaque aurum dum custodit, oblitus cibi
fame est consumptus: quem stans vulturius super
fertur locutus : 'o canis, merito iaces,
qui concupisti subito regales opes,   10
trivio conceptus, educatus stercore !'

XXVIII. VVLPES ET AQVILA.

Quamvis sublimes debent humiles metuere,
vindicta docili quia patet sollertiae.
Vulpinos catulos aquila quondam sustulit
nidoque posuit pullis, escam ut carperent.
hanc prosecuta mater orare incipit, 5
ne tantum miserae luctum importaret sibi.
contempsit illa, tuta quippe ipso loco.
vulpes ab ara rapuit ardentem facem
totamque flammis arborem circumdedit,
hosti dolorem damno miscens sanguinis. 10
aquila ut periclo mortis eriperet suos,
incolumes natos supplex vulpi tradidit.

XXX. RANAE METVENTES TAVRORVM PROELIA.

Humiles laborant, ubi potentes dissident.
Rana in palude pugnam taurorum intuens :
'heu quanta nobis instat pernicies !' ait.
interrogata ab alia, cur hoc diceret,
de principatu cum illi certarent gregis 5
longeque ab ipsis degerent vitam boves :
'est statio separata ac diversum genus ;
sed pulsus regno nemoris qui profugerit,
paludis in secreta veniet latibula
et proculcatas obteret duro pede. 10
ita caput ad nostrum furor illorum pertinet.'

XXXI. MILVVS ET COLVMBAE.

Qui se committit homini tutandum improbo,
auxilia dum requirit, exitium invenit.
  Columbae saepe cum fugissent miluum
et celeritate pinnae vitassent necem,
consilium raptor vertit ad fallaciam   5
et genus inerme tali decepit dolo :
'quare sollicitum potius aevum ducitis,
quam regem me creatis icto foedere,
qui vos ab omni tutas praestem iniuria ?'
illae credentes tradunt sese miluo ;   10
qui regnum adeptus coepit vesci singulas
et exercere imperium saevis unguibus.
tunc de relicuis una : 'merito plectimur,
quae nostram vitam tali credidimus duci.'

LIBER SECVNDVS.

AVCTOR.

  Exemplis continetur Aesopi genus ;
nec aliud quicquam per fabellas quaeritur,
quam corrigatur error ut mortalium
acuatque sese diligens industria.
quicumque fuerit ergo narrandi iocus,   5
dum capiat aurem et servet propositum suum,
re commendatur, non auctoris nomine.

equidem omni cura morem servabo senis ;
sed si libuerit aliquid interponere,
dictorum sensus ut delectet varietas,   10
bonas in partes, lector, accipias velim
ita, si rependet illam brevitas gratiam.
    Cuius verbosa ne sit commendatio,
attende, cur negare cupidis debeas,
modestis etiam offerre, quod non petierint.   15

I. IVVENCVS, LEO ET PRAEDATOR.

Super iuvencum stabat deiectum leo.
praedator intervenit partem postulans.
' darem,' inquit, ' nisi soleres per te sumere ' :
et improbum reiecit.   forte innoxius
viator est deductus in eundem locum   5
feroque viso rettulit retro pedem.
cui placidus ille : ' non est quod timeas,' ait ;
' sed, quae debetur pars tuae modestiae,
audacter tolle !' tunc diviso tergore
silvas petivit, homini ut accessum daret.   10
    Exemplum egregium prorsus et laudabile ;
verum est aviditas dives et pauper pudor.

II. ANVS DILIGENS IVVENEM, ITEM PVELLA.

A feminis utcumque spoliari viros,
ament, amentur, nempe exemplo discimus.

B

Aetatis mediae quendam mulier non rudis
tenebat annos celans elegantia,
animosque eiusdem pulchra invenis ceperat.   5
ambae, videri dum volunt illi pares,
capillos homini legere coepere invicem.
qui se putaret fingi cura mulierum,
calvus repente factus est ; nam funditus
canos puella, nigros anus evellerat.   10

III. AESOPVS AD QVENDAM DE SVCCESSV
IMPROBORVM.

Laceratus quidam morsu vehementi canis
tinctum cruore panem misit malefico,
audierat esse quod remedium vulneris.
tunc sic Aesopus : 'noli coram pluribus
hoc facere canibus, ne nos vivos devorent,   5
cum scierint esse tale culpae praemium.'
Successus improborum plures adlicit.

IV. AQVILA, FELES ET APER.

Aquila in sublimi quercu nidum fecerat ;
feles cavernam nancta in media pepererat ;
sus nemoris cultrix fetum ad imam posuerat.
tum fortuitum feles contubernium
fraude et scelesta sic evertit malitia.   5
ad nidum scandit volucris : 'pernicies,' ait,
'tibi paratur, forsan et miserae mihi ;

nam fodere terram quod vides cotidie
aprum insidiosum, quercum vult evertere,
ut nostram in plano facile progeniem opprimat. 10
terrore offuso et perturbatis sensibus
derepit ad cubile setosae suis :
'magno,' inquit, 'in periclo sunt nati tui ;
nam, simul exieris pastum cum tenero grege,
aquila est parata rapere porcellos tibi.' 15
hunc quoque timore postquam complevit locum,
dolosa tuto condidit sese cavo.
inde evagata noctu suspenso pede,
ubi esca se replevit et prolem suam,
pavorem simulans prospicit toto die. 20
ruinam metuens aquila ramis desidet ;
aper rapinam vitans non prodit foras.
quid multa ?   inedia sunt consumpti cum suis
felisque catulis largam praebuerunt dapem.

Quantum homo bilinguis saepe concinnet mali, 25
documentum habere stulta credulitas potest.

V. TI. CAESAR AD ATRIENSEM.

Est ardalionum quaedam Romae natio,
trepide concursans, occupata in otio,
gratis anhelans, multa agendo nil agens,
sibi molesta et aliis odiosissima.
hanc emendare, si tamen possum, volo 5
vera fabella : pretium est operae adtendere.

Caesar Tiberius cum petens Neapolim
in Misenensem villam venisset suam,
quae monte summo posita Luculli manu
prospectat Siculum et respicit Tuscum mare :   10
ex alticinctis unus atriensibus,
cui tunica ab umeris linteo Pelusio
erat destricta, cirris dependentibus,
perambulante laeta domino viridia
alveolo coepit ligneo conspargere   15
humum aestuantem, iactans officium leve ;
sed deridetur.   inde notis flexibus
praecurrit alium in xystum, sedans pulverem.
agnoscit hominem Caesar remque intellegit.
ille ut putaret esse nescio quid boni :   20
' heus ! ' inquit dominus.   ille enimvero adsilit,
donationis alacer certae gaudio.
tum sic iocata est tanti maiestas ducis :
' non multum egisti et opera nequiquam perit ;
multo maioris alapae mecum veneunt.'   25

VI. AQVILA ET CORNIX.

Contra potentes nemo est munitus satis ;
si vero accessit consiliator maleficus,
vis et nequitia quicquid oppugnant, ruit.
Aquila in sublime sustulit testudinem.
quae cum abdidisset cornea corpus domo   5
nec ullo pacto laedi posset condita,

venit per auras cornix et propter volans :
'opimam sane praedam rapuisti unguibus ;
sed nisi monstraro quid sit faciendum tibi,
gravi nequiquam te lassabit pondere.'   10
promissa parte suadet, ut scopulum super
altis ab astris duram inlidat corticem,
qua comminuta facili vescatur cibo.
inducta verbis aquila. monitis paruit,
simul et magistrae large divisit dapem.   15
sic tuta quae naturae fuerat munere,
impar duabus occidit tristi nece.

VII. MVLI DVO ET RAPTORES.

Muli gravati sarcinis ibant duo :
unus ferebat fiscos cum pecunia,
alter tumentes multo saccos hordeo.
ille onere dives celsa cervice eminet
clarumque collo iactat tintinnabulum :   5
comes quieto sequitur et placido gradu.
subito latrones ex insidiis advolant
interque caedem ferro in illum incursitant,
diripiunt nummos : neglegunt vile hordeum.
spoliatus igitur casus cum fleret suos :   10
'equidem,' inquit alter, 'me contemptum gaudeo,
nam nil amisi nec sum laesus vulnere.'
    Hoc argumento tuta est hominum tenuitas ;
magnae periclo sunt opes obnoxiae.

VIII. CERVVS ET BOVES.

Cervus nemorosis excitatus latibulis,
ut venatorum fugeret instantem necem,
caeco timore proximam villam petit
et opportuno se bovili condidit.
hic bos latenti: 'quidnam voluisti tibi,   5
infelix, ultro qui ad necem cucurreris
hominumque tecto spiritum commiseris?'
at ille supplex: 'vos modo,' inquit, 'parcite;
occasione rursus erumpam data.'
spatium diei noctis excipiunt vices.   10
frondem bubulcus adfert, nil ideo videt.
eunt subinde et redeunt omnes rustici:
nemo animadvertit.   transit etiam vilicus:
nec ille quicquam sentit.   tum gaudens ferus
bubus quietis agere coepit gratias,   15
hospitium adverso quod praestiterint tempore.
respondit unus: 'salvum te cupimus quidem;
sed ille, qui oculos centum habet, si venerit,
magno in periclo vita vertetur tua.'
haec inter ipse dominus a cena redit,   20
et quia corruptos viderat nuper boves,
accedit ad praesepe: 'cur frondis parum est?
stramenta desunt!   tollere haec aranea
quantum est laboris?'   dum scrutatur singula,
cervi quoque alta est conspicatus cornua;   25
quem convocata iubet occidi familia

praedamque tollit.--haec significat fabula,
dominum videre plurimum in rebus suis.

AVCTOR.

Aesopi ingenio statuam posnere Attici
servumque collocarunt aeterna in basi,
patere honoris scirent ut cuncti viam
nec generi tribui, sed virtuti, gloriam.
quoniam occuparat alter, ne primus forem,   5
ne solus esset, studui (quod superfuit):
nec haec invidia, verum est aemulatio.
quod si labori faverit Latium meo,
plures habebit, quos opponat Graeciae.
sin livor obtrectare curam voluerit,   10
non tamen eripiet laudis conscientiam.
si nostrum studium ad aures cultas pervenit
et arte fictas animus sentit fabulas,
omnem querelam submovet felicitas.
sin autem rabulis doctus occurrit labor,   15
sinistra quos in lucem natura extulit
[nec quicquam possunt nisi meliores carpere].
fatale vitium corde durato feram,
donec fortunam criminis pudeat sui.

LIBER TERTIVS.

PHAEDRVS AD EVTYCHVM.

Phaedri libellos legere si desideras,
vaces oportet, Eutyche, a negotiis,
ut liber animus sentiat vim carminis.
'verum,' inquis, 'tanti non est ingenium tuum
momentum ut horae pereat officiis meis.'   5
non ergo causa est manibus id tangi tuis,
quod occupatis auribus non convenit.
fortasse dices : 'aliquae venient feriae,
quae me soluto pectore ad studium vocent
legesne, quaeso, potius viles nenias,   10
impendas curam quam rei domesticae,
reddas amicis tempora, uxori vaces,
animum relaxes, otium des corpori,
ut adsuetam fortius praestes vicem ?'
mutandum tibi propositum est et vitae genus,   15
intrare si Musarum limen cogitas.
ego, quem Pierio mater enixa est iugo,
in quo Tonanti sancta Mnemosyne Iovi
fecunda novies artium peperit chorum,
quamvis in ipsa paene natus sim schola   20
curamque habendi penitus corde eraserim
et laude invicta vitam in hanc incubuerim,
fastidiose tamen in coetum recipior.
quid credis illi accidere, qui magnas opes

exaggerare quaerit omni vigilia, 25
docto labori vile praeponens lucrum ?
sed iam 'quodcumque fuerit' (ut dixit Sinon,
ad regem cum Dardaniae perductus foret),
librum exarabo tertium Aesopi stilo,
honori et meritis dedicans illum tuis. 30
quem si leges, laetabor; sin autem minus,
habebunt certe, quo se oblectent, posteri.
    Nunc, fabularum cur sit inventum genus,
brevi docebo.   servitus obnoxia,
quia quae volebat non audebat dicere, 35
adfectus proprios in fabellas transtulit
calumniamque fictis elusit iocis.
ego porro illius semita feci viam
et cogitavi plura quam reliquerat,—
in calamitatem deligens quaedam meam ! 40
quod si accusator alius Seiano foret,
si testis alius, iudex alius denique,
dignum faterer esse me tantis malis,
nec his dolorem delenirem remediis.
suspitione si quis errabit sua 45
et rapiet ad se, quod erit commune omnium,
stulte nudabit animi conscientiam.
huic excusatum me velim nihilo minus :
neque enim notare singulos mens est mihi,
verum ipsam vitam et mores hominum ostendere. 50
    Rem me professum dicet forsan quis gravem.
si Phryx Aesopus potuit, si Anacharsis Scytha

aeternam famam condere ingenio suo :
ego, litteratae qui sum propior Graeciae,
cur somno inerti deseram patriae decus ? 55
Threissa cum gens numeret auctores suos,
Linoque Apollo sit parens, Musa Orpheo,
qui saxa cantu movit et domuit feras
Hebrique tenuit impetus dulci mora.
ergo hinc abesto, Livor, ne frustra gemas, 60
quoniam sollemnis mihi debetur gloria.
 Induxi te ad legendum ; sincerum mihi
candore noto reddas iudicium peto.

I. ANVS AD AMPHORAM.

 Anus iacere vidit epotam amphoram,
adhuc Falerna faece e testa nobili
odorem quae iucundum late spargeret.
hunc postquam totis avida traxit naribus :
' o suavis anima ! quale in te dicam bonum 5
antehac fuisse, tales cum sint reliquiae ?'
 Hoc quo pertineat, dicet, qui me noverit.

II. PANTHERA ET PASTORES.

 Solet a despectis par referri gratia.
 Panthera imprudens olim in foveam decidit.
videre agrestes : alii fustes congerunt,
alii onerant saxis ; quidam contra miseriti

periturae quippe, neminem quae laeserat, 5
misere panem, ut sustineret spiritum.
nox insecuta est : abeunt securi domum,
quasi inventuri mortuam postridie.
at illa, vires ut refecit languidas,
veloci saltu fovea sese liberat 10
et in cubile concito properat gradu.
paucis diebus interpositis provolat,
pecus trucidat, ipsos pastores necat.
et cuncta vastans saevit irato impetu.
tum sibi timentes, qui ferae pepercerant, 15
damnum haud recusant, tantum pro vita rogant.
at illa : 'memini quis me saxo petierit,
quis panem dederit : vos timere absistite ;
illis revertor hostis, qui me laeserunt.'

IV. LANIVS ET SIMIVS.

Pendere ad lanium quidam vidit simium,
inter relicuas merces atque obsonia ;
quaesivit, quidnam saperet ? tum lanius iocans :
'quale,' inquit, ' caput est, talis praestatur sapor.'
Ridicule magis hoc dictum quam vere aestimo ; 5
quando et formosos saepe inveni pessimos,
et turpi facie multos cognovi optimos.

V. AESOPVS ET PETVLANS.

Successus ad perniciem multos devocat.
Aesopo quidam petulans lapidem impegerat.

'tanto,' inquit, 'melior !' assem deinde illi dedit,
sic prosecutus : 'plus non habeo me hercules,
'sed, unde accipere possis, monstrabo tibi.   5
venit ecce dives et potens : huic similiter
impinge lapidem, et dignum accipies praemium.'
persuasus ille fecit, quod monitus fuit ;
sed spes fefellit impudentem audaciam :
comprensus namque poenas persolvit cruce.   10

VI. MVSCA ET MVLA.

Musca in temone sedit et mulam increpans
'quam tarda es !' inquit, 'non vis citius progredi ?
vide ne dolone collum compungam tibi.'
respondit illa : 'verbis non moveor tuis ;
sed istum timeo, sella qui prima sedens   5
tergum flagello temperat lento meum
et ora frenis continet spumantibus.
quapropter aufer frivolam insolentiam ;
namque ubi tricandum et ubi currendum sit scio.'
    Hac derideri fabula merito potest,   10
qui sine virtute vanas exercet minas.

VII. LVPVS AD CANEM.

Quam dulcis sit libertas, breviter proloquar.
    Cani perpasto macie confectus lupus
forte occucurrit.   dein salutatum invicem
ut restiterunt : 'unde sic, quaeso, nites ?
aut quo cibo fecisti tantum corporis ?   5

'ego, qui sum longe fortior, pereo fame.'
canis simpliciter: 'eadem est condicio tibi,
praestare domino si par officium potes.'
'quod?' inquit ille. 'custos ut sis liminis,
a furibus tuearis et noctu domum.' 10
'ego vero sum paratus: nunc patior nives
imbresque in silvis asperam vitam trahens:
quanto est facilius mihi sub tecto vivere
et otiosum largo satiari cibo!'
'veni ergo mecum!' dum procedunt, aspicit 15
lupus a catena collum detritum canis.
'unde hoc, amice?' 'nihil est.' 'dic, quaeso, tamen!'
'quia videor acer, alligant me interdiu,
luce ut quiescam et vigilem, nox cum venerit:
crepusculo solutus, qua visum est, vagor. 20
adfertur ultro panis; de mensa sua
dat ossa dominus; frusta iactat familia
et, quod fastidit quisque, pulmentarium.
sic sine labore venter impletur meus.'
'age, si quo abire est animus, est licentia?' 25
'non plane est,' inquit. 'fruere, quae laudas, canis:
regnare nolo, liber ut non sim mihi.'

VIII. SOROR ET FRATER.

Praecepto monitus saepe te considera.
Habebat quidam filiam turpissimam
idemque insignem pulchra facie filium.

hi speculum in cathedra matris ut positum fuit
pueriliter ludentes forte inspexerunt.   5
hic se formosum iactat : illa irascitur
nec gloriantis sustinet fratris iocos,
accipiens quippe cuncta in contumeliam.
ergo ad patrem decurrit laesura invicem
magnaque invidia criminatur filium,   10
vir natus quod rem feminarum tetigerit.
amplexus ille utrumque et carpens oscula
dulcemque in ambos caritatem partiens :
'cotidie,' inquit, 'speculo vos uti volo :
tu formam ne corrumpas nequitiae malis ;   15
tu faciem ut istam moribus vincas bonis !'

IX. SOCRATES DE AMICIS.

Vulgare amici nomen, sed rara est fides.
  Cum parvas aedes sibi fundasset Socrates
(cuius non fugio mortem, si famam adsequar,
et cedo invidiae, dummodo absolvar cinis),
ex populo sic nescio quis, ut fieri solet :   5
'quaeso, tam angustam talis vir ponis domum?'
'utinam,' inquit, 'veris hanc amicis impleam !'

XII. PVLLVS AD MARGARITAM.

In sterculino pullus gallinaceus
dum quaerit escam, margaritam repperit.
'iaces indigno quanta res,' inquit, 'loco !

hoc si quis pretii cupidus vidisset tui,
olim redisses ad splendorem pristinum. 5
ego quod te inveni, potior cui multo est cibus,
nec tibi prodesse nec mihi quicquam potest.'
  Hoc illis narro, qui me non intellegunt.

XIII. APES ET FVCI VESPA IVDICE.

Apes in alta fecerant quercu favos :
hos fuci inertes esse dicebant suos.
lis ad forum deducta est, vespa iudice.
quae genus utrumque nosset cum pulcherrime,
legem duabus hanc proposuit partibus : 5
'non inconveniens corpus et par est color,
in dubium plane res ut merito venerit.
sed ne religio peccet imprudens mea,
alvos accipite et ceris opus infundite,
ut ex sapore mellis et forma favi, 10
de quis nunc agitur, auctor horum appareat.'
fuci recusant : apibus condicio placet.
tunc illa talem protulit sententiam :
'apertum est, quis non possit et quis fecerit.
quapropter apibus fructum restituo suum.' 15
  Hanc praeterissem fabulam silentio,
si pactam fuci non recusassent fidem.

XIV. DE LVSV ET SEVERITATE.

Puerorum in turba quidam ludentem Atticus
Aesopum nucibus cum vidisset, restitit

et quasi delirum risit. quod sensit simul
derisor potius quam deridendus senex,
arcum retensum posuit in media via :   5
'heus !' inquit, 'sapiens, expedi, quid fecerim !'
concurrit populus. ille se torquet diu
nec quaestionis positae causam intellegit.
novissime succumbit. tum victor sophus :
'cito rumpes arcum, semper si tensum habueris; 10
at si laxaris, cum voles, erit utilis.'
Sic lusus animo debent aliquando dari,
ad cogitandum melior ut redeat tibi.

XV. CANIS AD AGNVM.

Inter capellas agno palanti canis :
'stulte,' inquit, 'erras; non est hac mater tua,'
ovesque segregatas ostendit procul.
'non illam quaero, quae, cum libitum est, concipit,
verum illam, quae me nutrit admoto ubere   5
fraudatque natos lacte, ne desit mihi.'
'tamen illa est potior, quae te peperit.' 'non ita est.
unde illa scivit, niger an albus nascerer ?
age porro : parere si voluisset feminam,
quid profecisset, cum crearer masculus ?   10
beneficium magnum sane natali dedit,
ut exspectarem lanium in horas singulas !
cuius potestas nulla in gignendo fuit,

cur hac sit potior, quae iacentis miserita est
dulcemque sponte praestat benivolentiam ?   15
facit parentes bonitas, non necessitas.'
 His demonstrare voluit auctor versibus,
obsistere homines legibus, meritis capi.

XVI. CICADA ET NOCTVA.

Humanitati qui se non accommodat,
plerumque poenas oppetit superbiae.
 Cicada acerbum noctuae convicium
faciebat, solitae victum in tenebris quaerere
cavoque ramo capere somnum interdiu.   5
rogata est, ut taceret.   multo validius
clamare coepit.   rursus admota prece
accensa magis est.   noctua ut vidit sibi
nullum esse auxilium et verba contemni sua,
hac est adgressa garrulam fallacia :   10
'dormire quia me non sinunt cantus tui,
sonare citharam quos putas Apollinis,
potare est animus nectar, quod Pallas mihi
nuper donavit; si non fastidis, veni ;
una bibamus.'   illa, quae arebat siti,   15
simul cognovit vocem laudari suam,
cupide advolavit.   noctua egressa e cavo
trepidantem consectata est et leto dedit.
sic, viva quod negarat, tribuit mortua.

XVII. ARBORES IN DEORVM TVTELA.

Olim, quas vellent esse in tutela sua,
divi legerunt arbores. quercus Iovi,
at myrtus Veneri placuit, Phoebo laurea,
pinus Cybebae, populus celsa Herculi.
Minerva admirans, quare steriles sumerent,   5
interrogavit.   causam dixit Iuppiter :
'honorem fructu ne videamur pendere.'
'at, me hercules, narrabit quod quis voluerit.
oliva nobis propter fructum est gratior.'
tunc sic deorum genitor atque hominum sator :   10
'o nata, merito sapiens dicere omnibus !
nisi utile est quod facimus, stulta est gloria.'
    Nihil agere, quod non prosit, fabella admonet.

XVIII. PAVO AD IVNONEM DE VOCE SVA.

Pavo ad Iunonem venit indigne ferens,
cantus luscinii quod sibi non tribuerit ;
illum esse cunctis avibus admirabilem,
se derideri, simul ac vocem miserit.
tunc consolandi gratia dixit dea :   5
'sed forma vincis, vincis magnitudine ;
nitor smaragdi collo praefulget tuo,
pictisque pinnis gemmeam caudam explicas.'
'quo mi,' inquit, 'mutam speciem, si vincor sono ?'
'fatorum arbitrio partes sunt vobis datae :   10

tibi forma, vires aquilae, luscinio melos,
augurium corvo, laeva cornici omina,
omnesque propriis sunt contentae dotibus.'
 Noli adfectare quod tibi non est datum,
delusa ne spes ad querelam reccidat. 15

XIX. AESOPVS RESPONDET GARRVLO.

 Aesopus domino solus cum esset familia,
parare cenam iussus est maturius.
ignem ergo quaerens, aliquot lustravit domus
tandemque invenit, ubi lucernam accenderet.
tum circum eunti fuerat quod iter longius, 5
effecit brevius : namque recta per forum
coepit redire. et quidam ex turba garrulus :
'Aesope, medio sole quid cum lumine ?'
'hominem,' inquit, 'quaero,' et abiit festinans domum.
 Hoc si molestus ille ad animum rettulit, 10
sensit profecto se hominem non visum seni,
intempestive qui occupato adluserit.

POETA.

 Supersunt mihi quae scribam, sed parco sciens ;
primum esse videar ne tibi molestior,
distringit quem multarum rerum varietas ;
dein si quis eadem forte conari velit,
habere ut possit aliquid operis residui : 5

quamvis materiae tanta abundet copia,
labori faber ut desit, non fabro labor.
brevitati nostrae praemium ut reddas, peto,
quod es pollicitus : exhibe vocis fidem.
nam vita morti propior est cotidie,   10
et hoc minus perveniet ad me muneris,
quo plus consumet temporis dilatio.
si cito rem perages, usus fiet longior.
[fruar diutius, si celerius cepero.]
languentis aevi dum sunt aliquae reliquiae,   15
auxilio locus est ; olim senio debilem
frustra adiuvare bonitas nitetur tua,
cum iam desierit esse beneficium utile
et mors vicina flagitabit debitum.
stultum admovere tibi preces existimo,   20
proclivis ultro cum sit misericordia.
saepe impetravit veniam confessus reus :
quanto innocenti iustius debet dari ?
tuae sunt partes ; fuerunt aliorum prius ;
dein simili gyro venient aliorum vices.   25
decerne quod religio, quod patitur fides,
et graviter me tutare iudicio tuo.
excedit animus quem proposuit terminum ;
sed difficulter continetur spiritus,
integritatis qui sincerae conscius   30
a noxiorum premitur insolentiis.
qui sint, requires? apparebunt tempore.
ego, quondam legi quam puer sententiam

"palam muttire plebeio piaculum est,"
dum sanitas constabit, pulchre meminero.   35

LIBER QVARTVS.

POETA AD PARTICVLONEM.

Cum destinassem terminum operi statuere
in hoc, ut aliis esset materiae satis,
consilium tacito corde damnavi tamen.
nam si quis talis etiam tituli est appetens,
quovis pacto indagabit, quidnam omiserim,   5
ut illud ipsum cupiat famae tradere,
sua cuique cum sit animi cogitatio
colorque proprius.   ergo non levitas mihi,
sed certa ratio causam scribendi dedit.
quare, Particulo, quoniam caperis fabulis   10
(quas Aesopias, non Aesopi, nomino,
quia paucas ille ostendit, ego plures fero,
usus vetusto genere, sed rebus novis),
quartum libellum, dum vacabit, perleges.
hunc obtrectare si volet malignitas,   15
imitari dum non possit, obtrectet licet.
mihi parta laus est, quod tu, quod similes tui
vestras in chartas verba transfertis mea
dignumque longa iudicatis memoria.
inlitteratum plausum nec desidero.   20

I. ASINVS ET GALLI.

Qui natus est infelix, non vitam modo
tristem decurrit, verum post obitum quoque
persequitur illum dura fati miseria.
  Galli Cybebes circum in quaestus ducere
asinum solebant baiulantem sarcinas.   5
is cum labore et plagis esset mortuus,
detracta pelle sibi fecerunt tympana.
rogati mox a quodam, delicio suo
quidnam fecissent, hoc iocati sunt modo:
f putabat se post mortem securum fore;   10
ecce aliae plagae congeruntur mortuo!'

II. POETA.

Ioculare tibi videtur: et sane levi,
dum nihil habemus maius, calamo ludimus.
sed diligenter intuere has nenias:
quantam sub illis utilitatem reperies!
non semper ea sunt, quae videntur; decipit   5
frons prima multos: rara mens intellegit,
quod interiore condidit cura angulo.
hoc ne locutus sine mercede existimer,
fabellam adiciam de mustela et muribus.
  Mustela cum annis et senecta debilis   10
mures veloces non valeret adsequi,
involvit se farina et obscuro loco
abiecit neglegenter. mus escam putans

adsiluit et comprensus occubuit neci.
alter similiter periit, deinde et tertius.   15
aliquot secutis venit et retorridus,
qui saepe laqueos et muscipula effugerat ;
proculque insidias cernens hostis callidi :
' sic valeas,' inquit, ' ut farina es, quae iaces!'

III. DE VVLPE ET VVA.

Fame coacta vulpes alta in vinea
uvam adpetebat summis saliens viribus :
quam tangere ut non potuit, discedens ait :
' nondum matura est ; nolo acerbam sumere.'
    Qui, facere quae non possunt, verbis elevant,   5
adscribere hoc debebunt exemplum sibi.

IV. EQVVS ET APER.

Equus sedare solitus quo fuerat sitim,
dum sese aper volutat, turbavit vadum.
hinc orta lis est.   sonipes iratus fero
auxilium petiit hominis ; quem dorso levans
rediit ad hostem.   iactis hunc telis eques   5
postquam interfecit, sic locutus traditur :
' laetor tulisse auxilium me precibus tuis ;
nam praedam cepi et didici, quam sis utilis.'
atque ita coegit frenos invitum pati.
tum maestus ille : ' parvae vindictam rei   10
dum quaero demens, servitutem repperi.'

Haec iracundos admonebit fabula,
impune potius laedi quam dedi alteri.

VI. PVGNA MVRIVM ET MVSTELARVM.

Cum victi mures mustelarum exercitu
(historia quorum et in tabernis pingitur)
fugerent et artos circum trepidarent cavos,
aegre recepti tamen evaserunt necem.
duces eorum, qui capitibus cornua   5
suis ligarant, ut conspicuum in proelio
haberent signum, quod sequerentur milites,
haesere in portis suntque capti ab hostibus ;
quos immolatos victor avidis dentibus
capacis alvi mersit tartareo specu.   10
Quemcumque populum tristis eventus premit,
periclitatur magnitudo principum ;
minuta plebes facili praesidio latet.

VII. PHAEDRVS.

Tu, qui, nasute, scripta destringis mea
et hoc iocorum legere fastidis genus,
parva libellum sustine patientia,
severitatem frontis dum placo tuae.
en in coturnis prodit Aesopus novis.   5
'Vtinam nec umquam Pelii nemoris iugo
pinus bipinni concidisset Thessala,
nec ad professae mortis audacem viam

fabricasset Argus opera Palladia ratem,
inhospitalis prima quae ponti sinus   10
patefecit in perniciem Graium et barbarum !
namque et superbi luget Aeetae domus,
et regna Peliae scelere Medeae iacent,
quae saevum ingenium variis involvens dolis
illic per artus fratris explicuit fugam,   15
hic caede patris Peliadum infecit manus.'
　　Quid tibi videtur? hoc quoque insulsum est, ais,
falsoque dictum; longe quia vetustior
Aegaea Minos classe perdomuit freta
iustoque vindicavit exemplo improbos.   20
quid ergo possum facere tibi, lector Cato,
si nec fabellae te iuvant nec fabulae ?
noli molestus esse omnino litteris,
maiorem exhibeant ne tibi molestiam !
　　Hoc illis dictum est, qui stultitia nauseant   25
et, ut putentur sapere, caelum vituperant.

VIII. SERPENS AD FABRVM FERRARIVM.

Mordaciorem qui improbo dente adpetit,
hoc argumento se describi sentiat.
　　In officinam fabri venit vipera.
haec cum temptaret, si qua res esset cibi,
limam momordit. illa contra contumax :   5
'quid me,' inquit, 'stulta, dente captas laedere,
omne adsuevi ferrum quae conrodere?'

IX. VVLPES ET CAPER.

Homo in periclum simul ac venit callidus,
reperire effugium quaerit alterius malo.
   Cum decidisset vulpes in puteum inscia
et altiore clauderetur margine,
devenit hircus sitiens in eundem locum;   5
simul rogavit, esset an dulcis liquor
et copiosus?   illa fraudem moliens :
'descende, amice; tanta bonitas est aquae,
voluptas ut satiari non possit mea.'
immisit se barbatus.   tum vulpecula   10
evasit puteo, nixa celsis cornibus,
hircumque clauso liquit haerentem vado.

X. DE VITIIS HOMINVM.

Peras imposuit Iuppiter nobis duas :
propriis repletam vitiis post tergum dedit,
alienis ante pectus suspendit gravem.
   Hac re videre nostra mala non possumus;
alii simul delinquunt, censores sumus.   5

XI. FVR ET LVCERNA.

Lucernam fur accendit ex ara Iovis
ipsumque compilavit ad lumen suum.
qui sacrilegio onustus cum discederet,
repente vocem sancta misit Religio :

'malorum quamvis ista fuerint munera 5
mihique invisa, ut non offendar subripi.
tamen, sceleste, spiritu culpam lues,
olim cum adscriptus venerit poenae dies.
sed ne ignis noster facinori praeluceat,
per quem verendos excolit pietas deos, 10
veto esse tale luminis commercium.'
itaque hodie nec lucernam de flamma deum
nec de lucerna fas est accendi sacrum.

Quot res contineat hoc argumentum utiles,
non explicabit alius, quam qui repperit. 15
significat primo, saepe, quos ipse alueris,
tibi inveniri maxime contrarios ;
secundo ostendit scelera non ira deum,
fatorum dicto sed puniri tempore ;
novissime interdicit, ne cum malefico 20
usum bonus consociet ullius rei.

XII. MALAS ESSE DIVITIAS.

Opes invisae merito sunt forti viro,
quia dives arca veram laudem intercipit.

Caelo receptus propter virtutem Hercules
cum gratulantes persalutasset deos,
veniente Pluto, qui Fortunae est filius, 5
avertit oculos. causam quaesivit pater.
'odi,' inquit, 'illum, quia malis amicus est
simulque obiecto cuncta corrumpit lucro.'

XIII. . . .

'Vtilius homini nihil est quam recte loqui'
probanda cunctis est quidem sententia,
sed ad perniciem solet agi sinceritas

. . . .

. . . .

XIV. DE LEONE REGNANTE.

Cum se ferarum regem fecisset leo
et aequitatis vellet famam consequi,
a pristina deflexit consuetudine
atque inter illas tenui contentus cibo
sancta incorrupta iura reddebat fide.
postquam labare coepit paenitentia,

. . . .

. . . .

XVI. DE CAPRIS BARBATIS.

Barbam capellae cum impetrassent ab Iove,
hirci maerentes indignari coeperunt,
quod dignitatem feminae aequassent suam.
'sinite,' inquit, 'illas gloria vana frui
et usurpare vestri ornatum muneris,
pares dum non sint vestrae fortitudini.'
Hoc argumentum monet, ut sustineas tibi
habitu esse similes, qui sint virtute impares.

XVII. DE FORTVNIS HOMINVM.

Cum de fortunis quidam quereretur suis,
Aesopus finxit consolandi gratia :
' Vexata saevis navis tempestatibus
inter vectorum lacrimas et mortis metum,
faciem ad serenam subito ut mutatur dies,   5
ferri secundis tuta coepit flatibus
nimiaque nautas hilaritate extollere.
factus periclo tum gubernator sophus :
'parce gaudere oportet et sensim queri,
totam quod vitam miscet dolor et gaudium.''   10

XIX. SERPENS MISERICORDI NOCIVA.

Qui fert malis auxilium, post tempus dolet.
Gelu rigentem quidam colubram sustulit
sinuque fovit, contra se ipse misericors ;
namque ut refecta est, necuit hominem protinus.
hanc alia cum rogaret causam facinoris,   5
respondit : ' ne quis discat prodesse improbis.'

XX. VVLPES ET DRACO.

Vulpes, cubile fodiens, dum terram eruit
agitque plures altius cuniculos,
pervenit ad draconis speluncam intimam,
custodiebat qui thesauros abditos.
hunc simul aspexit : ' oro, ut imprudentiae   5

des primum veniam ; deinde si pulchre vides,
quam non conveniens aurum sit vitae meae,
respondeas clementer.   quem fructum capis
hoc ex labore, quodve tantum est praemium,
ut careas somno et aevum in tenebris exigas ?'   10
'nullum,' inquit ille, 'verum hoc a summo mihi
Iove adtributum est.'   'ergo nec sumis tibi
nec ulli donas quicquam ?'   'sic fatis placet.'
'nolo irascaris, libere si dixero :
dis est iratis natus, qui est similis tibi.'   15
    Abiturus illuc, quo priores abierunt,
quid mente cacca miserum torques spiritum ?
tibi dico, avare, gaudium heredis tui,
qui ture superos, ipsum te fraudas cibo,
qui tristis audis musicum citharae sonum,   20
quem tibiarum macerat iucunditas,
obsoniorum pretia cui gemitum exprimunt,
qui, dum quadrantes aggeras patrimonio,
caelum fatigas sordido periurio,
qui circumcidis omnem impensam funeris,   25
Libitina ne quid de tuo faciat lucri.

XXI. PHAEDRVS.

Quid iudicare cogitet livor modo,
licet dissimulet, pulchre tamen intellego.
quicquid putabit esse dignum memoria,
Aesopi dicet ; si quid minus adriserit,

a me contendet fictum quovis pignore.   5
quem volo refelli iam nunc responso meo :
sive hoc ineptum sive laudandum est opus,
invenit ille, nostra perfecit manus.
sed exsequamur coeptum propositi ordinem.

XXII. DE SIMONIDE.

Homo doctus in se semper divitias habet.
Simonides, qui scripsit egregium melos,
quo paupertatem sustineret facilius,
circum ire coepit urbes Asiae nobiles,
mercede accepta laudem victorum canens.   5
hoc genere quaestus postquam locuples factus est,
redire in patriam voluit cursu pelagio ;
erat autem, ut aiunt, natus in Cia insula.
ascendit navem, quam tempestas horrida
simul et vetustas medio dissolvit mari.   10
hi zonas, illi res pretiosas colligunt,
subsidium vitae.   quidam curiosior :
' Simonide, tu ex opibus nil sumis tuis ?'
' mecum,' inquit, ' mea sunt cuncta.'   tunc pauci
          enatant,
quia plures onere degravati perierant.   15
praedones adsunt, rapiunt, quod quisque extulit,
nudos relinquunt.   forte Clazomenae prope
antiqua fuit urbs ; quam petierunt naufragi.
hic litterarum quidam studio deditus,

Simonidis qui saepe versus legerat   20
eratque absentis admirator maximus,
sermone ab ipso cognitum cupidissime
ad se recepit; veste, nummis, familia
hominem exornavit.   ceteri tabulam suam
portant rogantes victum.   quos casu obvios   25
Simonides ut vidit : 'dixi,' inquit, 'mea
mecum esse cuncta; vos quod habuistis, perit.

XXIII. MONS PARTVRIENS.

Mons parturibat, gemitus immanes ciens,
eratque in terris maxima exspectatio.
at ille murem peperit.—Hoc scriptum est tibi,
qui, magna cum minaris, extricas nihil.

XXIV. FORMICA ET MVSCA.

[Nihil agere quod non prosit, fabella admonet.]
  Formica et musca contendebant acriter,
quae pluris esset.   musca sic coepit prior :
'conferre nostris tu potes te laudibus ?
ubi immolatur, exta praegusto deum ;   5
moror inter aras, templa perlustro omnia ,
in capite regis sedeo, cum visum est mihi,
et matronarum casta delibo oscula.
laboro nihil, atque optimis rebus fruor.
quid horum simile tibi contingit, rustica ?'   10
    .   .   .   .

'est gloriosus sane convictus deum,
sed illi, qui invitatur, non qui invisus est.
aras frequentas: nempe abigeris, cum venis.
reges commemoras et matronarum oscula:
super etiam iactas, tegere quod debet pudor.   15
nihil laboras: ideo cum opus est, nihil habes.
ego granum in hiemem cum studiose congero,
te circa murum pasci video stercore.
aestate me lacessis: cum bruma est, siles
mori contractam cum te cogunt frigora,   20
me copiosa recipit incolumem domus.
satis profecto rettudi superbiam.'

Fabella talis hominum discernit notas
eorum, qui se falsis ornant laudibus,
et quorum virtus exhibet solidum decus.   25

XXV. SIMONIDES A DEIS SERVATVS.

Quantum valerent inter homines litterae,
dixi superius: quantus, nunc, illis honos
a superis sit tributus, tradam memoriae.
Simonides idem ille, de quo rettuli,
victori laudem cuidam pyctae ut scriberet,   5
certo conductus pretio secretum petit.
exigua cum frenaret materia impetum,
usus poeta moris est licentia
atque interposuit gemina Ledae pignera,
auctoritatem similis referens gloriae.   10

D

opus adprobavit; sed mercedis tertiam
accepit partem. cum relicuam posceret :
'illi,' inquit, 'reddent, quorum sunt laudis duae.
verum, ut ne irate te dimissum censeas,
ad cenam mihi promitte ; cognatos volo   15
hodie invitare, quorum es in numero mihi.'
fraudatus quamvis et dolens iniuria,
ne male dimissus gratiam corrumperet,
promisit. rediit hora dicta, recubuit.
splendebat hilare poculis convivium,   20
magno adparatu laeta resonabat domus :
repente duo cum iuvenes sparsi pulvere,
sudore multo diffluentes, corpora
humanam supra formam, cuidam servulo
mandant, ut ad se provocet Simonidem ;   25
illius interesse, ne faciat moram.
homo perturbatus excitat Simonidem.
unum promorat vix pedem triclinio :
ruina camarae subito oppressit ceteros ;
nec ulli iuvenes sunt reperti ad ianuam.   30
ut est vulgatus ordo narratae rei,
omnes scierunt numinum praesentiam
vati dedisse vitam mercedis loco.

POETA AD PARTICVLONEM.

Adhuc supersunt multa, quae possim loqui,
et copiosa abundat rerum varietas;

sed temperatae suaves sunt argutiae,
immodicae offendunt.   quare, vir sanctissime,
Particulo, chartis nomen victurum meis,   5
Latinis dum manebit pretium litteris,
si non ingenium, certe brevitatem adproba,
quae commendari tanto debet iustius,
quanto poetae sunt molesti validius.

___

LIBER QVINTVS.

IDEM POETA.

Aesopi nomen sicubi interposuero,
cui reddidi iam pridem quicquid debui,
auctoritatis esse scito gratia :
ut quidam artifices nostro faciunt saeculo,
qui pretium operibus maius inveniunt novis,   5
si marmori adscripserunt Praxitelen suo,
trito Myronem argento, tabulae Zeuxidem.
adeo fucatae plus vetustati favet
invidia mordax quam bonis praesentibus.
sed iam ad fabellam talis exempli feror.   10

___

I. DEMETRIVS REX ET MENANDER POETA.

Demetrius, qui dictus est Phalereus,
Athenas occupavit imperio improbo.

ut mos est vulgi, passim et certatim ruit.
'feliciter!' succlamant.   ipsi principes
illam osculantur, qua sunt oppressi, manum,   5
tacite gementes tristem fortunae vicem
quin etiam resides et sequentes otium,
ne defuisse noceat, repunt ultimi ;
in quis Menander, nobilis comoediis,
(quas ipsum ignorans legerat Demetrius   10
et admiratus fuerat ingenium viri),
unguento delibutus, vestitu fluens,
veniebat gressu delicato et languido.
hunc ubi tyrannus vidit extremo agmine :
'quisnam cinaedus ille in conspectum meum   15
audet venire ?'   responderunt proximi :
'hic est Menander scriptor.'   mutatus statim :
'homo,' inquit, 'fieri non potest formosior !'

II. DVO MILITES ET LATRO.

Duo cum incidissent in latronem milites,
unus profugit, alter autem restitit
et vindicavit sese forti dextera.
latrone occiso timidus accurrit comes
stringitque gladium, dein reiecta paenula :   5
'cedo,' inquit, 'illum ; iam curabo sentiat,
quos adtemptarit.'   tunc, qui depugnaverat :
'vellem istis verbis saltem adiuvisses modo ;
constantior fuissem, vera existimans.

nunc conde ferrum et linguam pariter futilem,   10
ut possis alios ignorantes fallere.
ego, qui sum expertus, quantis fugias viribus,
scio, quam virtuti non sit credendum tuae,'
   Illi adsignari debet haec narratio,
qui re secunda fortis est, dubia fugax.   15

IIL CALVVS ET MVSCA.

Calvi momordit musca nudatum caput;
quam opprimere captans alapam sibi duxit gravem.
tunc illa inridens: ' punctum volucris parvulae
voluisti morte ulcisci; quid facies tibi,
iniuriae qui addideris contumeliam?'   5
respondit: ' mecum facile redeo in gratiam,
quia non fuisse mentem laedendi scio.
sed te, contempti generis animal improbum,
quae delectaris bibere humanum sanguinem,
optem necare vel maiore incommodo.'   10
   Hoc argumentum venia donari docet,
qui casu peccat. nam qui consilio est nocens,
illum esse quavis dignum poena iudico.

IV. ASINVS ET PORCELLVS.

Quidam immolasset verrem cum sancto Herculi,
cui pro salute votum debebat sua,
asello iussit reliquias poni hordei.
quas aspernatus ille sic locutus est:

'tuum libenter prorsus adpeterem cibum,   5
nisi, qui nutritus illo est, iugulatus foret.'
    Huius respectu fabulae deterritus
periculosum semper vitavi lucrum.
sed dices : 'qui rapuere divitias, habent.'
'numeremus agedum, qui deprensi perierunt :   10
maiorem turbam punitorum reperies.'—
paucis temeritas est bono, multis malo.

V. SCVRRA ET RVSTICVS.

Pravo favore labi mortales solent
et, pro iudicio dum stant erroris sui,
ad paenitendum rebus manifestis agi.
    Facturus ludos quidam dives nobilis
proposito cunctos invitavit praemio,   5
quam quisque posset ut novitatem ostenderet.
venere artifices laudis ad certamina ;
quos inter scurra, notus urbano sale,
habere dixit se genus spectaculi,
quod in theatro numquam prolatum foret.   10
dispersus rumor civitatem concitat.
paullo ante vacua turbam deficiunt loca.
in scaena vero postquam solus constitit
sine adparatu, nullis adiutoribus,
silentium ipsa fecit exspectatio.   15
ille in sinum repente demisit caput
et sic porcelli vocem est imitatus sua,

verum ut subesse pallio contenderent
et excuti iuberent. quo facto simul
nihil est repertum, multis onerant laudibus   20
hominemque plausu prosequuntur maximo.
hoc vidit fieri rusticus. 'non me hercules
me vincet,' inquit : et statim professus est
idem facturum melius se_postridie.
fit turba maior. iam favor mentes tenet,   25
et derisuri, non spectaturi, sedent.
uterque prodit.   scurra degrunnit prior
movetque plausus et clamores suscitat.
tunc simulans sese vestimentis rusticus
porcellum obtegere (quod faciebat scilicet,   30
sed, in priore quia nil compererant, latens),
pervellit aurem vero, quem celaverat,
et cum dolore vocem naturae exprimit.
acclamat populus, scurram multo similius
imitatum, et cogit rusticum trudi foras.   35
at ille profert ipsum porcellum e sinu,
turpemque aperto pignore errorem probans :
'en hic declarat, quales sitis iudices !'

VI. CALVVS ET QVIDAM AEQVE PILIS DEFECTVS.

Invenit calvus forte in trivio pectinem.
accessit alter, aeque defectus pilis.
'heia!' inquit, 'in commune, quodcumque est lucri !'

ostendit ille praedam et adiecit simul :
'superum voluntas favit; sed fato invido   5
carbonem, ut aiunt, pro thesauro invenimus.'
    Quem spes delusit, huic querela convenit.

VII. PROCAX TIBICEN.

    Vbi vanus animus aura captus frivola
adripuit insolentem sibi fiduciam,
facile ad derisum stulta levitas ducitur.
    Princeps tibicen notior populo fuit,
operam Bathyllo solitus in scaena dare.   5
is forte ludis (non satis memini quibus)
dum pegma rapitur, concidit casu gravi
necopinus et sinistram fregit tibiam,
duas cum dextras maluisset perdere.
inter manus sublatus et multum gemens   10
domum refertur.   aliquot menses transeunt,
ad sanitatem dum venit curatio.
ut spectatorum molle est et lepidum genus,
desiderari coepit, cuius flatibus
solebat excitari saltantis vigor.   15
    Erat facturus ludos quidam nobilis.
ut publicum incipiebat Princeps ingredi,
adducit pretio precibus, ut tantummodo
ipso ludorum ostenderet sese die.
qui simul advenit, rumor de tibicine   20
fremit in theatro.   quidam adfirmant mortuum,

quidam in conspectum proditurum sine mora.
aulaco misso devolutis tonitribus
di sunt locuti more translaticio.
tunc chorus ignotum modo reducto canticum   25
insonuit, cuius haec fuit sententia :
'laetare, incolumis Roma, salvo "principe"!'
in plausus consurrectum est.   iactat basia
tibicen; gratulari fautores putat.
equester ordo stultum errorem intellegit   30
magnoque risu canticum repeti iubet.
iteratur illud.   homo meus se in pulpito
totum prosternit.   plaudit inludens eques.
rogare populus hunc coronam existimat.
ut vero cuneis notuit res omnibus,   35
Princeps, ligato crure nivea fascia,
niveisque tunicis, niveis etiam calceis,
superbiens honore divinae domus,
ad universis capite est protrusus foras.

VIII. TEMPVS.

Cursu volucri, pendens in novacula,
calvus, comosa fronte, nudo corpore
(quem si occuparis, teneas; elapsum semel
non ipse possit Iuppiter reprehendere),
occasionem rerum significat brevem.   5
Effectus impediret ne segnis mora,
finxere antiqui talem effigiem Temporis.

IX. TAVRVS ET VITVLVS.

Angusto in aditu taurus luctans cornibus
cum vix intrare posset ad praesepia,
monstrabat vitulus quo se pacto flecteret.
'tace,' inquit; 'ante hoc novi, quam tu natus es.'
　　Qui doctiorem emendat, sibi dici putet.　　　5

X. CANIS ET SVS ET VENATOR.

Adversus omnes fortis et velox feras
canis cum domino semper fecisset satis,
languere coepit annis ingravantibus.
aliquando obiectus hispidi pugnae suis
adripuit aurem : sed cariosis dentibus　　　　5
praedam dimisit.　hoc tunc venator dolens
canem obiurgabat.　cui senex contra Lacon :
'non te destituit animus, sed vires meae.
quod fuimus lauda, si iam damnas quod sumus.'
　　Hoc cur, Philete, scripserim, pulchre vides.　　10

NOTES.

TITLE.

Augusti, C. Octavius Augustus, the first Roman Emperor; see Introd., p. vii.

Fabularum Aesopiarum, see iv. Prol. 11 note.

BOOK I.

PROLOGUE.

1. **Aesopus,** see Introd., p. xii.

2. **polivi,** cf. iv. 21. 8, "invenit ille, nostra perfecit manus."

3. **dos,** so Pliny, *Nat. Hist.*, xxxvii. 5, 'dos smaragdi'; and Ovid, 'dos oris' of eloquence, 'dos formae,' 'dos ingenii,' etc.; cf. Ovid, *Am.* i. 10. 60, "est quoque carminibus meritas celebrare puellas Dos mea," i.e. *my gift*.

4. **prudenti,** abl. with 'consilio,' rather than dat., as some editors take it.

6. **arbores loquantur,** subj., because 'virtual' oratio obliqua, '*because* (as they say) *trees speak.*' But in the fables which have been preserved no trees speak; this therefore refers to a lost portion of Phaedrus' works; see Introd., p. ix.

FABLE I.

1. **lupus et agnus,** proverbial foes. Cf. *Isaiah*, xi. 6, "The wolf also shall dwell with the lamb, and the leopard shall lie down with the kid ...." Lessing criticises the improbability

59

of a wolf and lamb coming to drink at the same stream.
But see Introd., p. xiv.

4. **iurgii causam intulit,** '*adduced the grounds for a quarrel,*'
modelled on legal phrase for bringing an action, 'inferre litem';
cf. Caesar, *Bell. Gall.* 1. 39, "alia causa illata."

6. **laniger,** *sc.* inquit, a very frequent omission in Phaedrus.
He uses an uncommon word 'laniger' to give freshness and
variety ; see 'auritulus,' i. 11. 6 ; 'barbatus,' iv. 9. 10 ; see
iv. 4. 3 note.

7. **qui,** '*how?*'

10. **ante hos sex menses,** the 'hos added just as in colloquial
Eng., '*these six months ago.*'

13. **correptum,** *sc.* agnum ; 'correptum lacerat,' '*seizes and
tears to pieces.*'

15. **qui fictis causis** ..., this line is often referred to Tiberius
or Sejanus, or both. But Phaedrus had not yet been attacked
by Sejanus ; see Introd., p. vii. It is better, therefore, to
suppose no special person aimed at.

<h3 style="text-align:center">FABLE II.</h3>

1. **aequis legibus,** *i.e.* under a democracy.

2. **libertas ... licentia,** cf. Milton, "Licence they mean when
they cry liberty." **frenum,** common metaphor from bridling
horses ; cf. Hor. *Odes,* iv. 15. 4 foll., "Tua Caesar actas ...
ordinem rectum et vaganti frena licentiae iniecit."

4. **conspiratis,** middle use ; see Vocab. Cf. 'iuratus,'
having sworn ; 'cenatus,' *having supped,* etc.

5. **Pisistratus,** see *Classical Dict.* He became 'tyrant' of
Athens 560 B.C. ; was driven out twice, but returned and
retained his power till his death, 527 B.C., when he was
succeeded by his son Hippias. **arcem,** the acropolis at
Athens, from which he commanded the city.

8. **insuetis,** always scanned 'insŭĕtis' in Phaedrus.

10. **liberis paludibus,** the epithet '*free*' is transferred from
frogs to marshes ; called hypallage by grammarians.

12. **qui ... compesceret,** final, '*to restrain ....*'

16. **hoc** = pavidum genus, *i.e.* the frogs, subject of lateret ;
'hoc' cannot be the log because if it had been hidden in mud
the frogs could not have seen it and crawled on to it.

22. **rogantes,** either nom., '*they sent to J. asking for another king,*' or acc., '*they sent to J. (ambassadors) asking for another king.*'

FABLE III.

Graculus, is a *jackdaw,* not La Fontaine's 'geai.' or jay. Horace, *Ep.* I. iii. 19, transfers the fable to the crow, 'cornicula.' Some editors treat the fable as a prophecy of the fall of Sejanus; others as aimed at Phaedrus' imitators.

1. **Ne gloriari ...,** construe, Aesopus prodidit hoc exemplum nobis, ne libeat gloriari alienis bonis (ut)que (libeat) potius degere vitam suo habitu; with 'suoque' understand 'ut libeat' from previous 'ne libeat.' Note 'libeat' pres. subj. because 'prodidit,' pres. perf., '*has* handed down.'

11. **notam,** '*brand,*' either referring to the brand with which foreheads of criminals were branded, or to the mark placed by censors against the names of unworthy citizens on census roll, the 'nota censoria.'

16. **tua calamitas = tu** calamitosus, '*your unhappy self*'; so in next fable, l. 5, 'aviditas' = 'avidus canis'; use of abstract for concrete very common in Phaedrus. Cf. also i. 5. 11, 'improbitas'; i. 13. 12, 'stupor,' etc., and our English, 'His Majesty'; see ii. 5. 23 note.

FABLE IV.

Lessing criticises this fable also on the ground that the ripple made by the dog would destroy the reflection.

1. **Amittit ...,** construe, qui adpetit alienum, merito amittit proprium, '*he who seeks another's property, deservedly loses his own.*'

5. **aviditas,** '*the greedy creature*'; see i. 3. 16 note.

FABLE V.

This fable also is criticised by Lessing, because a cow, etc., would not hunt with a lion! From it comes our expression 'lion's share.'

7. **primam**, *sc.* partem, '*first portion*'; so l. 8, 'secundam'; l. 9, 'tertia'; l. 10, 'quartam.' At meals and banquets a portion was assigned to each guest called his '*pars.*' **nominor quoniam leo**, *i.e.* 'because I am king of beasts.'

9. **me sequetur**, regular legal term for inheriting; cf. Hor. *Sat.* i. viii. 13, "heredes monimentum ne sequeretur."

11. **improbitas**, '*the rapacious creature*'; see i. 3. 16 note.

Fable VI.

Those who seek political meaning in the fables refer this to the crimes of Sejanus and his projected marriage with Livia or Livilla, sister of Germanicus, wife of Drusus, see Introd., p. viii.

2. **Aesopus**, see Introd., p. xii.

7. **unus**, *sc.* sol, '*one sun.*'

8. **arida sede**, better abl. of cause, '*because our home is dried up*,' than abl. of place, '*in our dried up home.*'

9. **crearit** for 'creaverit,' fut. perf.

Fable VII.

This fable is referred by some to the great men at Court.

1. **personam**, see *Dict. of Antiq.* The ancient mask, unlike ours, covered the whole head.

4. **sensum communem**, our '*common sense*' or '*good sense*,' Gr. κοινὸς λογισμός, cf. Juv. *Sat.* viii. 71 foll., "rarus enim ferme sensus communis in illa Fortuna"; and Hor. *Sat.* i. iii. 66, "communi sensu plane caret."

Fable VIII.

3. **impune** ..., construe, deinde quia iam non potest abire impune.

7. **persuasa est**, see iii. 5. 8, a violation of the rule that verbs which govern a dative in active are used impersonally in passive. But Phaedrus has good authority, for Ovid, *A. A.* iii. 679, has 'persuasus erit,' Verg. uses 'credor,' Hor. 'invideor' and 'imperor.'

12. **abstuleris**, subj. after 'quae' causal. **et**, '*and yet ....*'

Fable IX.

1. **Sibi ...**, construe, ostendemus paucis versibus stultum esse non cavere sibi et dare consilium aliis.

9. **securus**, note that 'securus' = *careless, unconcerned* ; 'tutus' = *safe, secure.*

Fable X.

5. **culpae proximam**, '*guilty*'; lit. *associated with* or *connected with* the fault; no exact parallels for this phrase. Cicero uses 'affinis culpae,' 'facinori,' etc.; Ovid, for its opposite, 'culpâ abesse' (Ovid, *Tris.* ii. 98); so Terence, "culpa a me est procul."

7. **causam perorassent**, '*had pleaded their cause to the end*' (per), *i.e.* '*had finished their pleadings.*'

9. **videris**, the legal phrase in giving judgment ; the Roman judge declared not that a man *was* guilty of so and so, but that he *seemed* or *was held* to be guilty, 'videris fecisse.'

Fable XI.

2. **ignotos ... notis**, see Vocab. both in active sense, '*those who do not know him...those who do know him*'; cf. i. 14. 2, 'ignoto loco'; cf. similar act. and pass. use of Gr. ἄγνωστος. For double dative, **notis est derisui**, cf. Hor. *Odes*, i. 28. 18, "exitio est avidum mare nautis," '*the greedy sea is a destruction to sailors*,' and below, v. 4. 12.

6. **auritulus**, cf. Phaedrus' use of 'laniger,' i. 1. 6 note ; 'barbatus,' iv. 9. 10, etc.

Fable XII.

1. **Laudatis ...**, construe, haec narratio eruit (ea) quae contempseris '*elicits* or *reveals that what you have despised*,' saepe inveniri utiliora laudatis, '*is often found more useful than what is praised*'; 'laudatis,' abl. of comparison ; 'contempseris,' subj. because rel. 'quae' is indef., '*anything which ...*.'

10. **retentis**, caught by the trees.

11. **lacerari coepit,** a violation of rule that 'coepi' is used with active inf., but ' coeptus est' with pass.

15. **luctus,** partitive gen. after 'quantum.'

Fable XIII.

1. **Qui ...,** construe (Is) qui gaudet se laudari subdolis verbis, dat turpes poenas serâ paenitentiâ.

3. **fenestra,** simply an *opening in the wall.*

6. **qui,** interrog. '*what* is the brilliance!' *i.e.* '*how great,*' or '*how splendid the brilliance !*'

7. **decŏris,** from '*decor*'; distinguish 'decŏris'from 'decus.' **geris,** used especially of what attracts attention ; cf. Verg. *Aen.* i. 315, "virginis os habitumque gerens."

12. **corvi stupor,** '*the stupid raven*'; see i. 3. 16 note.

Fable XIV.

2. **ignoto,** see i. 11. 2 note.

3. **falso antidotum nomine,** abl. of description, '*an antidote falsely so called,*' lit. *with a false name,* false because it would not really counteract poison.

4. **strophis,** from stropha, Gr. στροφή, properly a *turning* or *twist* of any sort, used especially of the turning of the chorus in a Greek play towards one side of the orchestra, and the song sung during this movement : but also of the *twists* made by wrestlers, etc., to elude adversary : and then of any *slippery dodge* or *trick* : so here.

5. **hic,** best '*hereupon,*' though it might be '*here,*'*i.e.* 'ignoto loco.'

7. **fusa ...,** construe, dein, aquâ fusâ, simulans se miscere toxicum antidoto illius, '*that he was mixing a poison with his antidote,*' iussit ipsum ebibere, '*bade the fellow himself drink (it) up,*' posito praemio, '*offering him a reward*' (for doing so).

11. **non artis ...,** construe, se factum nobilem non ulla prudentia medicae artis, verum stupore vulgi.

18. **stultitia**, nom. rather than abl. of cause, '*whose folly is a profit to ...*,' cf. i. 21. 2, 'iocus est.'

FABLE XV.

Referred by editors to the civil war between Caesar and Pompeius, or that between Octavian and Antony.

5. **subito**, better adv. than adj. qualifying 'clamore.'

6. **suadebat ... fugere**, in prose would be 'suadebat ut fugeret,' but the inf. is common enough in poetry.

7. **binas**, the distributive, not cardinal numeral, is employed with substantives which are used only in plur. (as 'clitellas' here), or in a different sense in plur., *e.g.* 'bina castra.'

10. **meas** = solitas, '*my regular ....*'

FABLE XVI.

1. **vocat sponsum**, legal term ; '*asks worthless men to become his security*,' 'spousum' is supine expressing purpose after verb implying motion ; cf. Hor. *Ep.* ii. 2. 67, "hic sponsum vocat."

2. **rem expedire**, '*seeks not to settle the business*' (so that thereafter no dispute may arise or loss fall on either party), '*but to do mischief*,' *i.e.* means not business but mischief.

FABLE XVII.

Referred by commentators to the 'delatores' or professional accusers who flourished under Tiberius.

1. **malefici** = maleficii, gen. after 'poenas'; cf. 'oti' for 'otii,' Verg. *Georg.* iv. 564 ; 'preti' for 'pretii,' etc.

2. **Calumniator** ..., construe, cum calumniator canis peteret ab ove panem, quem contenderet se commodasse, ...

FABLE XIX.

4. **ut deponeret**, '*to be allowed to place....*'

5. **reposcenti**, construe, dein admovit preces reposcenti locum '*to it when it asked for the place back again*'; 'reposcenti' is the other dog, the owner of the kennel.

E

7. ducere, *i.e.* secum ducere, '*lead her pups away with her, when they were stronger.*'

Fable XXI.

2. iocus, here the *thing joked at,* object of mirth ; cf. similar use of 'ludus' and 'ludibrium'; cf. Shak. *M. W.* iii. 3. 161, 'let me be your jest.'

5. fulmineis, favourite epithet in ancient and modern writers for boars' tusks, suggesting as much their swiftness and force as their gleaming whiteness.

10. fortes ... insultare mihi, acc. and inf. after 'indigne tuli,' which = 'indignatus sum.'

Fable XXII.

5. supplici, usually taken as dat. from 'supplex' = 'tibi supplici,' '*to you a suppliant*'; L. Müller, however, prefers it as gen. from 'supplicium,' cf. 'malefici,' i. 17. 1, in which case 'veniam supplici' = '*pardon from punishment.*'

7. rosuri, *sc.* mures '*at which the mice would nibble*' ; **simul et ipsos,** *sc.* ut, '*and that you may ... the mice themselves.*'

11. quorum privata ..., a variation of the usual phrase, 'qui serviunt utilitati privatae' or 'suae,' '*who are serving their own private interests.*'

Fable XXIII.

1. Repente liberalis, '*a man who is unexpectedly generous....*'

Fable XXIV.

This fable is given by Hor. *Sat.* ii. 3. 312 foll., and referred to by Martial, x. 79.

8. quis, for the usual 'uter,' '*which of the two.*'

Fable XXV.

3. currentes, *i.e.* running along bank and making dashes at water, not standing still.

4. **cŏrcŏdĭlis**, usual poetical form, made by 'metathesis' (or *transposition* of letters) from crŏcŏdīlus, κροκόδειλος, in order to lengthen the first syllable for metrical reasons.

6. **quamlibet**, either adv. or pron., from quilibet, *sc.* aquam, '*lap up as much as you like at your leisure.*'

This story about dogs and Nile is told in Pliny, *Nat. Hist.* viii. 40, and other ancient writers and became proverbial. Hence the story told by Macrobius—*Saturn,* i. 2.—when they asked what Antony was doing after his flight from Mutina, one of his friends said, "quod canis in Aegypto: bibit et fugit."

FABLE XXVI.

1. **nulli**, rarely used for 'nemini,' but 'nullius' and 'nullo' or 'nulla' are regularly used for gen. and abl.

7. **intrito cibo**, a common country dish made of crumbled bread, soaked in milk or curd, flavoured with cheese, garlic, oil, vinegar, etc., called also 'mŏrētum' (from 'mordeo,' *bite*), or 'alliātum' (from 'allium,' *garlic*).

11. **peregrinam**, because a bird of passage.

12. **sua exempla**, the example he himself sets, *i.e.* you must not mind being treated by others as you have treated them.

FABLE XXVII.

2. **et qui** = et eis qui, '*and to those who ....*'

3. **thesaurum**, numerous references in ancient writers, as well as the discoveries of modern archaeologists and diggers, prove how common was the practice of burying gold and silver ornaments, vessels and coins with the dead.

4. **Manes deos**, see *Class. Dict.* Manes is the name by which the Romans designated the souls of the departed; but as it is a natural tendency to consider the souls of departed friends as blessed spirits, the Manes were regarded as gods and worshipped with divine honours.

6. **Religio** personified; cf. Verg. *Aen.* iii. 362, "omnis cursum mihi prospera dixit Religio...."

8. **quem**, governed by 'super.'

Fable XXVIII.

1. **Quamvis ...,** '*men in however high a station ought to fear the humble, because revenge is easy to quick-witted cunning,*' lit. '*cunning which is quick to learn.*'

4. **escam,** '*as food.*'

10. **hosti ...,** either (1) lit. '*preparing grief for her foe by the loss of her offspring*' (sanguinis); 'miscens dolorem,' metaphor from mixing wine or a drink of any sort; cf. phrases 'miscere bella,' 'mala,' 'seditiones,' etc. ; 'damno,' abl. of means ; 'sanguinis'=eagle's brood ; or (2) '*mingling her foe's grief with the loss of her own offspring,*' i.e. killing her own litter as well as eagle's brood ; 'sanguinis' then=fox's own cubs. This would naturally require 'hostis.'

Fable XXX.

1. **laborant,** cf. Horace, *Ep.* i. 2. 14, "Quicquid delirant reges, plectuntur Achivi."

7. **statio.** Cf. Verg. *Georg.* iv. 8, "principio sedes apibus statioque petendae."

8. **regno,** so Verg., of conquered bull, *Georg.* iii. 228, "regnis excessit avitis."

Fable XXXI.

2. **auxilia dum requirit,** but the doves did not ask the kite for aid against another foe, and therefore the fable is pointless, as Jacobs and others have pointed out.

9. **praestem,** subj. after 'qui' final, '*to render you ....*'

BOOK II.

Prologue.

1. **Exemplis ...,** a difficult and much disputed passage. '*Aesop's style* (or the style of writing which Aesop used) *is confined to* (lit. by) *examples* (i.e. fictitious stories), *nor is any other object sought by fables than that men's mistakes should*

be corrected, and that careful search (into the meaning of the
fable) *should be encouraged* (lit. make itself more keen).
*Whatever, therefore, be the entertainment in the story, pro-
vided it charms the ear and serves its purpose, it wins praise
by that mere fact* (re) *not because of the author's name.'* I will
do my best to keep to Aesop's principles, but if I, for variety's
sake, introduce anything besides 'fables' do not be offended,
provided that I repay your kindness by brevity.

At beginning of Book I. Prol. 1. 2. Phaedrus had professed
to merely polish the material found by Aesop. But in this
and later books he introduces stories of real and even con-
temporary life (*e.g.* Fable V. below). These prefatory remarks
are a defence against hostile criticism. 'Aesop is still my
model,' he says; 'our objects are the same; it matters not
whether the stories be true or false provided they profit and
please our audience.'

1. **Exemplis**, 'exempla'=fabulae fictae, as often in Phaedrus,
cf. i. 3. 3; ii. 1. 11; iv. 3. 6.

4. **industria** = industry shown in trying to find out the
meaning and lesson of the fable.

7. **re**, refers to the previous line; '*by the mere fact*' of
charming the ear and serving its purpose of instructing.

8. **senis** = Aesop, a common title of respect for sages and
teachers. Cf. iii. 19. 11.

11. **bonas in partes**, for constr. cf. iii. 8. 8 note, "accipiens
cuncta in contumeliam"; and for phrase, Cic. *ad Att.* xi. 7.
"quod rogas, ut in bonam partem accipiam, ..."

Fable I.

2. **praedator** = '*hunter*.' Cf. Ovid. *Met.* xii. 306, "Abas
praedator aprorum."

9. **tergore**, used of the whole carcase, the '*meat*,' not the
back only. Cf. Verg. *Aen.* i. 211, "tergora deripiunt costis."

Fable II.

2. **ament, amentur**, '*let them love them, or be loved by them*'
= 'sive ament, sive amentur.'

8. **putarèt**, subj. after 'qui' concessive, '*though he thought....*'
fingi, often used of trimming or dressing hair, cf. Verg.
Aen. iv. 148, "mollique fluentem Fronde premit crinem
fingens."

FABLE III.

3. **remedium**, no parallels are quoted for this superstition,
but cf. the ancient 'hair of the same dog' superstition, viz.,
that the burnt hair of a dog is an antidote to its bite.

FABLE IV.

1. **in sublimi quercu**, '*on the top of an oak,*' usually 'in
summa quercu.'

2. **in media**, *sc.* quercu; so **ad imam**, next line, *sc.* quercum.

8. **quod ...**, a slightly irregular construction. Phaedrus
begins, '*for the fact that you see the treacherous pig daily
rooting up the earth,*' and then instead of continuing, 'is a
proof that it wishes,' he says, '*he wishes to ....*'

18. **suspenso pede**, so Ter. *Phormio*, v. 5. 28, "suspenso
gradu placide ire perrexi."

24. **praebuĕrunt**, note quantity; in perfect 3rd plur. the *e*
of -erunt is occasionally short, but of -ere always long.
For -ĕrunt cf. iii. *Epil.* 24; iv. 16. 2; iv. 20. 16. So Hor.
Epod. ix. 17, 'vertĕrunt.'

25. **Quantum ...**, construe, stulta credulitas potest habere
documentum ('*can have this as a proof,*' or '*can herein have
a proof*') quantum mali bilinguis homo saepe concinnet.
bilinguis = '*double-tongued,*' speaking one thing and meaning
another, cf. Verg. *Aen.* i. 665, "Tyriosque bilingues,"
which Servius explains as 'fallaces'; and among other
parallels in Plaut. cf. *Pers.* ii. iv. 28, "tamquam proserpens
bestia, est bilinguis et scelestus."

FABLE V.

2. **occupata in otio**, an "oxymoron." Cf. Hor. *Ep.* i. 11.
28, "strenua nos exercet inertia."

8. **Misenensem villam**, this villa on 'the top of the hill' at
Cape Misenum in Campania was really built by C. Marius,

and after passing through the hands of Cornelia, purchased by Lucullus, who may have rebuilt it, hence ' posita Luculli manu.' For **Lucullus** see *Class. Dict.* Lucius Licinius Lucullus, born about 110 B.C., died 57 or 56 B.C., famous as the conqueror of Mithridates and for his luxurious tastes which the treasures he amassed in Asia enabled him to gratify. His gardens in the immediate suburbs of the city were laid out in a style of extraordinary splendour; but still more remarkable were his villas at Tusculum and in the neighbourhood of Neapolis (Naples). Pompeius in derision called him the Roman Xerxes. His banquets were fabulously magnificent, a single supper is said to have cost him 50,000 denarii (about £1700 in our silver, but the purchasing value of money being higher then, it really represents a much greater sum).

11. **alticinctis**, with his tunic tucked up so as to move about his work more quickly. Cf. the Biblical phrase, ' with his loins girded'; cf. Hor. *Sat.* ii. 6. 107, " velut succinctus cursitat hospes."

12. **Pelusio**, Pelusium, a town on the Delta of the Nile, famous for the fineness of its linen stuffs.

14. **domino**, Tiberius the Emperor.

18. **xystum**, see Smith's *Dict. of Antiq.* under Hortus. " We have a very full description of a Roman garden in a letter of the younger Pliny, in which he describes his Tuscan villa. (Pliny, *Epist.* v. 6.) In front of the *porticus* there was generally a *xystus*, or flat piece of ground, divided into flowerbeds of different shapes by borders of box. There were also such flower-beds in other parts of the garden. Sometimes they were raised so as to form terraces, and their sloping sides planted with evergreens or creepers. The most striking features of a Roman garden were lines of large trees, among which the plane appears to have been a great favourite, planted in regular order; alleys or walks (*ambulationes*) formed by closely clipped hedges of box, yew, cypress, and other evergreens; beds of acanthus, rows of fruit-trees, especially of vines, with statues, pyramids, fountains, and summer-houses (*diaetae*) .... Attached to the garden were places for exercise .... An ornamental garden was called *viridarium*, and the gardener *topiarius* or *viridarius* ...." The *viridia* of l. 14 are the green shrubs or plants.

22. **donationis gaudio**, subjective genitive, '*joy caused by the gift*'; see below ii. 8. 2 note.

23. **tanti maiestas ducis**, '*the mighty sovereign's majesty*'; 'majestas,' just as we talk of ' His Majesty ' ; grammatically the phrase is parallel to '**corvi stupor**' in i. 13. 12 ; see i. 3. 16 note.

25. **maioris**, gen. of price. **alapae**, in freeing a slave by the form called 'vindicta,' the master turned him round and struck him lightly; hence 'alapae' here equals 'your freedom.' Cf. our tap of the sword in conferring knighthood.

FABLE VI.

3. **vis et** ..., construe, quicquid vis et nequitia oppugnant (id) ruit, '*whatever ... assail, falls.*'

11. **scopulum**, governed by 'super.' That eagles do thus treat reptiles is a familiar fact of natural history. It recalls the story of the poet Aeschylus' death, at Gela in Sicily, 456 B.C. An eagle, mistaking the poet's bald head for a stone, let a tortoise fall on it, and so fulfilled the oracle which declared that he would die by a blow from heaven.

FABLE VII.

2. **fiscos**, see Vocab. and Smith's *Dict. of Antiq.* under Fiscus.

10. **spoliatus**, the plundered mule.

FABLE VIII.

2. **venatorum necem**, '*death inflicted by the hunters,*' subjective genitive, see ii. 5. 22, 'donationis gaudio.' Cf. Verg. *Aen.* xii. 5, "saucius venantum vulnere."

5. **hic**, adverb, ' *hereupon.*'

7. **cucurreris**, subj. after 'qui' causal.

11. **frondem**, for food. In many of the poorer parts of Europe, *e.g.* Norway, at the end of summer you may see the peasants stripping the trees of leaves to provide food in winter for their cattle.

15. **quietis**, with 'bubus,' *silent* because they had not betrayed him.

18. **ille**, the master.   **oculos centum**, description taken from Argus, the 100-eyed monster, guardian of Io, whose eyes, when he was killed by Hermes, were transplanted by Hera into the tail of her peacock.

24. **quantum est laboris**, we say '*what a labour it would be*'; cf. 'longum est,' '*it would be tedious.*'

28. **dominum videre** ..., cf. Aristotle, *Oeconomics*, "the eyes of the master fatten the horse."

EPILOGUE.

1. **ingenio**, '*to*' or '*in honour of* the genius of Aesop.'

2. **servum**, see Introd., p. xii.

3. **patere** ..., construe, ut cuncti scirent viam honoris patere, nec gloriam tribui generi sed virtuti.

5. **occuparat ... ne primus forem**, lit. '*had anticipated me to prevent me being first*'; cf. use of Gr. φθάνω.   **alter** = Aesopus.

6. **ne solus** ..., '*I endeavoured to prevent him being the only one (i.e.* only writer of fables), *which alone was left for me.*'

7. **invidia**, bad sense, Gr. φθόνος, '*envy.*'   **aemulatio**, good sense, ζῆλος, '*rivalry,*' '*emulation.*'

9. **opponat**, subj. after 'quos' consecutive.

10. **curam**, '*my work*': properly my fables written with care ; cf. Tac. *Ann.* iv. 11, "quorum in manus cura nostra venerit," and cf. 'studium' in l. 12 below.

17. **nec quicquam**, *sc.* 'qui' from previous 'quos,' '*and who can do nothing but find fault with their betters.*'

BOOK III.

PROLOGUE.

2. **Eutychus**, generally identified with a Eutychus who was a charioteer and great favourite of Caligula.   The Greek name suggests that he was a freedman.   He may have held some public office of a judicial nature (this Prologue and the Epilogue to Book III. speak of him as being immersed in public duties), which would explain the tone of Phaedrus' complaints and appeals, l. 41 foll., and Epilogue, l. 20 foll.

4. **tanti**, gen. of price, '*worth so much*,' cf. Ovid, *Heroid.* i. 4, "vix Priamus tanti totaque Troia fuit."

10. **nenias**, cf. iv. 2. 3; 'neniae,' Gr. *νηνίαι*, were properly rough songs chanted in honour of the dead at funerals to the sound of the flute, then used of any common or unpolished songs. Here used modestly by Phaedrus of his own fables.

14. **adsuetam**, scanned, 'adsŭētam,' cf. i. 2. 8. **vicem**, lit. the *turn* of duty after holiday and rest, hence *duty*, *work*; cf. Tac. *Ann.* iv. 8, "vestram meamque vicem explete," and Livy, i. 20, "ne sacra regiae vicis desererentur."

17. **Pierio**, Mons Pierius, sacred to the Muses, who are hence called Pierides; it was partly in Macedonia, partly in Thessaly; in line 20 Phaedrus says he was *almost* born in Greece, "paene in ipsa natus sim schola"; therefore he was born on the Macedonian or non-Greek side, see Introd., p. vii.

18. **Mnemosyne**, the mother of the nine Muses (fecunda novies) by Jupiter.

21. **habendi**, of '*having*' property, *i.e.* of being a rich man; cf. Gr. οἱ ἔχοντες=*the rich.* **eraserim**, metaphor from scratching out writing, cf. Horace, *Odes*, iii. 24. 51, "eradenda cupidinis pravi sunt elementa."

23. **fastidiose**, *i.e.* only after careful and fastidious examination, '*I find but jealous admission.*' **in coetum**, sc. Musarum, the *company* of the Muses.

27. **Sinon**, see Verg. *Aen.* ii. 77, "cuncta equidem tibi, rex, fuerit quodcumque fatebor Vera inquit …."

28. **regem** D., Priam, King of Troy. called Dardania, from Dardanus, the traditional founder of the Trojan kingdom.

34. **servitus** = servus, abstract for concrete; cf. i. 3. 16 note; he means Aesop, see Introd., p. xii.

38. **semita**, '*narrow path*'; 'viam,' '*broad road.*' '*I in my turn have made a road on his narrow path, and have invented more than he had left …,*' cf. Prol. iv. 12. For phrase cf. Martial, *Ep.* vii. 61., "et modo quae fuerat semita facta via est."

40. **deligens**, lit. '*choosing some to my hurt*,' *i.e.* 'which have afterwards brought trouble upon me'; because his enemies gave them a political turn and got him into trouble with Tiberius and Sejanus, see Introd., p. vii.

41. Seiano, abl. of comparison after 'alius,' '*another than Sejanus.*' **Aelius Seianus,** as commander of the Praetorian troops, became the close friend and confidant of Tiberius. For many years he practically governed Tiberius, and at last seems to have aimed at imperial power. He poisoned Drusus by the aid of Livia or Livilla, Drusus' wife, whom he promised to marry (23 A.D.), and obtained the banishment of several other members of the imperial family. At length Tiberius' suspicions were aroused, and Sejanus was suddenly arrested and executed, 31 A.D. See *Class. Dict.*

44. his remediis, *i.e.* by writing fables.

49. notare, '*brand*'; see i. 3. 11 note.

52. Phryx Aesopus, see Introd., p. xii. **Anacharsis,** see *Class. Dict.*, "A Scythian of princely rank, who left his native country to travel in pursuit of knowledge and came to Athens about B.C. 594. He became acquainted with Solon, and by his talents and acute observations he excited general admiration. The fame of his wisdom was such that he was even reckoned by some among the seven sages. He was killed by his brother Saulius on his return to his native country."

54. propior, nearer by birth (see line 17 above) to literary Greece than Aesop who was born in Phrygia in Asia Minor, and Anacharsis who was born in Scythia.

57. Linus, see *Class. Dict.* "The personification of a dirge or lamentation, and therefore described as a son of Apollo by a Muse (Calliope) .... Both Argos and Thebes claimed the honour of his birth ...." **Orpheus,** see *Class. Dict.* A mythical personage, regarded by the Greeks as the most celebrated of the early poets before Homer. According to the common story he was the son of Oeagrus and the Muse Calliope. Apollo gave him the lyre, and instructed by the Muses he became so skilled in its use that he enchanted not only the wild beasts but even the trees and rocks on Olympus. He went on the famous Argonautic expedition after the golden fleece, and lulled the Colchian dragon to sleep. On his return he lived for a while in a cave in Thrace, and employed himself in civilizing the wild inhabitants. His wife Eurydice died from the bite of a serpent. Orpheus followed her to Hades, and by the charm of his playing obtained permission for her to return to earth, on condition that he should not look back at her till they had reached the upper world. He looked

round to see if she were really following, and saw her snatched
away from him for ever. His grief for the loss of Eurydice
led him to treat the Thracian women with contempt. In
revenge they tore him to pieces whilst in the frenzy of their
Bacchanalian orgies.

FABLE I.

2. **F. faece**, abl. of cause.

5. **suavis anima**, better (1) '*oh sweet fragrance*' than (2)
'*dear soul*,' as lovers often address their loved ones; but
either is possible.

7. **Hoc quo ...,** '*anyone who knows me will be able to tell the
application of this fable.*' Intentionally ambiguous and therefore no wonder many explanations have been given, *e.g.* (1)
'Those who like this work of my old age will understand what
far better poetry I might have produced when younger'; (2)
'The Ass = Tiberius, who in old age has to content himself
with the dregs of his former pleasures'; (3) 'he who likes the
fables of me, a mere imitator of Aesop, can guess how good
were Aesop's original ones.'

FABLE II.

Often referred to Tiberius in exile at Rhodes, and on his
return venting his wrath on those who had slighted him.

5. **periturae**, *sc.* 'pantherae,' better gen. after 'miseriti'
than dat. after 'misere'; 'p. quippe,' '*since it was doomed to
perish*,' the 'quippe' giving a causal force, see i. 28. 7, iii. 8. 8.

16. **damnum**. *i.e.* the '*loss*' of their cattle.

FABLE IV.

1. **Pendere ...,** a dead monkey hanging up for sale in
a butcher's shop for food. This is the natural meaning; but
monkeys are never mentioned as eaten by the Romans, and
so some have explained it of a live monkey simply exposed
for sale or hanging by a chain; or again of a fish called
πίθηκος, '*monkey fish*'. found in the Atlantic; but there is
no sufficient proof of the existence of such a fish.

4. **caput ... sapor,** the somewhat far-fetched joke seems to lie in the double meaning of both 'caput' and 'sapor'; 'caput,' either '*man's head*' or '*monkey's head*'; 'sapor,' either '*flavour*' or '*wit*.'

Fable V.

3. **tanto melior,** *sc.* es ; equivalent to our 'good !' or 'bravo !'

8. **persuasus,** 'persuadeo' with acc. of person is scarcely classical, and the personal use of pass. (as opposed to impers.) is very rare till later Latin, the rule being that verbs which govern a dat. in act. are used impersonally in the pass ; but see i. 8. 7 note.

Fable VI.

2. **non vis,** '*wont you go on?*' common in threats, or rebukes.

3. **vide,** note scansion 'vĭdĕ,' so in Plaut. *Ps.* i. 1. 46 ; cf. 'căvĕ' from 'caveo,' frequently in Plaut.

Fable VII.

5. **fecisti tantum corporis,** our '*have made so much flesh*' ; for 'corpus'='*flesh*,' cf. Ovid, *Am.* i. 6. 6, "Aptaque subducto corpore membra dedit." For this phrase cf. *Celsus de Medic.* vii. 3, "cibi potionesque corpori faciendo aptae" ; no exact parallel is quoted from earlier writers.

10. **a furibus ...,** construe, et (ut) tuearis noctu domum a furibus.

16. **a catena,** the use of the prep. instead of the simple abl. of instrument is poetical.

27. **liber ... ut,** '*on the condition of not being my own master.*'

Fable VIII.

3. **idem,** often used idiomatically in Lat. where we prefer an adv., '*and also.*'

4. **cathedra,** see *Dict. of Antiq.* for illustration : generally applied to a softly upholstered chair with a back, used by

women. **ut positum fuit,** lit. '*as it had been placed there,*' *i.e.* '*which happened to be lying there.*'

8. **accipiens ... in contumeliam,** see above, ii. Prol. 11 note, cf. Ter. *Adelph.* iv. 3. 15, "ad contumeliam omnia accipiunt." For **quippe,** giving causal force to participle, '*since she ...,*' cf. iii. 2. 5, i. 28. 7.

9. **laesura invicem,** '*to mortify him in her turn,*' *i.e.* apparently her brother ; but the object of 'laesura' might be her father.

11. **tetigerit,** subj. in virtual oratio obliqua, '*because* (as she said) *he ....*'

FABLE IX.

4. **cedo invidiae,** '*submit to envy,*' so "cedere fortunae," Caesar, *Bell. Gall.* vii. 89 ; 'cedere tempori,' etc.

FABLE XII.

Compare our 'casting pearls before swine.'

4. **hoc,** acc. object of 'vidisset,' '*this thing,*' *i.e.* '*you here.*'

6. **ego quod ...,** '*the fact that I have found you, I to whom food is much more precious, can neither profit you nor me in any way.*' The subj. of 'potest' is the clause 'quod ego te inveni.'

FABLE XIII.

This fable is, by some, supposed to be aimed at Phaedrus' imitators.

2. **hos,** *i.e.* fucos. **inertes,** cf. Vergil's "ignavum fucos pecus," '*the drones a lazy tribe,*' *Georg.* iv. 168.

8. **religio** = religio iurisiurandi, '*scrupulousness in the fulfilment of my oath,*' *i.e.* the oath to judge impartially. Cf. Cic. *Font.* 9. 20, "religione iurisiurandi ac metu deorum in testimoniis dicendis commoveri."

14. **possit,** *sc.* facere favos.

FABLE XIV.

Said to have been written by Phaedrus to justify the childish amusements of his late patron Augustus, of whom Suetonius (c. 83) writes, "animi laxandi causa modo piscabatur hamo, modo talis, aut ocellatis nucibusque ludebat cum pueris."

1, 2. **ludentem** ... **nucibus**, common boy's game, though how played we are not told ; cf. Hor. *Sat.* ii. 3. 171.

7. **torquet**, a common word for worrying over a difficult problem or subject.

9. **sophus**, '*the sage*,' Gr. σοφός, a '*learned man*,' especially applied to the professed philosophers or sophists.

10. **arcum**, cf. Hor. *Odes*, ii. 10. 20, "neque semper arcum tendit Apollo." All work and no play makes Jack a dull boy.

Fable XV.

Referred by commentators to mothers who either abandon their children or put them out to nurse.

9. **potior**, see iii. 12. 6, '*dearer*,' or perhaps ' *has a stronger claim on you*.'

10. **niger an albus**, perhaps a special application, because white lambs were esteemed more highly, black sent to the butcher. But the phrase, ' albus an ater sis nescio,' ' *I don't know whether you are black or white*,' seems to be proverbial for '*I know nothing about you*'; cf. Cic. *Phil.* ii. 16, etc.

18. **necessitas**, '*the order*' or '*laws of nature*,' called by Cicero "necessitas naturae" (Cic. *de Fato*, c. 30), to which the lamb owed its birth.

20. **legibus** = necessitas of l. 18, '*the laws of nature*.'

Fable XVI.

3. **noctuae**, dat. incommodi after 'acerbum.'

8. **accensa**, '*excited*,' *i.e.* 'ad clamandum.'

12. **sonare** ..., construe, quos putas citharam Apollinis sonare, '*sound like*' or '*ring with the sound of A.'s lyre*.' For the acc. cf. Verg. *Aen.* i. 328, "nec vox hominem sonat," '*rings with no mortal sound*.' Burmann points out that at the feasts of the gods, when the first course was removed and nectar was set on the table, it was the duty of Apollo and the Muses to play to the drinking gods.

13. **Pallas** ... **donavit**, because the owl was the sacred bird of Pallas Athene.

FABLE XVII.

3. **myrtus** ..., cf. Verg. *Ecl.* vii. 61, 62, " Populus Alcidae gratissima, vitis Iaccho, Formosae myrtus Veneri, sua laurea Phoebo."

4. **Cўbēbe**, parallel form of 'Cўbĕle,' always used by Phaedrus for sake of rhythm ; so in Gr. Κυβήβη and Κυβέλη.

7. **honorem** ..., '*lest we should seem to sell the honour*' (*i.e.* of choosing them as our special trees) '*for their fruit.*'

8. **me hercules**, is properly a man's oath, not a woman's ; see *Aul. Gell.* xi. c. 6.   **narrabit** ..., '*any one shall say what he likes.*'

10. **sator**, cf. Verg. *Aen.* i. 254, "Olli subridens hominum sator atque deorum."

11. **dicere**, probably present passive 'dicĕre,' not future 'dicēre.'

· FABLE XVIII.

1. **Pavo**, sacred to Juno.

2. **tribuerit**, subj. in virtual oratio obl., '*because* (as it said),... .'

3. **illum esse** ..., acc. and inf. after verb of saying implied in 'indigne ferens,' line 1.

9. **quo mi ... mutam speciem**, *sc.* dedisti, '*wherefore has thou given me* (mi=mihi)... .' Cf. Hor. *Ep.* i. 5. 12, "quo mihi fortunam, si non conceditur uti ?"

10. **partes**, metaphor from the stage, the *part* one has to play, and so duty, office, function, a common sense of 'partes' in the plural.

12. **laeva cornici omina**, a crow (cornix) on the left was a lucky omen, on the right unlucky ; a raven (corvus) lucky on right, unlucky on left. Cf. Cic. *Div.* 1. 39, "quid habet augur cur a dextra corvus, a sinistra cornix faciat ratum."

FABLE XIX.

3. **ignem quaerens**, it was a serious business to light a fire before the days of matches, and even of flint and steel and

tinder box. To refuse a request for a light was regarded as inhuman. Cf. Plaut. *Trin.* iii. 2. 53, "datur ignis, tametsi ab inimicis petas."

4. **accenderet,** subj. after 'ubi' consecutive, '*a place to light ....*'

9. **hominem,** one worthy of the name of man ; cf. the famous story of Diogenes the Cynic. Diog. Laert. vi. 41. (ed. Didot) λύχνον μεθ' ἡμέραν ἅψας περιῄει λέγων, ἄνθρωπον ζητῶ.

11. **seni,** the regular title of respect for Aesop in Phaedrus ; cf. ii. Prol. 8.

EPILOGUE.

3. **distringit,** ... , '*much business of different sorts engrosses.*'

21. **proclivis,** '*your compassion is ready, even without my asking for it* (ultro).'

24. **partes,** see iii. 18. 10 note. **fuĕrunt,** for ĕ short see ii. 4. 24 note.

26. **religio,** see iii. 13. 8 note.

34. **palam,** etc., from the Telephus of Ennius. See Introd., p. vii.

BOOK IV.

PROLOGUE.

In MSS. this is wrongly placed after iv. 26., *i.e.* at beginning of Bk. V. That it ought to come at beginning of Bk. IV. is proved by line 14.

2. **in hoc** = ideo, '*for this reason,*' explained by the next words ' ut ... satis.'

4. **talis tituli,** the title of Fabulist.

7. **sua cuique ...** , '*Since each man has his own opinions ana characteristics.*

10. **Particulo,** nothing is known about him.

11. **Aesopias, non Aesopi,** *i.e.* written in the style of Aesop, not copied or taken from Aesop ; explained more fully in next two lines. Note quantity, Aesopias.

F

18. **vestras in chartas** ..., '*transfer my words to your pages* ...'; this may mean, (1) constantly quote my lines in your writings, or (2) quote whole fables, or (3) write them in your 'common-place' books; or, which is less probable, (4) take down my poems when I recite them to circles of friends.

FABLE I.

1. **natus est infelix**, explained as '*malo astro natus*,' '*born under an unlucky star*,' for according to astrologers a man's fate was determined by the position of the stars at the hour of his birth; cf. iv. 20. 15, '**dis iratis natus**.'

4. **Cÿbēbe**, see above, iii. 17. 4 note.

8. **delicio**, '*what they had done with their pet*'; delicio, abl., cf. Ter., *Andria*, iii. 614, "nec quid me nunc faciam scio," '*I don't know what to do with myself*'; and *Id*. iv. 709, "quid me fiet," '*what will be done with me?*'

FABLE II.

This fable is generally told of the cat and mice.

1. **Ioculare tibi videtur**, *i.e.* the fable I have just told you, viz., Fable I.

3. **nenias**, see iii. Prol. 10 note.

5. **ea ... quae videntur**, '*that which they seem*,' *i.e.* '*what they seem to be*.'

6. **rara mens**, since 'rara' by position is opposed to 'multos,' tr. '*rarely does the mind*' or '*but few minds*,' cf. Ovid, *A. A.* iii. 261, "rara tamen facies menda caret"; and Verg. *Aen.* i. 118, "apparent rari nantes." Otherwise 'rara' might be taken '*uncommon*,' '*exquisite*,' cf. Ovid, *Met.* xiv. 337, "rara quidem facie sed rarior arte canendi."

17. **laqueos**, '*springes*' of hair or string. **muscipula**, '*traps*.'

19. **sic valeas ... ut farina es**, a simple passage of which much unnecessary difficulty has been made. 'Vale' or 'valeas' is the usual expression in leavetaking, 'adieu' or 'farewell': here it has the full force, '*may you fare well*'; sic ... ut, '*on this condition ... that*,' *i.e.* '*only ... if*.' '*Farewell, if you are a meal sack, who lie there*': but you are not, and therefore 'fare ill.'

FABLE III.

1. **famē**, note long ē, fifth decl. form ; cf. the double forms 'plebes' and 'plebs.'

6. **adscribere**, a common metaphor from book-keeping.

FABLE IV.

This fable is given in full by Hor. *Ep.* x. 34-8.

1. **Equus ...**, construe, aper, dum volutat sese, turbavit vadum, quo equus solitus fuerat sedare sitim.

3. **sonipes**, the use of a grand word to give dignity, cf. i. 1. 6 note, 'laniger': i. 6. 6, 'stagni incola'; for 'sonipes' see Verg. *Aen.* iv. 135 ; ix. 600.

4. **dorso**, properly abl. of instrument.

13. **potius**, *sc.* esse, '*that it is preferable to be ... .*'

FABLE VI.

2. **in tabernis**, probably here '*taverns*'; some however take it of booksellers' shops. So Hor. mentions rude sketches of popular gladiators painted or chalked on the walls, Hor. *Sat.* ii. 7. 98, "proelia rubrica picta aut carbone," '*painted with red chalk or charcoal.*'

4. **recepti**, see Vocab. in middle sense; the participle is concessive '*although they ... .*'

5. **capitibus cornua**, a common ornament of helmets among barbarous tribes, cf. *Herod.* vii. 76, etc.

9, 10. **immolatos ... tartareo specu**, grandiloquent and mock heroic.

13. **praesidio**, abl. of instrument after 'latet,' because it = 'are protected by': cf. Verg. "cadet hostia dextrâ," and Cic. "iacent suis testibus," '*are overthrown by their own witnesses*' (Walpole).

FABLE VII.

6-16. **Vtinam ... manus**, an imitation of Ennius' paraphrase of Euripides' *Medea.* For story see *Class. Dict.* under *Medea.* Medea, daughter of Acetes king of Colchis : celebrated for her skill in magic. When Jason came to Colchis in quest of the golden fleece, she fell in love with him and helped him to win it. She then fled with him to Greece, and, when followed by her father, cut up her brother Absyrtus and strewed his limbs on the way to delay the pursuers. On returning to Iolchos Jason found that his father Aeson had been killed by Pelias his half-brother. To punish Pelias, Medea persuaded the daughters of Pelias to cut their father up and boil the pieces, in order to restore him to youth and vigour, as she had shown them that she could change a ram into a lamb. For this crime she and Jason were expelled from Iolchos and went to Corinth. In time Jason grew weary of Medea and married the daughter of Creon, king of Corinth. In revenge Medea murdered the two children whom she had borne to Jason, and destroyed the young wife by a poisoned garment. She then fled in a chariot drawn by winged dragons.

15. **illic**, in Colchis.

16. **hic**, in Thessaly.

17. **Quid tibi videtur**, *i.e.* 'what do you think of this specimen of Euripides tragic style?'

18. **vetustior**, so says Thucydides, i. 4.

21. **lector Cato**, '*you reader, stern and censorious as Cato,*' who was proverbial for his censoriousness. See *Class. Dict.* M. Porcius Cato, surnamed Censor or Censorinus, B.C. 234-149; a strong opponent of the growing luxury and refinement of his age, and the influence of Greek literature and manners: Censor in 184, when he strove most earnestly but unsuccessfully to stem the tide of culture.

Fable VIII.

4. **temptaret, si**, '*was trying to see if...,*' so Caesar, *Bell. Gall.* ii. 9, "hanc si nostri transirent, hostes exspectabant."

Fable IX.

3. **inscia**, like 'imprudens' in iii. 2. 2.

10. **barbatus**, cf. 'laniger,' i. 1. 6 note.

FABLE X.

For this fable cf. *Catul.* xxii. 21, " sed non videmus manticae quod in tergo est," '*but we do not see that part of the wallet which is behind us*' : and Hor. *Sat.* ii. 3. 299 ; Pers. iv. 24.

FABLE XI.

2. **ipsum,** Jupiter himself, *i.e.* his temple.

4. **Religio,** '*the Holiness,*' *i.e.* the statue or altar of Jupiter, which is Jupiter himself.

12. **itaque hodie,** no other reference in ancient writers to this rule.

19. **fatorum dicto tempore,** lit. '*at the stated time of the fates*' = '*at the time appointed by the fates.*' For 'dicto,' cf. iv. 25. 19, 'hora dicta.'

20. **interdicit…,** construe, interdicit ne bonus consociet usum ullius rei cum maletico ; **consociet usum,** lit. '*unite the enjoyment of anything*' = '*join in using anything.*'

FABLE XII.

3. **Caelo receptus … Hercules,** cf. Hor. *Odes,* iii. 3. 9-10.

5. **Pluto,** abl. of Plutus.

6. **pater** = Jupiter.

FABLES XIII. AND XIV.

The MSS. are here hopelessly corrupt and deficient.

FABLE XVI.

2. **coepĕrunt,** note quantity of e, see ii. 4. 24 note.

3. **feminae,** nominative.

5. **usurpare vestri ornatum muneris,** lit. '*to appropriate the decoration of your gift,*' *i.e.* '*the adornment which has been given to you,*' viz., the beard given to you by the gods.

FABLE XVII.

2. **finxit**, *sc.* hanc fabulam, '*made up this story.*'
6. **tuta**, agreeing with subject 'navis,' in l. 3.
9. **parce**, adverb.

FABLE XIX.

5. **hanc**, *sc.* colubram; construe, cum alia rogaret hanc (*asked it*), causam facinoris (*the reason for its cruel deed*); 'hanc' and 'causam' double acc. after 'rogaret.'
6. **improbis**, the commentators point out that the snake 'gives itself away' by classing itself among the 'improbi.'

FABLE XX.

10. **careas somno**, the sleepless dragon of legend.
11. **nullum**, *sc.* praemium ; '*no reward, but this (duty) has been ....*'
15. **dis iratis natus**, proverbial expression for a luckless man, our 'born under an unlucky star,' cf. Hor. *Sat.* ii. 3. 8 ; see iv. 1. 1 note.
16. **abiĕrunt**, for short ĕ see ii. 4. 24 note.
26. **Libitina**, the goddess of funerals, here = 'libitinarii,' the undertakers.   **de tuo**, cf. Martial, *Ep.* vii. 46. 4. " Et tua de nostro, Prisce, Thalia tacet," '*and your muse, Priscus, is silent at our expense.*'

FABLE XXI.

4. **Aesopi**, *sc.* esse, '*that it is Aesop's.*' **adriserit**, '*if anything finds less favour in its eyes*' ; cf. Hor. *Sat.* i. 10. 89, "quibus haec, sunt qualiacumque, Arridere velim," '*in whose eyes I should wish that these should find favour, be they what they may.*'
5. **quovis pignore**, cf. *Catull.* xliv. 4, "quovis Sabinum pignore esse contendunt," '*are ready to stake anything to prove you are Sabine.*'
8. **ille**, Aesop.

Fable XXII.

2. Simonides, see *Class. Dict.* Simonides of Ceos, one of the most celebrated lyric poets of Greece, born at Iulis, in Ceos, 556 B.C. From Ceos he went to Athens, thence to Thessaly, and again to Athens. In 489 he conquered Aeschylus in the contest for the prize offered by the Athenians for an elegy on the warriors who fell at Marathon. Ten years later he composed the epigram inscribed on the tomb of the Spartans who fell at Thermopylae. When about 80 he was invited to Syracuse by Hiero, at whose court he lived till his death in 467. Fragments only of his poems have come down to us.

5. mercede accepta, abl. absol., '*for a fee*,' not necessarily '*when he had received his fee*,' though Simonides is said to have been notorious for his avarice. Pindar and other lyric poets used to write triumphal odes for winners in the great public games of Greece.

13. Simonide, Greek vocative; cf. 'hercle,' i. 1. 12.

14. mecum mea sunt cuncta, this saying is generally attributed to Bias, one of the seven sages of Greece (about B.C. 550). His native city was attacked by enemies, and he had to flee: the other citizens tried to carry off some of their goods, but he took nothing. When they asked him to try to save something he said, "I am doing so; for I carry all my wealth about me: omnia mea mecum porto" (*Val. Max.* vii. 2).

22. sermone ab ipso ..., construe, cupidissime recepit ad se (Simonidem) cognitum ab ipso sermone. For 'ab' cf. Verg. *Aen.* ii. 65, "crimine ab uno disce omnes."

24. tabulam, picture of the shipwreck carried round to excite compassion and extract alms. Cf. Juv. *Sat.* xiv. 301, "mersa rate naufragus assem Dum rogat et picta se tempestate tuetur"; Pers. i. 89-90, "cum fracta te in trabe pictum Ex umero portes."

Fable XXIII.

1. parturibat, for 'parturiebat'; so 'audibam,' Ovid, *Ep.* xiv. 36; 'lenibat,' Verg. *Aen.* vi. 468, etc.

Fable XXIV.

4. **conferre.** construe, tu potes conferre te nostris laudibus, '*compare yourself to our praises,*' *i.e.* compare the esteem in which you are held with the praise given to us.

12. **qui invisus est,** *sc.* 'illi' before the 'qui.'

Fable XXV.

2. **superius,** viz. in Fable xxii.; a rare word in this sense.

9. **gemina Ledae pignera,** Leda's sons, Castor and Pollux, famous for skill in boxing.

13. **duae,** *sc.* partes ; lit. '*of whom there are ...,*' *i.e* '*who have two-thirds of the praise.*'

15. **ad cenam mihi promitte,** regular form of invitation, *sc.* '*te venturum.*'

16. **es ... mihi,** '*you are in my eyes.*'

19. **recubuit,** the guests reclined, not sat, at table.

22. **sparsi pulvere,** the traditional way of representing them when appearing to encourage the Romans in battle.

23. **corpora,** in apposition with 'iuvenes,' '*... their bodies above ....*'

31. **ordo,** '*complete version.*' Cf. Tac. *Ann.* iv. 69, "ordinem fraudis ... narravere"; Suet. *Claud.* 37, "ordinem rei gestae perferre ad senatum."

Epilogue.

In the MSS. this is wrongly placed after V. 5.

BOOK V.

3. **auctoritatis,** gen. after 'gratiâ,' '*for the sake of ....*'

6. **Praxiteles, Myron, Zeuxis,** see *Class. Dict.* **Praxiteles,** a famous Athenian sculptor who lived about 364 B.C. Nothing is known of his personal history. His two chief works were a statue of Aphrodite at Cnidos and of Eros at Thespiae. **Myron,** a sculptor and engraver, born about 480 B.C. in Boeotia.

but called an Athenian because his birthplace Eleutherae had
been admitted to the Athenian franchise. His chief works
were the *Discobulus*, of which a probable copy is in the British
Museum, and his Cow. Zeuxis, Greek painter, flourished
about 424-400 B.C., a native of Heraclea. His most famous
picture was one of Helen, painted for the temple of Juno at
Croton.

FABLE I.

1. **Demetrius,** see *Class. Dict.* Demetrius, called Phalereus
from the Attic deme of Phalerus in which he was born about
345 B.C. His parents were poor, but he rose to a high position
by his talents. In 317 the government of Athens was en-
trusted to him by Cassander (son of Antipater, to whom, after
the death of Alexander the Great, fell the Macedonian and
Greek part of Alexander's dominions). He performed the
duty so well for 10 years that the Athenians conferred every
kind of honour upon him. On the approach of Demetrius
Poliorcetes to attack Athens, 307, he fled to Alexandria, and
ended his days in Egypt.

5. **illam osculantur manum,** cf. Pope, *Essay on Man,* "And
licks the hand just raised to shed his blood."

8. **ne defuisse,** subject of 'noceat'; after 'noceat' *sc.* 'sibi,'
lit. *'lest to have been away should injure them.'*

9. **Menander.** see *Class. Dict.* Menander, the most distinguished poet of the 'New Comedy,' born 342 B.C. at Athens,
died 291 B.C. His poems were imitated by the Romans, and
adapted by Terence.

13. **gressu delicato,** cf. i. *Samuel,* xv. 32, "Agag came
unto him delicately."

18. This line is missing in the MSS., and variously supplied
by editors.

FABLE II.

1-2. These lines are not in the old MSS.; supplied from the
Perottine MS. See Introd., p. x.

6. **cĕdŏ ... illum,** 'cĕdŏ,' old imperat. form, see Vocab., *'give
me the fellow'*; for the acc. with 'cedo,' cf. Ter. *Hec.* iv. 4.
86, "puerum, Philippe, mihi cedo, ego alam." **curabo**

sentiat = curabo ut sentiat, '*I'll make him feel,*' cf. 'vellem adinvisses,' l. 8 below.

9. **vera,** *sc.* esse verba tua, '*if I had thought they were true.*'

10. **conde ferrum et linguam,** a zeugma ; '*hold your sword and tongue.*'

14. **adsignari,** metaphor from book-keeping, see 'adscribere' above, iv. 3. 6.

15. **dubiā,** *sc.* re, a euphemism for '*misfortune*'; the plural in this sense is more common.

Fable III.

7. **mentem,** '*intention,*' so in Eng., 'I have a *mind* to do so and so.'

Fable IV.

1. **verrem,** offered to Hercules because of his victory over the Erymanthine boar.

2. **votum debebat,** to 'owe a vow' is to have made one and not yet paid it ; a person in this position was called 'voti reus,' cf. Verg. *Aen.* v. 237.

10. **qui,** antecedent is 'eos' understood as object of 'num-cremus,' '*let us count those who ....*'

12. **paucis ... bono,** for double dative see i. 11. 2 note, '*notis est derisui.*'

Fable V.

1. **favore,** abl. of cause.

2. **pro iudicio ... stant erroris sui,** '*stand up for their erroneous judgment*'; '*pro,*' '*in defence of*' ; 'stant pro iud.,' military metaphor ; 'iudicio erroris' evidently = 'erranti' or ' falso iudicio,' cf. l. 33, 'vocem naturae' = 'natural voice'; no parallels are quoted for this singular expression.

6. **quam quisque ...,** construe, ut quisque ostenderet novi-tatem quam posset (ostendere); for novitas, used like our '*novelty*' for something new, cf. Horace, *A. P.* 223, "illece-bris erat et grata novitate morandus spectator."

12. **turbam deficiunt loca,** the dat. after 'deficiunt' is more common, but acc. quite classical, cf. Horace, *Sat.* ii. 1. 13, "cupidum, pater optime, vires deficiunt"; *Id.* 3. 153, etc.

17. **sua,** *sc.* voce.

18. **verum,** *sc.* porcellum, '*a real pig.*'

19. **excuti,** *sc.* pallium, '*order his cloak to be searched,*' lit. '*shaken out*'; a common phrase for searching thieves, etc.

31. **in priore,** *sc.* homine, '*in the case of the former one.*'

32. **vero,** dative, *sc.* porcello, '*pulls the real pig's ear.*'

33. **vocem naturae,** '*natural voice*'; see above, note on l. 2, 'iudicio erroris.'

35. **cogit,** '*tries* to compel;' by shouts and hissing they try to force the attendants to turn out the rustic.

FABLE VI.

2. **defectus pilis,** cf. *Tibul.* ii. v. 75, "solem defectum lumine vidit"; contrast different use in i. 21. 3, "defectus annis."

3. **in commune,** *sc.* confer, '*make common, divide*'; transl. '*shares in ...*'; a common phrase, cf. *Seneca, Epist.* 120 (119), "Quoties aliquid inveni, non exspecto donec dicas 'in commune'; ipse mihi dico."

6. **carbonem ... pro thesauro,** a proverb from the Greek ἄνθρακες ὁ θησαυρός.

FABLE VII.

4. **Princeps,** proper name, common at Rome.

5. **Bathyllus,** celebrated pantomimist of the day, native of Alexandria; freedman and favourite of Maecenas; mentioned in Juvenal; see *Class. Dict.*

7. **pegma,** see Smith's *Dict. of Antiq.* "Pegma (πῆγμα), an edifice of wood consisting of two or more stages (*tabulatae*) which were raised or depressed at pleasure by means of balance-weights. These great machines were used in the Roman amphitheatres, the gladiators who fought on them being called *pegmares.* They were supported upon wheels so

as to be drawn into the circus, glittering with silver and profusion of wealth."

8. **tibiam**, here '*leg*,' lit. shin bone ; in next l. **dextras**, *sc.* tibias, '*his two right pipes*'; Phaedrus puns on this double meaning of 'tibia.' For tibia see *Dict. Antiq.*; the 'dextra tibia' was base ; 'sinistra tibia,' treble.

18. **pretio precibus**, '*by bribes and prayers*'; a common phrase. Cf. Ter. *Eun.* v. ix. 24, "perfice hoc precibus pretio."

23. **misso**, because, contrary to the modern custom, the curtain was lowered for the performance ; and raised when the performance was over. **devolutis**, because the stage thunder was produced by rolling down balls behind the scenes.

28. **consurrectum est**, *sc.* a turba, '*the audience rose in a body to applaud.*'

30. **equester ordo**, sat in fourteen rows of seats set apart for them by the Law of Otho ; Horace and Juvenal constantly refer to the fact.

38. **divinae domus**, the '*royal house*,' called 'divinus' because of the deification of the Emperors, 'divus Caesar.'

FABLE VIII.

3. **quem si occuparis, teneas**, '*if you catch him, you should hold him*'; 'occuparis,' fut. perf., lit. '*if you shall have caught him.*'

FABLE IX.

5. **dici**, *sc.* 'hoc' as subject, '*that this is said to him.*'

FABLE X.

Some editors think that in this fable Phaedrus refers to his own old age.

1. **Adversus** ..., construe, cum canis, fortis et velox adversus omnes feras, semper satis fecisset domino ... .

4. **pugnae**, with 'obiectus.' **hispidi suis** = 'apri.'

5. **cariosis dentibus**, abl. of cause '*because his teeth ....*'

7. **Lacon**, may be the dog's name, or simply '*Spartan hound*'; the breed was very famous, cf. Soph. *Ajax*, 8, κυνὸς Λακαίνης ὥς τις εὔρινος βάσις, "keen scenting as a Laconian hound's"; Shakespeare *Mid. N. Dream*, "my hounds are bred out of the Spartan kind."

9. **fuimus and sumus**, emphatic, 'what I *was* but now *am*.'

10. **Philete**, uncertain who this man was, but identified by some editors with a Tib. Claudius Philetus, a freedman of the Emperor Claudius.

VOCABULARY.

a, ab, prep. with abl., *from, by;* of agent *by;* a catena detritum, iii. 7. 16 note.

abdĭtus, -a, -um, perf. part. of abdo, as adj., *hidden.*

abdo, -ĕre, -dĭdi, -dĭtum, v. tr., *put away, hide, conceal.*

ăbeo, -īre, -īvi and -ii, -ĭtum, v. intr., *go away, depart, go off, escape,* i. 8. 3; abiturus, iv. 20. 16, *since you will soon depart.*

ăbĭcio (for abiĭcio), -ĕre, -iēci, -iectum, v. tr., *throw away* or *down.* [iacio.]

ăbĭgo, -ĕre, -ēgi, -actum, v. tr., *drive away* or *off.* [ago.]

absens, -entis, part. fr. absum as adj., *absent.*

absisto, -ĕre, -stĭti, no sup., v. intr., *withdraw, stand aloof from;* with inf., *cease to.*

absolvo, -ĕre, -vi, -sŏlūtum, v. tr., *release, acquit.*

abstuli, see aufero.

absum, -esse, āfui, v. intr., *am away from, absent;* hinc abesto, iii. Prol. 60, *go hence, away with you.*

abundo, -āre, -āvi, -ātum, v. intr., *overflow, abound, am plentiful.*

ac, conj., see atque.

accēdo, -ĕre, -cessi, -cessum, v. intr., *approach, come up to, go to; am added.*

accendo, -ĕre, -ndi, -nsum, v. tr., *kindle, set light to, inflame, excite.*

accessus, -ūs, m., *a going near, approach; safe approach,* ii. 1. 10.

accĭdo, -ĕre, -cĭdi, no sup., *fall upon; happen.* [cădo.]

accĭpio, -ĕre, -cēpi, -ceptum, v. tr., *take, receive, get; hear;* in contumeliam accipiens, iii. 8. 8, *treating as an insult.*

accĭpĭter, -tris, m., *hawk, falcon.*

acclāmo, -āre, -āvi, -ātum, v. tr. and intr., *cry* or *shout at, applaud.*

accommŏdo, -āre, -āvi, -ātum, v. tr., *fit, adjust, adapt.*

94

accurro, -ĕre, -curri rarely -cŭcurri, -cursum, v. intr., *run up, run to, hasten to.*

accūsātor, -ōris, m., *accuser, plaintiff.* [accuso.]

ācer, -cris, -cre. adj., *sharp, keen, severe, fierce.* [rt. ac. cf. acerbus, acuo, acies.]

ăcerbus, -a, -um, adj., *harsh to the taste, bitter, hostile, grievous, annoying,* iii. 16. 3. [see acer.]

ācrĭter, adv., *sharply, keenly.* [acer.]

ăcuo, -ĕre, -ui, -ūtum, v. tr., *sharpen, whet, stimulate, excite, arouse.*

ăd, prep. with acc., *to, towards; at, by, near;* ad lanium, iii. 4. 1, *at a butcher's shop.*

addo, -ĕre, -dĭdi, -dĭtum, v. tr., *put to, join to, add.*

addūco, -ĕre, -xi, -ctum, v. tr., *lead to, lead on to, induce.*

ădeō, adv., *to such an extent, so much, so very, so.*

adeptus, see adipiscor.

adfecto,-āre,-āvi,-ātum,v. tr., *aim at, strive after, pretend to, claim.* [freq. of adficio.]

adfectus, -ūs, m., *feeling or emotion of mind, personal feeling,* iii. Prol. 36.

adfero, -ferre, -tŭli, -lātum, v. tr., *bring to, offer to.*

adfĭcio, -ĕre, -fēci, -fectum, v. tr., *do something to a person, work upon; influence, affect; visit with punishment, fear, joy, etc.;*

malo adf., i. 5. 10, *he will suffer for it.* [facio.]

adfirmo, -āre, -āvi, -ātum, v. tr., *affirm, declare, assert, maintain.*

adflictus, -a, -um, perf. part. of adfligo as adj., *damaged, shattered, crushed, in affliction,* i. 2. 28.

adflīgo, -ĕre, -ixi, -ictum, v. tr., *dash to the ground, strike down.*

adgrĕdior, -grĕdi, -gressus, v. dep. tr. and intr., *go to, approach, accost,* iii. 16. 10.

ădhuc, adv., *up to this point, as yet, still.*

ādĭcio, (for adiĭcio), -ĕre, -iēci, -iectum, *throw to, put to, add.* [iacio.]

ădĭpiscor, -sci, -eptus, v. dep. tr., *attain to, obtain.*

ădĭtus, -ūs, m., *approach, access, entrance.*

adiŭtor, -ōris, m., *aider, assistant.* [adiuvo.]

adiŭvo, -āre, -iūvi, -iūtum, v. tr., *aid, help, assist.*

adlĭcio, -ĕre, -lexi, -lectum, v. tr., *attract, allure, entice on, encourage,* ii. 3. 7. [obsolete lacio.]

adlūdo, -ĕre, -si, -sum, v. tr. and intr., *play with; do a thing in sport, jest; mock at,* iii. 19. 12.

admīrābĭlis, -e, adj., *worthy of wonder or admiration, admired.*

admīrātor, -ōris, m., *an admirer.*

admīror, -āri, -ātus, v. dep.
tr., *wonder at, admire.*

admŏneo, -ēre, -ui, -ĭtum, v.
tr., *warn, admonish, suggest.*

admŏveo, -ēre, -mōvi, -mōtum,
v. tr., *move to, apply to,
give to,* iii. 15. 7; *use, employ,* preces adm., i. 19. 6;
iii. Ep. 20.

adnăto, -āre, -āvi, no sup.,
v. intr., *swim up to.*

adpărātus, -ūs, m., *preparation, arrangement; magnificence, luxury.*

adpĕto, -ĕre, -īvi or -ii, -ītum,
v. tr., *strive after, seek, try
to get, aim at, attack.*

adprŏbo, -āre, -āvi, -ātum, v.
tr., *assent to, favour, approve of, gain approval for,*
iv. 25. 11.

adquīro, -ĕre, -sīvi, -sītum, v.
tr., *get in addition, gain.*
[quaero.]

adrīdeo, -ēre, -si, -sum, v. tr.
and intr., *laugh at; smile
upon, favour; find favour
with, please,* iv. 21. 4.

adrĭpio, -ĕre, -rĭpui, -reptum,
v. tr., *snatch up, snatch at,
seize, appropriate;* adr.
fiduciam, *assume ...* v. 7. 2.
[răpio.]

adscrībo, -ĕre, -psi, -ptum, v.
tr. and intr., *write in addition; inscribe on: write
down to, assign to, apply
to;* adscriptus dies, iv. 11.
8, *appointed day.*

adsĕquor, -sĕqui, -sĕcūtus, v.
dep. tr., *follow up, pursue;*

overtake, *catch,* iv. 2. 11;
attain to, win, iii. 9. 3.

adsigno, -āre, -āvi, -ātum, v.
tr., *mark out, assign to,
impute, ascribe.*

adsĭlio, -īre, -ui, -ultum, v.
intr., *leap upon, on to;
dash or run quickly up,*
ii. 5. 21.

adsuesco, -ĕre, -suēvi, -suētum,
v. tr. and intr., *accustom,
grow accustomed;* adsuevi,
I am accustomed, i. 16. 5.

adsuētus, -a, -um, part. of
adsuesco as adj., *accustomed, usual.*

adsum, -esse, adfui, v. intr.,
am at or near, am at hand.

adtempto, -āre, -āvi, -ātum,
v. tr., *strive after, essay;
assail, attack.*

adtendo, -ĕre, -tendi, -tentum, v. tr. and intr., *stretch
to, turn towards;* with
animum expressed or
understood, *give attention
to, attend.*

adtestor, -āri, -ātus, v. dep.
tr., *bear witness to, testify.*

adtribuo, -ĕre, -ui, -ūtum, v.
tr., *assign, allot.*

advĕnio, -īre, -vēni, -ventum,
v. intr., *come to.*

adversus, prep. with acc. and
adv., *opposite to, against.*

adversus, -a, -um, part. of
adverto as adj., *fronting,
opposite; adverse, hostile;*
adverso tempore, ii. 8. 16,
in adversity.

advŏco, -āre, -āvi, -ātum, v.
tr., *call to, summon.*

advŏlo, -āre, -āvi, -ātuin, v.
intr., *fly to, fly up to, fly
against; dash up, hurry
up to.*

aedes, -is, f., *dwelling of gods,
temple;* pl., *house.*

Aeētēs, -ae, in., King of
Colchis, father of Medea,
iv. 7. 12. [Αἰήτης.]

Aegaeus, -a, -um, adj., *Aegean,
of the Aegean Sea,* now the
Archipelago, iv. 7. 19.
[Αἰγαῖος.]

aegrē, adv., *with trouble or
difficulty, scarcely.* [aeger.]

aemŭlātĭo, -ōnis, f., *emulation, rivalry.*

aequē, adv., *equally.* [aequus.]

aequĭtas, -ātis, f., *equality,
justice, fairness.*

aequo, -āre, -āvi, -ātum, v. tr.,
*make even or equal; come
up to a level with, attain
equally to, equal.*

aequus, -a, -um, adj., *even,
level, fair; equal* laws, i. 2.
1 ; aequo animo, i. 26. 12,
with equanimity.

Aesōpĭus, -a, -um, adj., *of
Aesop; in the manner of
Aesop,* iv. Prol. 11.

Aesōpus, -i, m., see note,
page 81.

aestas, -ātis, f., *summer.* [αἴθω,
burn.]

aestĭmo, -āre, -āvi, -ātum, v.
tr., *estimate, value, reckon,
regard, consider.*

aestuo, -āre, -āvi, -ātum, v.
intr., *am in violent agitation, boil, surge; am hot,
glow.*

aetas, -ātis, f., *period of life,
age.*

aeternus, -a, -um, adj., *eternal,
lasting.*

aevum, -i, n., *lifetime, life;
age; time, eternity.* [αἰών.]

ăgĕdum, interj., *come now!
now then!*

aggĕro, -āre, -āvi, -ātum, v.
tr., *heap* or *pile up.* [agger.]

agmen, -ĭnis, n., *band, troop,
column.* [lit. *moving body*
of anything, from ago.]

agnosco, -ĕre, -nōvi, -nĭtum,
v. tr., *recognise.*

agnus, -i, m., *lamb.* [cf. ἀμνός.]

ăgo, -ĕre, ēgi, actum, v. tr.,
*put in motion, drive, lead,
perform, do; push forward,
extend,* of tunnel, iv. 20. 2 ;
ag. gratias, *return or give
thanks;* agitur de, iii. 13.
11, *the question is about;*
age, as interj., *come!*

ăgrestis, -e, adj., *of the country, rustic:* as subst., *a
rustic.* [ager.]

aio, v. defect., *say, affirm.*

ălăcer, -cris, -cre, adj., *lively,
brisk, quick, eager.*

ălăpa, -ae, f., *cuff, slap, box
on the ear,* of manumission
of slave, ii. 5. 25 n.

albus, -a, -um, adj., *white.*

āles, -ĭtis, adj., *winged;* as
subst., m. and f., *a bird.*
[ala.]

ălĭēnus, -a, -um, adj., *of
another, of others.* [alius.]

ălĭquando, adv., *at some time
or other, once, formerly,
sometimes.*

ălĭqui, -qua, -quod, indef. pron. adj., *some, any.*

ălĭquis, -quid, indef. pron., *some* or *any one* or *thing.*

ălĭquot, indef. adj., indecl., *some, a few, several.*

ălĭus, -a, -ud, pron. adj., *another, other ; other than, different ;* alius Seiano, iii. Prol. 41, *different from S. ;* alii ... alii, *some ... others.*

allĭgo, -āre, -āvi, -ātum, v. tr., *bind* or *fasten to, tie up.*

ălo, -ĕre, -ui, ălĭtum and altum, v. tr., *nourish, feed; rear; cherish.*

altē, adv., *on high, aloft ; deeply, deep ;* comp. altius, superl. altissime. [altus.]

alter, -ĕra, -ĕrum, pron. adj., *the one* or *other* of two, *another, second.*

altĭcinctus, -a, -um, adj., *high girded,* hence *busy,* ii. 5. 11 n. Not found elsewhere.

altus, -a, -um, adj., *high, lofty, tall, deep.* [alo.]

alveŏlus, -i, m., *small tub* or *trough* or *vessel.* [dim. of alveus.]

alvus, -i, f., *stomach ; bee-hive,* iii. 13. 9.

ambo, -ae, -o, num. adj., *both.* [ἄμφω.]

ămīcus, -a, -um, adj., *friendly.* [amo.]

ămīcus, -i, m., *friend.* [amo.]

ămitto, -ĕre, -si, -ssum, v. tr., *send away; lose;* am. fidem, i. 10. 2, *is not believed.*

ămo, -āre, -āvi, -ātum, v. tr., *love.*

amphŏra, -ae, f., *an amphora,* large earthenware vessel, with handle on each side of neck, and pointed bottom, for wine, etc., iii. 1. 1. [ἀμφορεύς.]

amplector, -i, -plexus, v. dep. tr., *embrace.*

an, conj., *or ; whether, if ;* prop. used in second part of disjunct. interrog.

Ănăcharsis, -is, m., *a famous* Scythian, see note, iii. Prol. 52. ['Ανάχαρσις.]

angŭlus, -i, m., *angle, corner, nook.* [cf. ἀγκύλος.]

angustus, -a, -um, adj., *narrow, close, small.* [ango, squeeze.]

ănhēlo, -āre, -āvi, -ātum, v. intr., *breathe hard, pant.*

ănĭma, -ae, f., *air, breath ; vital principle, life, soul ; vapour, fragrance,* see iii. 1. 5.

animadverto, -ere, -ti, -sum, v. tr., *pay attention to, notice.* [animus : adverto.]

ănĭmal, -ālis, n., *living creature, animal.*

ănĭmus, -i, m., *mind, intellect ; feelings, disposition, inclination ;* est animus, iii. 16. 13, *I am minded to ; heart, affection ;* ad animum rettulit, iii. 19. 10, *took to heart ; courage ; your spirit,* i.e. *cowardice,* i. 11. 15.

annus, -i, m., *year ; age ;* defectus annis, i. 21, 3, *weakened by age.*

antĕ, prep. with acc. and adv., *before, in front of;* ante hos sex menses, i. 1. 10, *these six months ago;* ante…quam, see antequam, *before that.*

antĕhāc, adv., *till now, hitherto, formerly.*

antĭdŏtum, -i, n., *a counter-poison, specific against poison, antidote, remedy.*

antīquus, -a, -um, adj., *of former times, ancient;* pl., antiqui, *the ancients.*

ănus, -ūs, f., *old woman.*

ăper, -pri, m., *wild boar* or *pig,* used of female, ii. 4. 9. [cf. κάπρος.]

ăperio, -īre, -ui, -ertum, v. tr., *lay open, open, display, expose to view.*

ăpertus, -a, -um, part. of aperio as adj., *open, evident, manifest.*

ăpis, -is, f., *bee.*

Apollo, -ĭnis, m., *Apollo* or Phoebus, son of Jupiter and Latona, brother of Diana, god of the sun, of archery, divination, eloquence, poetry, music, etc., iii. Prol. 57; iii. 16. 12.

appāreo, -ēre, -ui, -ĭtum, v. intr., *appear, am visible, plain.*

appĕtens, -entis, part. fr. appeto or adpeto as adj., *desirous of, eager for,* with gen.

ăqua, -ae, f., *water.*

ăquĭla, -ae, f., *eagle.*

ăra, -ae, f., *altar.*

ărāneum, -i, n., *spider's web, cobweb.* [ărānea, *spider.*]

arbĭtrium, -i, n., *judgment, decision, will.*

arbor, -ŏris, f., *tree.*

arca, -ae, f., *chest, coffer;* esp. *money-chest* or -*box.*

arcus, -ūs, m., *bow.*

ardălio, -onis, m., *a busy, officious person, busy-body.* [ardelio, fr. ardeo.]

ardens, -entis, part. of ardeo as adj., *burning, blazing, hot, eager.*

ardeo, -ēre, -arsi, no sup., v. intr., *am on fire, blaze; am inflamed* with passion, etc.

argentum, -i, n., *silver.* [cf. ἀργός, *white.*]

argūmentum, -i, n., *argument, evidence, proof; subject* of play, etc. ; *play, fable,* etc., ii. 7. 13 ; iv. 11. 14, etc. [arguo.]

arguo, -ĕre, -ui, -ūtum, v. tr., *make clear, show, prove; accuse, charge with,* i. 10. 4.

Argus, -i, m., the builder of the ship Argo, son of Phrixus, iv. 7. 9.

argūtiae, -ārum, f. pl., *liveliness, witty remarks, wit, subtlety.*

ărĭdus, -a, -um, adj., *dry, parched.* [areo.]

ars, artis, f., *skill, art.*

artĭfex, -ĭcis, m. and f., *artist, workman, artificer; artiste,* v. 5. 7.

artus, -ūs, m., generally in pl., *limb.*

artus, -a, -um, adj., *narrow, confined.*

arx, arcis, f., *fortress, citadel; acropolis* at Athens, i. 2. 5.

as, assis, m., a copper coin, about ⅔d. English.

ascendo, -ĕre, -ndi, -nsum, v. tr. and intr., *ascend, mount; embark* on ship, iv. 22. 9.

ăsellus, -i, m., *little* or *contemptible* or *young ass.* [dim. of ăsĭnus.]

Ăsia, -ae, f., *Asia.* (1) town in Lydia and country around ; (2) Asia Minor or Roman province of Asia, which included Mysia, Lydia, Caria, and Phrygia, iv. 22. 4. ; (3) the continent of Asia.

ăsĭnus, -i, m., *ass.*

asper, -ĕra, -ĕrum, adj., *rough, rugged, wild, fierce, cruel.*

aspernor, -āri, -ātus, v. dep. tr., *cast off, disdain, scorn.* [ab : sperno.]

aspĭcio, -ĕre, -xi, -ctum, v. tr., *gaze on, behold, see, catch sight of.*

astrum, -i. n., *star.* [ἄστρον.]

at or **ast,** conj. adversative, *but, yet, on the other hand ;* at ille, iv. 23. 3, *and after all he.* [cf., ἀτάρ.]

Ăthēnae, -ārum, f., pl. *Athens,* capital of Attica. ['Αθῆναι.]

atque, or **ac** before consonants only, conj., *and also, and moreover, and ;* simul ac, *as soon as.* [ad : que.]

ătriensis, -e, adj., *of the*

atrium ; as subst., m., *an overseer of the atrium* or *hall, a house-steward,* ii. 5. 11.

attendo, -ĕre, -tendi, -tentum, v. tr. and intr., *stretch to, turn towards ;* with animum expressed or understood, *give attention to, listen.* [ad : tendo.]

Attĭcus, -a, -um, adj., *of Attica, Attic, Athenian ;* as subst. pl., *the Athenians.* ['Αττικός.]

attingo, -ĕre, -tĭgi, -tactum, v. tr., *touch, reach, get to ; affect, concern.* [ad: tango.]

auctor, -ōris, m., *one who produces, creator, maker, author, poet, inventor, originator.* [augĭo.]

auctōrĭtas, -ātis, f., *advice, opinion, personal weight, influence; weighty precedent* or *example,* iv. 25. 10.

audācia, -ae, f., *boldness, daring, audacity.* [audax.]

audacter, adv., *boldly, recklessly.* [audax.]

audax, -ācis, adj., *daring, bold ;* in bad sense, *rash, reckless, audacious.* [audeo.]

audeo, -ēre, ausus, v. tr. and intr., semi-dep., *dare, venture.*

audio, -īre, -īvi or -ii, -ītum, v. tr., *hear, listen to.*

aufĕro, -ferre, abstŭli, ablātum, v.tr., *carry off* or *away, remove, take away, leave without,* i. 7, 4. aufer, iii. 6. 8, *away with.* [ab: fero.]

augŭrium, -ii, n., *augury,*
science of divination from
observing feeding, cries, or
flight of birds. [ăvis.]

Augustus, -i, m., lit. *venerable, august,* title taken by
Octavius Caesar, B.C. 27,
and afterwards assumed by
all the Roman Emperors.
[augeo.]

aulaeum, -i, n., *piece of tap-
estry, hanging, curtain,* v.
7. 23. [α'λαία.]

aura, -ae, f., *air, breeze,
breath; breeze of popular
favour, applause,* v. 7. 1.
[αὔρα.]

auris, -is, f., *ear.* [οὖς,
audio.]

auritŭlus, -i, m., *the long-
eared one, Master Long-
Ears,* of ass, i. 11. 6
[auris.]

aurum, -i, n., *gold.*

aut. conj., *or;* aut ... aut,
either ... or.

autem, conj., *but, however,
now, moreover.* [aut.]

auxĭlium, -i, n., *help, aid.*

ăvārus, -a, -um, adj., *greedy,
avaricious, miserly.* [aveo,
covet.]

āverto, -ĕre, -ti, -sum, v. tr.,
turn off or aside.

ăvĭdĭtas, -ātis, f., *eagerness,
greediness, greed; greedy
creature,* i. 4. 5. [aveo.]

ăvĭdus, -a, -um, adj., *greedy,
eager.* [aveo.]

ăvis, -is, f., *bird.*

bālŭlo, -āre, no perf. or sup.,
carry a load. [βαστάζω.]

barba, -ae, f., *beard.*

barbărus, -a, -um, adj.,
foreign, barbarian, i.e. not
Greek or Roman.

barbātus, -a, -um, adj., *with
a beard, bearded;* of goat,
Master Long-Beard, iv. 9.
10. [barba.]

băsis, -is, f., *pedestal, base,*
ii. Epil. 2. [βάσις.]

bāsium, -ii, n., *kiss.*

Băthyllus, -i, m., native of
Alexandria, famous panto-
mimist, v. 7. 5 note.

bĕnĕ, adv. *well;* comp. mĕlius,
better; superl. optĭmē, *best.*
[bŏnus.]

bĕnĕfĭcium, -ii, n., *kindness,
favour, good service, benefit.*
[bene : facio.]

bĕnignĭtas, -ātis, f., *friendli-
ness, kindness.* [benignus.]

bĕnĭvŏlentia, -ae, f., *goodwill,
favour, benevolence.*

bestia, -ae, f., *beast.*

bĭbo, -ĕre, bibi, no sup., v.
tr., *drink.* [πίνω.]

bĭdens, -entis, f., two-year-
old *sheep,* from the two
prominent cutting teeth
which mark that age. [bis :
dens.]

bĭlinguis, -e, adj., *having two
tongues, double-tongued;
false, treacherous.* [bis :
lingua.]

bīni, -ae, -a, num. adj. distrib., *two each, two.* [bis].

bĭpennis, -is, f., *double-edged
axe, battle axe.* [bis : pinna
or penna.]

bis, num. adj., *twice.*

blandītia, -ae, f., *flattery, coaxing;* pl., *blandishments, charms.*

bŏnĭtas, -ātis, f., *goodness, excellence, kindness.* [bonus.]

bŏnum, -i, n., *a good thing, blessing, gain ; advantage, good fortune,* i. 2. 29 ; est bono, *is a blessing,* v. 4. 12 ; pl., *good things, good fortune, wealth, property.*

bŏnus, -a, -um, adj., *good, honest, advantageous;* comp. mēlior ; superl. optĭmus.

bos, bŏvis, pl., boum, abl., bobus or bubus, m. and f., *ox, bull, cow.*

bŏvĭle, -is, n., *ox-stall, cow-house.* [bos.]

brĕvi, adv., *in a short time, shortly, briefly.*

brĕvis, -e, adj., *short, brief.*

brĕvĭtas, -ātis, f., *shortness, brevity.*

brĕvĭter, adv., *shortly, concisely.*

brūma, -ae, f., *the shortest day,* i.e. winter solstice, hence *winter.* [for brevima fr. brevis.]

bŭbulcus, -i, m., *beast-herd, cowherd, herdsman.* [bos.]

bubus, see bos.

caecus, -a, -um, adj., *blind ; hidden, secret ; blinding.*

caedes, -is, f., *cutting; slaughter.* [caedo.]

caelum, -i, n., *heaven.*

Caesar, -ăris, m., cognomen of Gens Iulia, to which belonged C. Iulius Caesar.

After him it was used as title by the Emperors. Caesar Tiberius, ii. 5. 7 ; 5. 19.

călămĭtas, -ātis, f., *disaster, misfortune ;* tua cal., i. 3. 16 n., *your unhappy self.*

călămus, -i, m., *cane, reed ; reed pen.* [κάλαμος.]

calceo, -āre, -āvi, -ātum, v. tr., *furnish with shoes ;* calceandos, i. 14. 16, *to be shod.*

calceus, -i, m., *shoe.* [calx, *heel.*]

callĭdus, -a, -um, adj., *experienced, skilful, cunning.* [calleo.]

călumnia, -ae, f., *intrigue, trickery ; false accusation, slander, libel,* iii. Prol. 37.

călumniātor, -ōris, m., *one who makes a business of bringing false charges, false accuser,* i. 17. 2.

călumnior, -āri, -ātus, v. dep. tr. and intr., *falsely accuse, slander, disparage, cavil at.*

calvus, -a, -um, adj., *bald ;* as subst., *a bald-headed man,* v. 3. 1.

calx, calcis, f., *heel.* [λάξ.]

cămăra, -ae, f., *vaulted roof or ceiling, vaulted building, vault.*

campus, -i, m., *plain.*

candor, -ōris, m., *whiteness, brilliance; fairness, purity.*

cănis, -is, m. and f., *dog, hound.*

căno, -ĕre, cĕcĭni, cantum, v. tr., *sing, sing of, celebrate.*

canticum, -i, n., *solo*, in Roman comedy, accompanied by music and dancing; *song, air*, v. 7. 25. 31. [cano.]

cantus, -ūs, m., *song.* [cano.]

cānus, -a, -um, adj., *white, hoary, white-haired.*

căpax, -ācis, adj., *able to hold, large, capacious.* [capio.]

căpella, -ae, f., *she-goat.* [dim. of caper.]

căper, -pri, m., *he-goat, goat.* [κάπρος, *wild boar.*]

căpillus, -i, m., *hair.*

căpio, -ĕre, cēpi, captum, v. tr., *take, seize, capture; win over, captivate, ensnare, please; receive, gain profit; enjoy sleep.*

capto, -āre, -āvi, -ātum, v. tr., *try to catch, snatch at, aim at, try to,* v. 3. 2. [freq. of capio.]

căput, -itis, n., *head, life;* play on words, iii. 4. 4. capite, v. 7. 39, *headlong.*

carbo, -ōnis, m., *charcoal, coal,* v. 6. 6.

cāreo, -ēre, -ui, -itum, v. intr. with abl., *am without, free from, lack, am deprived of, miss.*

căriōsus, -a, -um, adj., *decayed, rotten.*

cărĭtas, -ātis, f., *dearness, high price; affection.* [cārus.]

carmen, -inis, n., *poem, poetry, song.* [for casmen, cf. Casmenae or Camenae,

old Italian goddesses of song and literature; cano.]

cāro, carnis, f., *flesh; piece of meat,* i. 4. 2.

carpo, -ĕre, -psi, -ptum, v. tr., *pick, pluck, take; pull to pieces, find fault with,* ii. Epil. 17; carpens oscula, iii. 8. 12, *kissing.*

cāsĕus, -i, m., *cheese, piece of cheese,* i. 13. 3.

castus, -a, -um, adj., *chaste, virtuous.*

cāsu, adv., *by chance or accident.* [cāsus.]

cāsus, -ūs, m., *fall, chance, plight, misfortune.* [cado.]

cătēna, -ae, f., *chain, fetter.*

căthēdra, -ae, f., *chair, used esp. by women.* [καθέδρα.]

Căto, -ōnis, m., Roman cognomen; in iv. 7. 21 n., of M. Porcius Cato surnamed Censor.

cătŭlus, -i, m., *puppy, cub, whelp, kitten.*

cauda, -ae, f., *tail.*

causa, -ae, f., *cause, reason, pretext; legal, charge, case, pleadings,* i. 10. 7; meâ causâ, *for my sake;* nec quaestionis positae causam intelligit, iii. 14. 8, *does not understand the reason of,* i.e. *cannot solve the problem which has been set.*

cautus, -a, -um, part. of caveo as adj., *made safe, secure, careful, cautious.*

căveo, -ēre, cāvi, cautum, v. tr. and intr., *am on my guard, cautious;* with dat., *take precaution for* a person, *provide for, take heed to the interests of.*

cǎverna, -ae, f., *cave, cavern, hollow, hole.*

cǎvus, -a, -um, adj., *hollow.*

cǎvus, -i, m., and cǎvum, -i, n., *a hollow, hole.*

cēdo, -cre, cessi, cessum, v. intr., *go away, withdraw, yield ; retire from, give up,* with abl., i. 19. 10 ; with dat., *submit to,* iii. 9. 4, n.

cēdŏ, old imperat. form ; pl., cedite or cette, *pray tell me ; just give me, grant.*

cĕlĕber, -bris, -bre, adj., *crowded, attended by a large company,* i. 6. 1 ; *famous.*

cĕlĕrĭtas, -ātis, f., *quickness, speed.*

cĕlĕrĭter, adv., *quickly,* comp. celerius.

cēlo, -āre, -āvi, -ātum, v. tr., *conceal, hide.* [καλύπτω.]

celsus, -a, -um, adj., *high, lofty, tall ; held high,* of head, ii. 7. 4.

cēna, -ae, f., *principal Roman meal taken about 3 o'clock, dinner.*

censeo, -ēre, -ui, -sum, v. tr., *take an estimate, register ; value, reckon ; think, consider.*

censor, -ōris, m., *censor,* (1) Roman magistrate: two appointed every five years to register and rate the citizens, superintend public morals, and arrange public

revenue and works ; (2) *a critic, censurer,* iv. 10. 5.

centum, num. adj. indecl., *hundred.*

cēra, -ae, f., *tablet covered with wax ;* in pl. poet. *wax cells* in bee hive, iii. 13. 9.

cĕrĕbrum, -i, n., *brain.* [κάρα, *head.*]

cerno, -ĕre, crēvi, crētum, v. tr., *separate, discern, perceive.* [κρίνω.]

certāmen, -ĭnis, n., *contest, rivalry.* [certo.]

certātim, adv., *in rivalry, eagerly.* [certo.]

certē, adv., *certainly, surely, atleast,at any rate.* [certus.]

certo, -āre, -āvi, -ātum, v. intr., *contend, strive, fight.*

certus, -a, -um, adj , *determined, fixed, sure, certain.* [cerno.]

cervix, -īcis, f., *nape of neck, neck.* [cerebrum, κάρα.]

cervus, -i, m., *stag, deer.* [κέρας, *horn.*]

cesso, -āre, -āvi, -ātum, v. intr., *linger, loiter, cease.*

[cētĕrus], -a, -um, adj., *rare in sing., not in nom. masc., the rest.*

charta, -ae, f., *leaf of papyrus, paper ; hence letter, poem,* etc., see iv. Prol. 18.; iv. Epil. 5. [χάρτης.]

chŏrus, -i, m., *choral dance ; band of dancers, chorus, choir.* [χορός.]

Cīa or Cēa, -ae, f., *island of Ceos,* in Cyclades, birth-

place of Simonides, iv. 22.
8. [Κέως.]

cĭbus, -i, m., *food.*

cĭcāda, -ae, f., *tree cricket,*
iii. 16. 3.

cĭcōnia, -ae, f., *stork,* i. 26. 3.

cieo, -ēre, cīvi, cĭtum, v.
tr., *put in motion, rouse;
cause; utter,* iv.23,1. [κινέω.]

cĭnaedus, -i, m., *blackguard,*
v. 1. 15. [κίναιδος.]

cĭnis, -ĕris, m., *rarely* f.,
generally in pl., *ashes;*
cinis, iii. 9, 4, *when dead.*

circā, prep. with acc. and
adv., *round, about.*

circum, prep. with acc. and
adv., *round, about.*

circumcīdo, -ĕre, -cīdi, -cīsum,
v. tr., *cut round, lop; re-
duce, retrench,* iv. 20. 25.
[caedo.]

circumdo, -āre, -dĕdi, -dătum,
v. tr., *place round;* with
acc. and abl., *surround,
enclose with,* i. 28. 9.

cirrus, -i, m., generally in
pl., *curl of* hair, *tuft of*
hair; *fringe.*

cĭthăra, -ae, f., *lute, lyre.*
[κιθάρα.]

cĭtō, adv., *quickly, speedily;*
comp. citius. [citus.]

cĭto, -āre, -āvi, -ātum, v. tr.,
*put into quick motion; call,
summon, cite* as witness,
i. 17, 4.

cīvis, -is, m. and f., *citizen.*

cīvĭtas, -ātis, f., *citizenship;
state.* [civis.]

clāmĭto, -āre, -āvi, -ātum, v.
tr. and intr., *call out loudly,*

cry out, proclaim. [freq.
of clamo.]

clāmo, -āre, -āvi, -ātum, v.
tr. and intr., *call* or *cry
out, shout; make a loud
noise* of cicada, iii. 16. 7,
[καλέω.]

clāmor, -ōris, m., *shout, cry;
noise,* of donkey's *bray,*
i. 11. 7.

clārus, -a, -um, adj., *bright,
conspicuous; loud, clear* of
sounds.

classis, -is, f., (1) a *muster* of
citizens, etc.; hence *class,
division;* (2) *fleet* or *army.*
[καλέω.]

claudo, -ĕre, -si, -sum, v. tr.,
shut, shut up, shut in.
[clavis, *key.*]

Clāzŏmĕnae, -ārum, f. pl.,
city in Ionia on coast,
iv. 22. 17.

clēmenter, adv., *gently, kindly.*
[clemens.]

clītellae, -ārum, f. pl., *pack-
saddle, saddle bags.*

coepi, -isse, coeptum, v. tr.
and intr. deflect., *begin;*
with pass. inf., i. 12. 11 n.

coetus, -ūs, m., *gathering,
meeting, company.* [coeo.]

cōgĭtātio, -ōnis, f., *thinking,
consideration, opinion.*

cōgĭto, -āre, -āvi, -ātum, v.
tr., *consider thoroughly,
ponder, meditate on; devise,
purpose, intend.* [co: agito.]

cognātus, -i. m., *blood relation, kinsman.* [co: gnascor.]

cognosco, -ĕre, -gnōvi, -gnĭ-
tum, v. tr., *become thor-*

oughly acquainted with, learn ; in perf., know.

cōgo, -ĕre, coēgi, coactum, v. tr., drive together, collect ; compel, force. [co : ago.]

collĭgo, -ĕre, -lēgi, -lectum, v. tr., gather together, collect. [lego.]

collŏco, -āre, -āvi, -ātum, v. tr., place, station, set.

collum, -i, n., neck or throat.

cŏlo, -ĕre, cŏlui, cultum, v. tr., cultivate, till.

cŏlor, -ōris, m., colour, hue ; characteristics, iv. Prol. 8.

cŏlŭbra, -ae, f., female snake. [coluber.]

cŏlumba, -ae, f., dove, pigeon.

cŏmĕdo, -edĕre or -esse, -ēdi, -ēsum, v. tr., eat up.

cŏmes, -ĭtis, m. and f., comrade, companion.

comesse, see comedo.

commĕmŏro, -āre, -āvi, -ātum, v. tr., recount, relate, tell of.

commendātio, -ōnis, f., recommendation.

commendo, -āre, -āvi, -ātum, v. tr., put into the hands of, commit to, entrust ; recommend. [mando : manus.]

commercĭum, -ii, n., commerce, traffic, interchange, relations with. [merx.]

commĭnuo, -ĕre, -ui, -ūtum, v. tr., crush, break in pieces, lessen, weaken. [minor, less.]

committo, -ĕre, -mīsi, -missum, v. tr., bring together, join, entrust, commit.

commŏdo, -āre, -āvi, -ātum,

v. tr., adjust ; lend, supply ; accommodate.

commūnis, -e, adj., shared in by all, common to, with gen., iii. Prol. 46 ; in commune, v. 6. 3, shares ! com. sensus, i. 7. 4, common sense, good sense.

commūto, -āre, -āvi, -ātum, v. tr., change completely.

cōmoedia, -ae, f., comedy. [κωμῳδία.]

cŏmōsus, -a, -um, adj., shaggy, hairy. [coma.]

compello, -ĕre, -pŭli, -pulsum, v. tr., drive together, collect ; compel.

compĕrio, -īre, -pĕri, -pertum, v. tr., find out with certainty, ascertain.

compesco, -ĕre, -scui, no sup., v. tr., restrain.

compĭlo, -āre, -āvi, -ātum, v. tr., pillage, rob.

compleo, -ĕre, -ēvi, -ētum, v. tr., fill up.

comprendo or comprĕhendo, -ĕre, -di, -sum, v. tr., lay hold of, seize, arrest.

compulsus, see compello.

compungo, -ĕre, -punxi, -punctum, v. tr., sting, prick.

concĭdo, -ĕre, -cĭdi, no sup., v. tr., fall together, fall, drop. [cădo.]

concieo, -ēre, -cīvi, -cītum, v. tr., put in violent motion, arouse.

concinno, -āre, -āvi, -ātum, v. tr., arrange ; devise ; produce, cause. [concinnus, well adjusted.]

concĭpio, -ĕre, -cēpi, -ceptum, v. tr., *take hold of; perceive; imagine; conceive.* [capio.]

concĭto, -āre, -āvi, -ātum, v. tr., *put in quick motion, arouse, excite.* [freq. of concieo.]

concĭtus, -a, -um, part. of concieo as adj., *quick, rapid.*

concŭpisco, -ĕre, -cŭpīvi or -ii, -cŭpĭtum, v. tr., *desire strongly, covet.* [con : incept. of cupio.]

concurro, -ĕre, -curri, -cursum, v. intr., *run or flock together.*

concurso, -āre, no perf. or sup., v. intr., *run or flock together, rush to and fro.*

condĭcio, -ōnis, f., *agreement, terms; condition, situation, way of life,* iii. 7. 7.

condo, -ĕre, -dĭdi, -dĭtum, v. tr., *put together, build; build up, store up; hide, bury; sheathe* sword.

condūco, -ĕre, -xi, -ctum, v. tr., *bring together; hire, engage.*

confectus, -a, -um, part. of conficio as adj., *done up, exhausted.*

confĕro, -ferre, -tŭli, collātum, v. tr., *bring together, collect; compare.*

confĭcio, -ĕre, fēci, fectum, v. tr., *do thoroughly, accomplish; exhaust.* See confectus. [facio.]

confĭteor, -ēri, -fessus, v. dep. tr. and intr., *acknowledge, admit, confess.* [făteor.]

confŏdio, -ĕre, -fodi, -fossum, v. tr., *dig thoroughly; gore,* i. 21. 7.

congĕro, -ĕre, -gessi, -gestum, v. tr., *carry together, collect, pile up.*

cōnor, -āri, -ātus, v. dep. tr. and intr., *endeavour, try, attempt.*

conrōdo, -ĕre, -si, -sum, v. tr., *gnaw to pieces.*

conscientia, -ae, f., *joint knowledge, with others, complicity: knowledge in or with oneself, consciousness;* laudis c., ii. Ep. 11, *consciousness of deserving praise.* [con : scio.]

conscius, -a, -um, adj., *aware of, conscious of,* with gen.

consector, -āri, -ātus, v. dep. tr., *follow eagerly, pursue.*

consĕquor, -qui, -cūtus, v. dep. tr., *follow up, pursue, overtake, obtain, win.*

consīdĕro, -āre, -āvi, -ātum, v. tr., *look at attentively. inspect.*

consĭlĭātor, -ōris, m., *counsellor,* i. 9, title; ii. 6. 2. post-Augustan and rare. [consilior.]

consĭlio, adv., *on purpose, intentionally.* [abl. of consilium.]

consĭlium, -ii, n., *deliberation; counsel, advice; plan, tactics.*

consisto, -ĕre, -stīti, -stĭtum, v. intr., *take my stand, stand firm.* [sto.]

consŏcio, -āre, -āvi, -ātum, v. tr., *share equally, associate;* cons. usum ullius rei, iv. 11. 21, *join in using anything.*

consōlor, -āri, -ātus, v. dep. tr., *console, comfort.*

conspargo, -ĕre, -si, -sum, v. tr., *sprinkle* thoroughly. [spargo.]

conspectus, -ūs, m., *sight, view.* [conspicio.]

conspĭcio, -ĕre, -xi, -ctum, v. tr., *observe, see, behold, catch sight of.* [-specio.]

conspĭcor, -āri, -ātus, v. dep. tr., *catch sight of.* [-specio.]

conspĭcuus, -a, -um, adj., *easy to see, visible, conspicuous.* [conspicio.]

conspīro, -āre, -āvi, -ātum, v. intr., *breathe together, agree together;* perf. part., conspiratus, with middle force, *having leagued together, entered into a conspiracy,* i. 2. 4.

constans, -utis, part. fr. consto as adj., *standing firm, firm, steady;* comp. constantior.

consto, -āre, -stīti, -stātum, v. intr., *stand firm, remain unmoved.*

consuētudo, -ĭnis, f., *habit.* [consuesco.]

consūmo, -ĕre, -mpsi, -mptum, v. tr., *take all in; devour,* consume, destroy, spend. [sumo.]

consurgo, -ĕre, -surrexi, -surrectum, v. intr., *rise up together;* in plausus consurrectum est, v. 7. 28, *the audience rose in a body to applaud.*

contĕgo, -ĕre, -texi, -tectum, v. tr., *cover up, conceal.*

contemno, -ĕre, -mpsi, -mptum, v. tr., *despise, disdain.*

contendo, -ĕre, -di, -tum, v. tr. and intr., *draw tight; hurl; strive after; assert strenuously, maintain.*

contentus, -a, -um, part. of contineo as adj., *contented, content, satisfied.*

conterreo, -ēre, -ui, -ītum, v. tr., *terrify, frighten greatly.*

contĭneo, -ēre, -ui, -tentum, v. tr., *contain, enclose, embrace, restrain;* pass. continetur as middle, ii. Prol. 1, *comprises, includes.* [teneo.]

contingo, -ĕre, -tĭgi, -tactum, v. tr., *touch, reach to, attain;* v. intr., *reach, happen to, fall to the lot of,* generally of good fortune. [tango.]

contĭnuo, adv., *forthwith, immediately.* [continuus.]

contio, -ōnis, f., *public meeting* summoned by magistrates.

contrā, prep. with acc., *opposite, contrary to ; against;* contra se ipsum misericors, iv. 19. 3, *show-*

ing pity to his own hurt; adv., *opposite, on the contrary, on the other hand, in turn, in reply.*

contrăho, -ĕrc, -xi, -ctum, v. tr., *draw together, assemble, contract; pinch up* with cold, iv. 24. 20.

contrārius, -a, -um, adj., *opposite, facing, hostile.* [contra.]

contŭbernium, -ii, n., lit. *tent companionship; comradeship, fellowship, association,* ii. 4. 4. [taberna.]

contŭmax, -acis, adj., *obstinate, stubborn, unyielding.*

contŭmēlla, -ae, f., *insult, affront;* in contumeliam accipens, iii. 8. 8, *treating as an insult.*

convĕnio, -īre, -vēni, -ventum, v. intr., *come together; agree with, suit.*

convĕniens, -entis, part. of convenio, as adj., *agreeing, suitable, applicable to,* i. 27. 1.

convīcium, -ii, n., *loud noise,* prop. of many voices together, *general clamour, outcry.* [vox.]

convictus, -ūs, m., *living together, intimacy.* [vivo.]

convīva, -ae, m. and f., *messmate, guest.* [vivo.]

convīvium, -ii, n., *banquet, feast.* [vivo.]

convŏco, -āre, -āvi, -ātum, v. tr., *call together, summon.*

cōpia, -ae, f., *abundance, plenty, supply.* [co : ops.]

cōpiōsus, -a, -um, adj., *well-supplied, plentiful, abundant.* [copia.]

cor, cordis, n., *heart.* [καρδία.]

cōram, prep. with abl. and adv., *in the presence of, before.*

corcŏdīlus, -i, m., poet. form of crocodilus, *crocodile;* i. 25. 4 note. [κροκόδειλος.]

cŏrium, -ii, n., *hide, leather.* [χόριον.]

cornĕus, -a, -um, adj., *of horn, horny; hard* as horn, iii. 6. 5, of shell. [cornu.]

cornix, -īcis, f., *crow.* [κορώνη.]

cornu, -ūs, n., *horn, antler.* [κέρας.]

cŏrōna, -ae, f., *wreath, chaplet, garland.* [κορώνη.]

corpus, -ŏris, n., *body; person; frame; size,* i. 5. 5.

corrĭgo, -ĕre, -rexi, -rectum, v. tr., *set straight, amend, correct.* [rego.]

corrĭpio, -ĕre, -rĭpui, -reptum, v. tr., *seize hold of, seize.* [rapio.]

corrumpo, -ĕre, -rūpi, -ruptum, v. tr., *spoil, ruin, demoralise, corrupt; weaken,* ii. 8. 21; gratiam cor., iv. 25. 18; *lose his favour or patronage.*

cortex, -īcis, m., rarely f., *bark* of tree; *shell* of tortoise, ii. 6. 12.

corvus, -i, m., *raven.* [cf. cornix, κόραξ.]

cōtīdiē, adv., *everyday, daily.* [quot: dies.]

cŏturnus, -i, m., *boot* with thick soles worn by tragic actors, *tragic buskin,* iv. 7. 5. [κόθορνος.]

crēdo, -ĕre, -dīdi, -dītum, v. tr. and intr., *trust, entrust, believe, think.*

crēdŭlītas, -ātis, f., *easiness of belief, credulity.*

creo, -āre, -āvi, -ātum, v. tr., *create, beget, make, produce, appoint.* [cresco.]

crēpuscŭlum, -i, n., *twilight, dusk.*

crīmen, -īnis, n., *charge, accusation ; fault, crime.*

crīmĭnor, -āri, ātus, v. dep. tr., *charge, accuse.*

crūdēlis, -e, adj., *cruel, hardhearted.* [crudus.]

cruor, -ōris, m., *blood* from wound, *gore.* [crudus.]

crus, crūris, n., *leg* below knee.

crux, crūcis, f., *cross,* instrument of torture on which criminals were impaled or hanged.

cŭbīle, -is, n., *couch ; bedchamber ; lair, den.*

culpa, -ae, f., *blame, fault, sin, misdeed ;* meâ culpâ, i. 23. 8, *through my fault ;* culpae proximam, i. 10. 5 note, *guilty.*

cultrix, -īcis, f., *female inhabitant,* ii. 4. 3.

cultus, -a, -um, part. of cŏlo as adj., *cultivated ;* of ears, ii. Epil. 12.

cum, prep. with abl., *together with, with.*

cum, conj., (1) temporal, *when,* with ind. or subj. ; (2) causal, with subj. *since ;* (3) concessive, with subj. *although.*

cunctus, -a, -um, adj., *all together, one and all.*

cŭnĕus, -i, m., *wedge ;* wedge-shaped *block of seats* in theatre or amphitheatre, v. 7. 35.

cŭnīcŭlus, -i, m., *rabbit ; subterranean gallery, burrow, tunnel.* [Spanish word.]

cŭpīdē, adv., *eagerly, earnestly ;* superl. cupidissime. [cupidus.]

cŭpīdĭtas, -ātis, f., *eager desire, longing, greed.*

cŭpīdus, -a, -um, adj., *eager, desirous of, greedy.*

cŭpio, -ĕre, -īvi, -ītum, v. tr. and intr., *desire, long for.*

cŭr, conj. *why, wherefore.* [quare.]

cūra, -ae, f., *care, anxiety ; object of care ; work,* ii. Epil. 10. [caveo.]

cūrātio, -ōnis, f., *management ;* in medicine, *method of treatment, means of cure,* v. 7. 12.

cūriōsus, -a, -um, adj., *full of care, careful ; inquisitive.* Comp. curiosior.

cūro, -āri, -āvi, -ātum, v. tr., *take care of, see to, see that,* with subj., v. 2. 6.

curro, -ĕre, cŭcurri, cursum, v. intr., *run, hasten.*

cursus, -ūs, m., *running, race, course, flight, march, voyage, speed, pace.* [curro.]

custōdio, -īre, -īvi or -ii, -ītum, v. tr., *guard, watch.*

custos, -ōdis, m. and f., *guardian, guard.*

cŭtis, -is, f., *skin,* generally of men.

Cўbēbĕ, -ēs, or -ae, f., *Cybĕle,* Phrygian goddess, also called Rhea, worshipped at Rome as Ops or the Magna Mater. Her priests were called Galli, Corybantes or Curetes, iii. 17. 4; iv. 1. 4.

damno, -āre, -āvi, -ātum, v. a., *condemn.*

damnum, -i, n., *loss, damage, harm.*

[daps], dăpis, f. defect. not in nom. sing., *sacrificial feast;* generally in plur., *banquet, feast.*

Dardănia, -ae, f., the *country of Dardanus;* hence poet. *Troy.*

de, prep. with abl., *down from, from, out of, of; concerning, about;* de tuo, iv. 20. 26, *at your expense.*

dēbeo, -ēre, -ui, -ītum, v. tr. and intr., *owe; am bound, due, ought.* [de: habeo.]

dēbĭlis, -e, adj., *disabled, feeble, weak.* [de: habilis.]

dēbĭtum, -i, n., *thing due, debt.* [debeo.]

dĕcem, num. adj. indecl., *ten.* [δέκα.]

dĕceptus, see decipio.

dēcerno, -ĕre, -crēvi, -crētum, v. tr. and intr., *decide, determine.*

dēcĭdo, -ĕre, -cĭdi, no sup. v. intr., *fall down* or *from.* [cădo.]

dēcĭpio, -ĕre, -cēpi, -ceptum, v. tr., *entrap, deceive.* [căpio.]

dēclāro, -āre, -āvi, -ātum, v. tr., *make clear, declare.*

dĕcor, -ōris, m., *what is becoming, beauty.* [deceo.]

dēcurro, -ĕre, -cŭcurri or -curri, -cursum, v. intr., *run down; run completely over, complete, spend.*

dĕcus, -ŏris, n., *ornament, beauty, glory, honour.* [deceo.]

dēdĕcus, -ŏris, n., *dishonour, disgrace.*

dēdĭco, -āre, -āvi, -ātum, v. tr., *declare; dedicate, consecrate.*

dēdo, -ĕre, dedĭdi, dedĭtum, v. tr., *give up, abandon, surrender.* Middle use dedi, iv. 4. 13, *surrender oneself;* deditus studio, iv. 22. 19, *devoted to study.*

dēdūco, -ĕre, -xi, -ctum, v. tr., *lead down, conduct to, bring* case *into* law courts, iii. 13. 3; est deductus, ii. 1. 5, *came.*

dēfĭcio, -ĕre, -fēci, -fectum, v. tr. and intr., *fail, am wanting, abandon, desert;* defectus, i. 21. 3, *worn out, weakened;* defectus pilis,

v. 6. 2, *destitute of hair.*
[făcio.]

deflecto, -ĕre, -xi, -xum, v.
tr. and intr., *bend* or *turn
aside.*

dēgo, -ĕre, dēgi, no sup. v.
tr., *spend, pass* time, etc.
[de : ago.]

dēgrăvo, -āre, no perf., -ātum,
v. tr., *weigh down.* [grăvis.]

dēgrunnio, -īre, no perf. or
sup. v. intr., *grunt* or
squeak loudly, v. 5. 27.

dein or deindĕ, adv., *from
there, thereafter, then, next,
secondly.*

dēïcio (for dŭïicio), -ĕre, -iēci,
-iectum, v. tr., *throw* or
cast down, hurl or *strike
down.* [de : iacio.]

dēïectus, see deicio.

delecto, -āre, -āvi, -ātum, v.
tr., *delight, amuse.*

dēlēnio, -īri, -īvi, -ītum, v.
tr., *soothe.* [lēnis.]

dēlĭbo, -āre, -āvi, -ātum, v.
tr., *taste of, sip, gather.*

dēlĭbūtus, -a, -um, perf. part.
from obsolete delibuo as
adj., *smeared with, drenched
with, reeking.*

dēlĭcătus, -a, -um, adj., *delightful, delicate, mincing*
step, v. 1. 13.

dēlĭcium, -ii, n., *anything that
delights; luxury, effemin-
acy; darling, pet,* iv. 1. 8.

dēlĭgo, -ĕre. -lēgi, -lectum,
v. tr., *pick out, select.* [lego.]

dēlinquo, -ĕre, -līqui, -lictum,
v. intr., *leave undone, fail
in duty, sin, offend.*

dēlīrus, -a, -um, adj., *crazy,
senseless, mad.*

dēlūdo, -ĕre, -si, -sum, v. tr.,
*make game of, mock, baffle,
disappoint.* [ludus.]

dēmens, -entis, adj. *out of
one's mind, mad, foolish.*

dēmentia, -ae, f., *madness,
folly.*

Dēmētrius, -ii, m., *Demetrius*
of Phalerum, v. 1. 1 note.
[Δημήτριος.]

dēmitto, -ĕre, -mīsi, -missum,
v. tr., *send down, lower.*

dēmonstro, -āre, -āvi, -ātum,
v. tr., *point out, show,
prove.*

dēmum, adv., *at length, at last.*

dēnĭquĕ, adv., *and then, in
short, finally.*

dens, dentis, m., *tooth, tusk.*
[ὀδούς.]

dēpendeo, ēre, no perf. or
sup., v. intr., *hang down.*

dēperdĭtus, -a, -um, part.
from deperdo as adj., *utterly
ruined.*

dēplōro, -āre, -āvi, -ātum, v.
tr. and intr., *lament, bewail,
deplore.*

dēpōno, -ĕre, -pŏsui, -pŏsĭtum,
v. tr., *set* or *place down,
place, deposit.*

deprendo or deprĕhendo, -ĕre,
-di, -sum, v. tr., *seize upon,
catch.*

dēprimo, -ĕre, -pressi, -pres-
sum, v. tr., *press down;*
depressus, *sunk,* i. 20. 3.

dēpugno, -āre, -āvi, -ātum,
v. intr., *fight it out, fight to
the end.*

dērēpo, -ĕre, -psi, no sup., v. intr., *creep* or *crawl down.*

dērīdeo, -ēre, -rīsi, -rīsum, v. tr., *laugh to scorn, mock at, deride.*

dērīsor, -ōris, m., *scoffer, mocker.*

dērīsus, -ūs, m., *mockery, scorn, derision;* derisui est, i. 11. 2, *is an object of scorn.*

descendo, -ĕre, -ndi, -nsum, v. intr. *climb down, come down, descend.* [scando.]

descrībo, -ĕre, -psi, -ptum, v. tr., *write of, describe.*

dēsĕro, -ĕre, -sĕrui, -sertum, v. tr., *disjoin; abandon, desert, betray.*

dēsertus, -a, -um, part. of descro as adj., *abandoned, desert.*

dēsīdĕro, -āre, -āvi, -ātum, v. tr., *yearn for* something, *look for* in vain, *long for, regret, miss, expect* in vain, i. 8. 1.

dēsīdo, -ĕre, -sēdi, no sup., v. intr., *settle down, sit still, perch,* ii. 4. 21. [sedeo.]

dēsīno, -ĕre, -sīvī or -sii, -sītum, v. intr., *leave off, cease.*

dēspīcio, -ĕre, -spexi, -spectum, v. tr., *look down at, despise, scorn.*

destīno, -āre, -āvi, -ātum, v. tr., *establish; resolve, determine.*

dēstītuo, -ĕre, -ui, -ūtum, v. tr., *set aside, abandon, desert.* [statuo.]

destrictus, see destringo.

destringo, -ĕre, -nxi, -ctum, v. tr., *draw off; strip off;* of dress. tunica ab umeris erat destricta, ii. 5. 13, *his tunic was stripped from his shoulders,* i.e. *left his shoulders bare; find fault with, attack,* iv. 7. 1.

dēsum, -esse, -fui, v. intr., *am wanting to, fail;* ne desit mihi, iii. 15. 8, *that I may not want.*

dētĕro, -ĕre, -trīvi, -trītum, v. tr., *rub* or *wear away.*

dēterreo, -ēre, -ui, -itum, v. tr., *frighten off, prevent.*

dētrāho, -ĕre, -xi, -ctum, v. tr., *draw off, take off, flay,* iv. 1. 7.

dētrītus, see detcro.

deus, -i, m., *God.*

dēvĕnio, -īre, -vēni, -ventum, v. intr., *come* or *go down.*

dēvōco, -āre, -āvi, -ātum, v. tr., *call away, lead on to, lure* or *allure to,* i. 20. 2, etc.

dēvolvo, -ĕre, -volvi, -vŏlūtum. v. tr., *roll down, roll off,* v. 7. 23 n., of thunder.

dēvŏro, -āre, -āvi, -ātum, v. tr., *swallow, devour.*

dextĕra or dextra, -ac, f., *right hand.* [prop. f. of adj. dexter, sc. manus.]

dīco, -ĕre, -xi, -ctum, v. tr., *say, speak, speak of as, call, name; appoint,* iv. 25. 19; *pronounce* sentence, i. 10. 8; male dicere, *with dat., speak ill of, slander.*

H

dictum, -i, n., *thing said, word, order, decree* of fate, iv. 11. 19. [dico.]

dies, -ēi, in sing. m. and f., pl. m., *day, daylight; climate, weather,* iv. 17. 5. *the day of payment,* i. 16. 7.

difficulter, adv., *with difficulty.* [difficilis.]

diffluo, -ēre, no perf. and sup., v. intr., *flow different ways, flow, drip* with perspiration, iv. 25. 23.

dignĭtas, -ātis, f., *work, merit, dignity, official rank, importance.* [dignus.]

dignus, -a, -um, adj., *worthy, deserving, suitable; worthy of,* with abl.

dīlātio, -ōnis, f., *delay, postponement.*

dīlĭgens, -entis, part. fr. diligo as adj., *careful, painstaking, exact, industrious.*

dīlĭgenter, adv., *carefully, accurately.*

dīlĭgo, -ēre, -lexi, -lectum, v. tr., *single out; love.* [lego.]

dīmitto, -ēre, -mīsi, -missum, v. tr., *send off, dismiss, let go.*

dīrĭpio, -ēre, -rĭpui, -reptum, v. tr., *tear asunder; pillage, plunder.* [rapio.]

discēdo, -ēre, -cessi, -cessum, v. intr., *go different ways, depart.*

discerno, -ēre, -crēvi, -crētum, v. tr., *separate, distinguish.*

disco, -ēre, dĭdĭci, no sup., v. tr., *learn.* [διδάσκω.]

dispergo, -ēre, -spersi, -spersum, v. tr., *scatter about, spread abroad.* [spargo.]

dispersus, see dispergo.

dissĭdeo, -ēre, -sēdi, -sessum, v. intr., *sit apart, am separated, disagree, quarrel.* [sedeo.]

dissĭmŭlo, -āre, -āvi, -ātum, v. tr., *conceal, hide.*

dissŏlūtus, -a, -um, part. of dissolvo, as adj., *loose, lax, licentious.*

dissolvo, -ēre, -solvi, -sŏlūtum, v. tr., *unloose, dissolve, destroy, break up,* iv. 22. 10.

distringo, -ēre, -nxi, -ctum, v. tr., lit. *draw asunder,* rare; *engage attention* from other things, *engross,* iii. Epil. 3.

diu, adv., *for a long time;* comp. diutius, *for longer, for some little while,* i. 2. 16. [dies.]

dīversus, -a, -um, part. of diverto as adj., *opposite, hostile, different.*

dīves, -ĭtis, adj., *rich; richly stocked,* iv. 12. 2.

dīvĭdo, -ēre, -vīsi, -vīsum, v. tr., *separate, divide, distribute.* [dis.]

dīvīnus, -a, -um, adj., *divine, celestial;* d. domus, v. 7. 38, *the royal house.* [divus.]

dīvīsus, see divido.

dīvĭtiae, -ārum, f. pl., *riches, wealth.* [dives.]

dīvus, -i, m., *god, deity.*
[deus.]

do, dăre, dĕdi, dătum, v.
tr., *give, offer, grant, afford,
assign;* accessum d., ii. 1.
10, *permit approach;* poenas d., i. 13. 2, *pay penalty;*
operam d., v. 7. 5, *assist;*
leto d., iii. 16. 18, *put to
death, kill.*

dŏceo, -ēre, -cui, -doctum, v.
tr., *teach, inform, state, explain.* [διδάσκω, disco.]

dŏcĭlis, -e, adj., *easily taught;
quick* of apprehension,
ready.

doctus, -a, -um, part. of doceo
as adj., *learned, educated,
skilled.*

dŏcŭmentum, -i, n., *lesson,
example, proof, instructive
instance.* [doceo.]

dŏleo, -ēre, -ui, -ĭtum, v. intr.
and tr., *feel pain* or *annoyance, grieve, grieve for, feel
indignant at.*

dŏlo or dŏlon, -ōnis, m., *pike*
with sharp iron point;
sword-stick; sting of fly,
etc., iii. 6. 3 n.

dŏlor, -ōris, m., *pain, grief.*

dŏlōsus, -a, -um, adj., *full of
cunning, crafty, deceitful,
treacherous.* [dolus.]

dŏlus, -i, m., *craft, guile,
trick.* [δόλος.]

dŏmestĭcus, -a, -um, adj., *of
the house* or *home, domestic;*
res d., iii. Prol. 11, *domestic
affairs.*

dŏmĭnus, -i, m., *master, lord;
the Master* of Euripides, ii.

5. 14; *the Sovereign* of
Emperor, ii. 5. 21.

dŏmo, -āre, -ui, -ĭtum, v. tr.,
tame, subdue. [δαμάω.]

dŏmum, adv., *to home, home-
wards.*

dŏmus, -ūs, f., irreg., *house,
home.* [δόμος.]

dōnātio, -ōnis, f., *gift, present,
reward.* [dono.]

dōnĕc, conj., *as long as, while:
until.*

dōno, -āre, -āvi, -ātum, v. tr.,
give, present.

dormio, -īre, -īvi or -ii, -ītum,
v. intr., *sleep.* [δαρθάνω.]

dorsum, -i, n., *back* of animal,
rarely of man; *ridge* of
rock.

dōs, dōtis, f., *dowry; en-
dowment, quality, special
gift, excellence,* i. Prol. 3.
[do.]

drāco, -onis, m., *serpent,
dragon.* [δράκων.]

dŭbĭto, -āre, -āvi, -ātum, v.
intr., *waver* in opinion,
hesitate, doubt. [duo.]

dŭbium, -ii, n., *doubt;* in
dubium venerit, iii. 13. 7,
has come to be disputed.

dŭbĭus, -a, -um, adj., *waver-
ing, doubtful;* res d., v.
2. 15, *misfortune.* [duo.]

dūco, -ĕre, -xi, -ctum, v. tr.,
*lead, guide: lead away,
take off,* i. 19. 7, etc.; *spend*
life, etc.; *marry* a wife;
give a blow, v. 3. 2.

dulcis, -e, adj., *sweet, pleasant,
charming, dear: fresh*
water, iv. 9. 6. [γλυκύς.]

dum, conj., *while, whilst, as long as, until*, generally with indic.; *provided that*, with subj., 1. 15. 10, etc.

dummŏdŏ, conj., *if only, provided only that*, with subj.

duŏ, -ae, -o, num. adj., *two*. [δύο.]

dŭplex, -ĭcis, adj., *twofold, double*.

dūro, -āre, -āvi, -ātum, v. tr., *make hard, harden*.

dūrus, -a, -um, adj., *hard; harsh; painful, disagreeable*.

dux, dŭcis, m. and f., *leader, chief, commander;* tanti maiestas ducis, ii. 5. 23, *the mighty sovereign's majesty*. [duco.]

e, prep. : see ex.

ēbĭbo, -ĕre, -bĭbi, -bĭbĭtum, v. tr., *drink up*.

eccĕ, demons. adv., *see / behold !*

ēdo, -ĕre, -dĭdi, -dĭtum, v. tr., *give forth, produce ; utter words*.

ēdūco, -ĕre, -xi, -ctum, v. tr., *lead forth or out*.

ēdūco, -āre, -āvi, -ātum, v. tr., *bring up, rear, educate*.

effectus, -ūs, m., *accomplishment, execution, operation, result*. [efficio.]

effĕro, -ferre, extŭli, ēlātum, v. tr., *carry out, bring forth*.

effĭcio, -ĕre, -fēci, -fectum, v. tr., *complete, effect, make*. [făcio.]

effĭgies, -ēi, f., *likeness, image, statue, reflection*.

effŏdio, -ĕre, -fōdi, -fossum, v. tr., *dig out*.

effŭgio, -ĕre, -fūgi, no sup., v. tr. and intr., *flee away, escape, escape from*.

effŭgium, -ii, n., *flight, escape*.

ĕgŏ, gen. mei, 1st pers. pron., *I*. [ἐγώ.]

egrēdior, -grĕdi, -gressus, v. dep. tr. and intr., *go or come out, pass out from, leave*. [gradior.]

ēgrēgius, -a, -um, adj., *distinguished, eminent, excellent*. [e : grex.]

ēlābor, -i, -lapsus, v. dep. intr., *slip away, escape*.

ēlĕgantia, -ae, f., *good taste, refinement, elegance*.

ēlĕvo, -āre, -āvi, -ātum, v. tr., *make light, lessen, disparage*. [levis.]

ēlūdo, -ĕre, -lūsi, -lūsum, v. tr., *elude blow, escape, avoid, baffle*. [prop. *win from a person at play,* ludus.]

ēmendo, -āre, -āvi, -ātum, v. tr., *free from faults, improve, correct*.

ēmĭneo, -ēre, -ui, no sup., v. intr., *stand out, project, am prominent;* celsa cervice eminet, ii. 7. 4, *carries his neck high*.

ēmitto, -ĕre, -mīsi, -missum, v. tr., *send out or forth ; let go*.

ēmŏrior, -mŏri, -mortuus, v. dep. intr., *die away, die out, perish utterly*.

ēn, interj., *lo! behold!*

ēnăto, -āre, -āvi, no sup. v. intr., *swim out, escape by swimming,* iv. 22. 14.

ēnim, conj., *in fact, indeed, for;* neque enim, *for indeed ... not.*

ēnimvēro, conj., *as a matter of course, yes indeed, naturally.*

ēnītor, -i, -nixus or -nisus, v. dep. tr. and intr., *struggle out, strive: give birth to.*

enixus, see enitor.

eo, īre, īvi or ii, itum, v. intr., *go;* pres. part., iens; gen. enntis. [εἶμι.]

ĕpīlŏgus, -i, m., *concluding remarks, poem, etc., epilogue.* [ἐπίλογος.]

ēpōto, -āre, -āvi, epōtum, v. tr., *drink up, drain;* epotus, *drained, emptied,* iii. 1. 1.

ēpōtus, see epoto.

ĕques, -ĭtis, m., *horseman: knight;* pl. Equites, *the Knights,* a Roman order, v. 7. 33. [ĕquus.]

ĕquester, -tris, -tre, adj., *of a horseman or knight;* eq. ordo, *the Order of Knights,* see eques, v. 7. 30. [eques.]

ĕquĭdem, adv., *verily, truly, indeed.* [e: quidem.]

ĕquus, -i, m., *horse.* [ἴππος.]

ērādo, -ĕre, -si, -sum, v. tr., *scrape off* or *out, efface, erase.*

ergŏ, adv., *therefore, then; and so,* often ironical, or

indicating surprise or grief, see iv. 20. 12.

ērĭpio, -ĕre, -rīpui, -reptum, v. tr., *snatch away, tear from, rescue from,* i. 28. 11. [răpio.]

erro, -āre, -āvi, -ātum, v. intr., *wander about; go wrong, err, make mistake, blunder.* [ἔρ-χομαι.]

error, -ōris, m., *wandering: error, mistake.* [erro.]

ērumpo, -ĕre, -rūpi, -ruptum, v. tr. and intr., *make to burst forth; break forth, dash forth.*

ēruo, -ĕre, -rui, -rūtum, v. intr., *dig out, tear out; draw forth, elicit, show,* i. 12. 2.

esca, -ae, f., *food; bait.* [ĕdo ēsum, *eat.*]

ēsŭrio, -īre, no perf., -ītum, v. tr. and intr., *desire to eat, am hungry.* [desid. of ĕdo, *eat.*]

ĕt, conj. and adv., *and, and also, also; and yet,* i. 8. 12; et ... et, *both ... and,* so et ... nec, i. 4. 7.

ĕtiam, conj., *and also, even.* [et : iam.]

eunti, see eo.

Eutўchus, -i, m., proper name, see iii. Prol. 2 note.

ēvādo, -ĕre, -si, -sum, v. tr. and intr., *go forth or out; get out of, escape from.*

ēvăgor, -āri, -ātus, v. tr. and intr., *wander forth, stray beyond.*

ēvello, -ĕre, -velli, rarely
-vulsi, -vulsum, v. tr., *tear
out, pluck out.*

ēventus, -ūs, m., *occurrence,
event.* [ēvĕnio, *happen.*]

ēverto, -ĕre, -ti, -sum, v. tr.,
overthrow, destroy.

ēvŏco, -āre, -āvi, -ātum, v. tr.,
call forth or *out.*

ex or e, prep. with abl., *out
of, from;* unus ex, *one of;
on the side of, instead of,
after.* [ἐκ, ἐξ.]

exaggĕro, -āre, -āvi, -ātum, v.
tr., *heap up.* [agger.]

exāro, -āre, -āvi, -ātum, v. tr.,
*plough up, furrow; scratch
on wax tablets,* i.e. *write,*
iii. Prol. 29.

excēdo, -ĕre, -cessi, -cessum,
v. tr. and intr., *go forth* or
out or *away : depart from,
leave; go beyond, overstep.*

excĭpio, -ĕre, -cēpi, -ceptum,
v. tr., *take out, exempt,
except ; take to oneself,
catch ;* as hunting term
capture, i. 11. 6; *take in
turn, receive next,* i. 12. 9;
come next to, succeed, ii. 8.
10. [capio.]

excĭto, -āre, -āvi, -ātum, v. tr.,
call out or *forth ; summon
forth ; excite, arouse, startle,
start* from lair, of stag, ii.
8. 1.

excŏlo, -ĕre, -cŏlui, -cultum,
v. tr., *cultivate well, improve ; honour, worship.*

excūso, -āre, -āvi, -ātum, v.
tr., *release from a charge*
or *from blame ; excuse ;* me

excuso, *apologise ;* huic excusatum me velim, iii.
Prol. 48, *I should wish to
apologise to him ; allege in
excuse, plead.*

excŭtio, -ĕre, -cussi, -cussum,
v. tr., *shake out* or *off.*
[quatio.]

exemplum, -i, n., *example,
instance, case, warning ;*
frequently of a fable or
story, e.g. ii. Prol. 1,
etc.

exeo, -īre, -īvi or -ii, -ĭtum, v.
intr., *go out* or *forth.*

exerceo, -ĕre, -ui, -ĭtum, *keep
in motion* or *at work, engage, occupy, practise,
maintain* rule, i. 31. 12 ;
employ, indulge in threats,
iii. 6. 11. [arceo.]

exercĭtus, -ūs, m., *drilled
body, army.* [exerceo.]

exhĭbeo, -ēre, -hĭbui, -hĭbitum,
v. tr., *hold forth, deliver,
display, show, exhibit ; produce, occasion,* iv. 7. 24.
[habeo.]

exĭgo, -ĕre, -ēgi, -actum, v.
tr., *drive forth ; enforce,
exact; bring to an end,
complete ; spend, pass* life
etc. [ago.]

exĭguus, -a, -um, adj., lit.
exactly measured, hence
scanty, little. [exigo.]

existĭmo, -āre, -āvi, -ātum, v.
tr., *value, judge, consider,
think.*

exĭtium, -ii, n., lit. *going
forth; disaster, destruction,
ruin.* [exeo.]

exĭtus, -ūs, m., *going forth,
way out, means of escape.*
[exeo.]

exōro, -āre, -āvi, -ātum, v.
tr., *move by entreaty, entreat earnestly.*

exorno, -āre, -āvi, -ātum, v.
tr., *furnish completely,
equip* thoroughly.

expēdio, -ire, -ivi or -ii, -itum,
v. tr., lit. *free the feet from,
disengage; make ready;
explain;* exp. rem, i. 16. 2,
settle the business. [ex:
pes.]

expĕrior, -iri, -pertus, v. dep.
tr., *put to the proof, make
trial of, experience, undergo,
find out.* [cf. comperio,
πεῖρα.]

expers, -ertis, adj., *having no
part in, without a share of,*
with gen. [pars.]

expēto, -ĕre, -ivi or -ii, -itum,
v. tr., *seek eagerly for.*

explĭco, -āre, -āvi and -ui,
-ātum and -itum, v. tr.,
unfold, open out, explain;
exp. fugam, iv. 7. 15, *open
out a way for* or *facilitate
flight.*

explōro, -āre, -āvi, -ātum, v.
tr., *bring to light, examine.*

exprĭmo, -ĕre, -pressi, -pres-
sum, v. tr., *press out, force
out, extort, extract.* [premo.]

exsĕquor, -qui, -cūtus, v. dep.
tr., *follow* or *pursue to the
end.*

exspectātio, -ōnis, f., *a looking out for, expectation.*
[exspecto.]

exspecto, -āre, -āvi, -ātum, v.
tr. and intr., *look out for,
wait for, expect; look out.*

exspīro, -āre, -āvi, -ātum, v.
tr. and intr., *breathe out,
breathe one's last, expire.*

exta, -ōrum, n. pl., *the outer
entrails,* heart, lungs, liver,
the *vitals,* of victim.

extollo, -ĕre, no perf. or sup.,
v. tr., *lift up* or *out, raise,
exalt, excite.*

extrăho, -ĕre, -xi, -ctum, v.
tr., *drag* or *draw out, extract.*

extrēmus, -a, -um, adj.,
superl. of exter and ex-
terus, *outermost, utmost,
last;* extremo agmine, v.
1. 14, *at the end of the band*
or *crowd.*

extrĭco, -āre, -āvi, -ātum,
v. tr., *disentangle, clear up;*
extricas nihil, iv. 23. 4,
*unravel, i.e. succeed in pro-
ducing nothing.*

extŭli, see effero.

extundo, -ĕre, -tŭdi, -tūsum,
v. tr., *beat out;* i. 21. 9, of
kicking.

exūro, -ĕre, -ussi, -ustum,
v. tr., *burn up.*

fābella, -ae, f., *short story,
tale,* or *fable.* [dim. of
fabula.]

făber, -bri, m., *workman* in
wood, iron, brass, etc.,
smith, etc.

făbrĭco, -āre, -āvi, -ātum, v.
tr., *construct, make, build.*
[faber.]

făbŭla, -ae, f., *story* true or false, *tale, legend, myth, fable, apologue.* [fari, *say.*]

făcies, -ēi, f., *form, figure, face, aspect, phase, beauty.*

făcĭlē, adv., *easily.* comp. facilius. [facilis.]

făcĭlis, -e, adj., *easy to do, easy, simple.* [făcio.]

făcĭnus, -ŏris, n., *deed, evil deed, crime.* [facio.]

făcio, -ĕre, fēci, factum, v. tr., *make, do, perform* ; *practise* art of medicine, i. 14. 2 ; *administer* remedy, i. 8. 9 ; *exhibit* games, v. 7. 16 ; f. lucrum, *make gain, profit,* i. 23. 8 ; *cause* delay, iv. 25. 26 ; partibus factis, i. 5. 6, *when it had been divided into shares;* fecisse ... satis for satisfecisse, see satisfacio, v. 10. 2.

factio, -ōnis, f., *a taking sides, combination, cabal, faction.*

faex, faecis, f., *dregs, sediment.*

Fălernus, -a, -um, adj., *Falernian,* of Falernian district in N. of Campania, famous for wine, iii. 1. 2.

fallācia, -ae, f., *deceit, trick, treachery.* [fallo.]

fallo, -ĕre, fĕfelli, falsum, v. tr., *deceive, trick.*

falso, adv., *falsely, erroneously.* [falsus.]

falsus, -a, -um, part. of fallo as adj., *false, erroneous.*

fāma, -ae, f., *report, rumour, reputation, fame.*[fari, *say.*]

fămēlĭcus, -a, -um, adj., *starving, famished, hungry.* [fāmes.]

fămes, -is, f.; abl. sing. famē, 5th decl. form, iv. 3. 1 n.; *hunger.*

fămĭlĭa, -ae, f., *the slaves of a household,household,family, establishment,* used of one man, iii. 19. 1. [famulus.]

fărīna, -ae, f., *flour of wheat, meal.* [far, *spelt, corn.*]

fas, n. indecl., *what is permitted by divine law;* fas est, *it is lawful* or *allowed.* [fari.]

fascia, -ae, f., *band, bandage.* [fascis.]

fastĭdio, -ire, -īvi or -ii, -ĭtum, v. tr., *feel disgust at, loathe, despise, scorn.* [fastidium.]

fastĭdĭōsē, adv., *with disgust, disdainfully, with disdainful niceness, critically ;* fastidiose recipior, iii. Prol. 23, *I find but jealous admission.*

fātālis, -e, adj., *ordained* or *destined by fate.* [fatum.]

făteor, -ēri, fassus, v. dep. tr., *confess, admit.* [fari.]

fătĭgo, -āre, -āvi, -ātum, v. tr., *weary, tire out.*

fātum, -i, n., *prophetic utterance; fate, destiny ;* personified plur., *the Fates.* [fari.]

fauces, -ium, f. pl.; abl. sing., fauce, only poetical, i. 8. 4 : i. 1. 3 ; upper part of *throat, gullet ; jaws ; appetite, voracity.*

fautor, -ōris, m., *one who favours, supporter.* [faveo.]

făveo, -ēre, favi, fautum, v. intr., *am favourable to, favour.*

făvor, -ōris, m., *favour, popularity; approval, partisanship.* [faveo.]

făvus, -i, m., *honey comb.* iii. 13. 1 ; 13, 10.

fax, făcis, f., *torch, firebrand.* [φάος.]

fēcundus, -a, -um, adj., *fruitful, fertile.* [rt. fe, see femina, felicitas, fetus.]

fēles and fēlis, -is, f., *cat.*

fēlīcĭtas, -ātis, f., *fertility; happiness, good fortune, success.* [rt. fe, see fecundus, felix.]

fēlīcĭter, adv., *fruitfully, happily, auspiciously.* In exclamations of greeting, *good luck to you ; hurrah ;* sc. vivas or sit tibi, v. 1. 4. [See felicitas.]

fēmĭna, -ae, f., *woman ; female* of lamb, iii. 15. 11 ; of goat, iv. 16. 3. [See fecundus.]

fēnestra, -ae, f., *opening* in wall, *aperture, window.* [φαίνω, *show.*]

fēra, -ae, f., *wild beast* or *animal.* [ferus.]

fērĭae, -ārum, f. pl., *holidays, festival.*

fēro, ferre, tŭli, lātum, v. tr., *bear, carry, bring, give* aid to ; *put up with, endure ;* indigne f., *am indignant at, take it ill, complain,* i.

21. 10, iii. 18. 1 ; *report, say ; exhibit, publish,* v. Prol. 12. Pass. feror, in middle sense, v. Prol. 10, *move on to ;* of ship, iv. 17. 6, *sail along, move onward.* [φέρω.]

ferrārius, -a, -um, adj., *of* or *belonging to iron ;* faber f., *a blacksmith,* iv. 8, title. [ferrum.]

ferrum, -i, n., *iron, steel,* iron *weapon* or *tool, sword,* etc.

fĕrus, -a, -um, adj., *wild, untamed.*

fĕrus, -i, m., *wild beast* or *animal.*

fessus, -a, -um, adj., *wearied, tired.* [fatiscor.]

festīno, -āre, -āvi, -ātum, v. tr. and intr., *hasten, make haste.*

fētus, -ūs, m., *brood, litter, offspring.* [rt. fe, see fecundus.]

fictus, -a, -um, part. of fingo as adj., *feigned, false, fictitious.* See fingo.

fĭdēlis, -e, adj., *trustworthy, faithful.* [fides.]

fĭdes, -ēi, f., *trust, faith, loyalty, good faith, belief ;* amittit fidem, i. 10. 2, *does not obtain credence ;* vocis fidem, iii. Epil. 9, *your promise, the fulfilment of your promise ;* pactam fidem, iii. 13. 17, *promise.*

fĭdūcia, -ae, f., *confidence, trust.* [fido.]

fīlia, -ae, f., *daughter.*

fīlius, -ii, m., *son.* [rt. fe, see fecundus.]

fingo, -ĕre, finxi, fictum, v. tr., *form, fashion; compose,* ii. Epil. 13; *imagine; represent,* v. 8. 7; *contrive, invent; arrange, trim, improve in appearance,* ii. 2. 8; absol. finxit, *composed a fable,* iv. 17. 2. [figura.]

fio, fĭĕri, factus, v. intr. semidep., used as pass. of facio, *am made, become, happen, turn into.*

firmus, -a, -um, adj., *firm, strong.* [fortis.]

fiscus, -i, m., *large osier basket; pannier,* ii. 7. 2, for carrying money; *money, public treasury, revenue.*

flăgellum, -i, n., *scourge, riding* or *driving whip.* [dim. of flagrum, *scourge.*]

flăgĭto, -āre, -āvi, -ātum, v. tr., *demand* eagerly, *clamour for.* [rt. flag, cf. flamma.]

flamma, -ae, f., *blaze, flame. fire.* [rt. flag, cf. flagito.]

flătus, -ūs, m., *blowing, breath, blast, breeze.* [flāre, *to blow.*]

flecto, -ĕre, -xi, -xum, v. tr. and intr., *bend, turn, direct.*

fleo, -ēre, flēvi, fletum, v. tr. and intr., *weep, weep for, bewail, lament.* [cf. fluo.]

flētus, -ūs, m., *weeping, lament.* [fleo.]

flexus, -ūs, m., *bending, turning, winding;* ii. 5. 17, *winding ways* or *side paths.* [flecto.]

flōreo, -ēre, -ui, no sup., v. intr., *blossom; prosper, flourish.* [flos.]

fluens, -entis, part. of fluo, *I flow,* as adj., *lax, effeminate;* fluens vestitu, v. 1. 12, *with flowing robes.*

flūmen, -ĭnis, n., *flowing water, river, stream.* [fluo.]

fluvius, -ii, m., *stream, river.* [fluo.]

fŏdio, -ĕre, fōdi, fossum, v. tr. and intr., *dig, dig up.*

foedus, -ĕris, n., *league, treaty.* [fides: fido.]

fons, fontis, m., *spring, fountain, source.*

fŏras, adv. with verbs of motion, *out of doors.* [acc. form : foris, abl. form.]

fŏret, see sum.

forma, -ae, f., *form, shape; good shape, beauty, shapeliness.*

formīca, -ae, f. *ant.*

formōsus, -a, -um, adj., *shapely, beautiful, handsome;* comp. formosior. [forma.]

forsan, adv., *may be, perhaps.* [fors-sit-an.]

fortassĕ, adv., *perhaps, possibly.* [forte.]

fortĕ, adv., *by chance, as chance would have it, it chanced that.* [abl. of fors.]

fortis, -e, adj., *strong, brave.* [firmus.]

fortĭter, adv., *strongly, stoutly, bravely, vigorously;* comp. fortius, sup. fortissime. [fortis.]

fortĭtūdo, -ĭnis, f., *strength,
courage.* [fortis.]
fortuītus, -a, -um, adj., *hap-
pening by chance, casual,
accidental.* [fors.]
fortūna, -ae, f., *luck, fortune,
good or bad.* Personified
as goddess Fortuna, iv. 12.
5. [fors.]
forŭm, -i, n., *public place,
market place,* in a town ;
esp. *the Forum* at Rome,
between Capitoline and
Palatine hills, surrounded
by the official and business
buildings; hence *law courts,*
iii. 13. 3. [cf. foras.]
fŏvea, -ae, f., *pitfall, snare,
trap.* [fodio, *dig.*]
fŏveo, -ēre, fōvi, fōtum, v.
tr., *warm, cherish.*
frango, -ĕre, frēgi, fractum,
v. tr., *break, smash.*
[ῥήγνυμι.]
frāter, -tris, m., *brother.*
[φράτηρ.]
fraudātor, -ōris, m., *one who
defrauds, cheat, impostor.*
[fraudo.]
fraudo, -āre, -āvi, -ātum, v.
tr., *cheat, defraud of,* with
acc. and abl., iv. 20. 19,
etc. [fraus.]
fraus, fraudis, f., *deceit,
treachery ; trick, artifice ;*
fraudem moliens, iv. 9. 7,
laying a trap.
frĕmo, -ĕre, -ui, -ĭtum, v.
intr., *make a low, dull noise,
mutter, roar, sound ;* rumor
fremit, v. 7. 21, *the report
buzzes* through the theatre.

frēno, -āre, -āvi, -ātum, v.
tr., *furnish with bridle ;
curb, restrain.* [frēnum.]
frēnum, -i, n., pl. freni or
frena ; *bridle, curb, bit ;
check, restraints,* i. 2. 3.
frĕquento, -āre, -āvi, -ātum,
v. tr., *resort to frequently,
frequent.* [frequens.]
frētum, -i, n., *strait, channel ;
sea.* [ferveo.]
frīgus, -ŏris, n., *cold.* [ῥῖγος.]
frīvŏlus, -a, -um, adj., *trifling,
vain, empty, silly ;* f. aura,
v. 7. 1, *empty,* i.e. *worthless breeze* of popularity.
frons, -ntis, f., *forehead,
brow ; appearance,* iv. 2. 6.
frons, -ndis, f., *leaf, bough,
foliage ; fodder,* ii. 8. 11.
fructus, -ūs, m., *enjoyment ;
produce ; fruit : result* of
toil, etc., *reward, profit,*
iii. 13. 15 ; iv. 20. 8.
[fruor.]
fruor, -i, fructus and fruĭtus,
v. dep. with abl., rarely
acc., *enjoy, have the benefit
of.* [fruges : fructus.]
frustrā, adv., *in error, in
vain.* [fraus.]
frustum, -i, n., *fragment,
morsel, bit, scrap.*
frutex, -ĭcis, m., *shrub, bush.*
fūcātus, -a, -um, part. fr.
fuco as adj., *painted, made
up, artificial.*
fūcus, -i, m., *drone bee.*
fŭga, -ae, f., *flight.* [fugio.]
fŭgax, -ācis, adj., *inclined to
flee, apt to run away.*
[fugio.]

fŭgio, -ĕre, fūgi, fŭgĭtum, v. intr. and tr., *flee, fly, run away; flee from, escape from; avoid, decline,* iii. 9. 3. [φεύγω : φυγή.]

fŭgĭto, -āre, -āvi, -ātum, v. intr. and tr., *flee hastily, flee from eagerly, shun.* [freq. of fugio.]

fŭgo, -āre, -āvi, -ātum, v. tr., *cause to flee, put to flight, chase away.*

fulmĭnĕus, -a, -um, adj., *belonging to lightning or a thunderbolt; lightning like, flashing* of boar's tusks, i. 21. 5. [fulmen.]

fundĭtus, adv., *from the bottom or foundation, utterly, completely.* [fundus.]

fundo, -ĕre, fūdi, fūsum, v. tr., *pour, pour out.*

fundo, -āre, -āvi, -ātum, v. tr., *lay the foundation of, found.*

fūnus, -ĕris, n., *burial, funeral: dead body.* [lit. *burning*, cf. fumus.]

fūr, fūris, m. and f., *thief.*

fŭror, -ōris, m., *frenzy, madness, passion.* [furo.]

furtim, adv., *by stealth, stealthily.* [fur.]

furtum, -i, n., *theft.* [fur.]

fustis, -is, m., *cudgel, bludgeon,* iii. 2. 3. [rt. fed, cf. offendo, etc.]

fūsus, see fundo.

fŭtĭlis, -e, adj., lit. *leaky; untrustworthy, worthless.* [fundo, *pour.*]

fŭtūrus, fut. part. fr. sum.

gallīnācĕus, -a, -um, adj., *of poultry;* pullus g., iii. 12. 1, *a barndoor chicken* or *pullet.* [gallīna, *hen.*]

Gallus, -i, m., a priest of Cybele, so called from the River Gallus in Phrygia, iv. 1. 4.

garrŭlus, -a, -um, adj., *chattering, talkative, noisy;* as subst., a *noisy fellow, chatterbox.* [garrio.]

gaudeo, -ēre, gāvisus, v. intr. and tr., semi-dep., *rejoice, rejoice at, am pleased.* [γαίω.]

gaudium, -ii, n., *joy, pleasure.* [gaudeo.]

gĕlus, -ūs, m., *cold, frost;* rare except in abl., gelu.

gĕmĭnus, -a, -um, adj., *twin-born, twin, double, two-fold,*

gĕmĭtus, -ūs, m., *sighing, groan.* [gemo.]

gemmĕus, -a, -um, adj., *set with precious stones, gem-like, spangled,* iii. 18. 8 [gemma.]

gĕmo, -ĕre, -ui, -itum, v. intr. and tr., *groan, wail, groan for, bewail.*

gĕnĭtor, -ōris, m., *begetter, father.* [gigno.]

gens, gentis, f., *race, tribe.* [gigno.]

gĕnus, -ĕris, n., *birth, descent; race, class, kind; folk,* i. 2. 15; *character, style* of writing, etc. [gigno : gens : γένος.]

gĕro, -ĕre, gessi, gestum, v. tr., *carry, bear; have, display,* i. 13. 7.

gigno, -ĕre, gĕnui, gĕnĭtum, v. intr., *beget, give birth to.* [genus : gens : γίγνομαι.]

glădius, -ii, m., *sword.*

glōria, -ae, f., *glory, fame, reputation.*

glōrior, -āri, -ātus, v. dep. intr., *boast, vaunt.* [gloria.]

glōriōsus, -a, -um, adj., *full of glory, famous, glorious : boastful.* [gloria.]

grăcŭlus, -i, m., *jackdaw.*

grădus, -ūs, m., *step, footstep, degree.* [gradior.]

Graecia, -ae, f., *Greece.*

Grāii or Grāi, -ōrum or -ûm, m. pl., *the Greeks.*

grānum, -i, n., *grain, seed, corn.*

grātia, -ae, f., *esteem, regard, favour;* redire in gratiam, v. 3. 6, *become reconciled to, forgive;* gratiam corrumperet, iv. 25. 18, *lose his favour* or *patronage; agreeableness, grace; thankfulness, gratitude, thanks,* with agere, always in pl., e.g. ii. 8. 15; abl. gratiā, *for the sake of.*

grātis, adv., *for nothing, gratuitously; to no profit* or *purpose.* [lit. *by way of favour,* opp. to *reward;* abl. of gratia.]

grātŭlor, -āri, -ātus, v. dep. intr., *express joy, congratulate.* [gratus.]

grātus, -a, -um, adj., *pleasing, agreeable, welcome, grateful;* gratum esset (sc. mihi), i. 22. 5, *I should have been grateful;* lit. *it would have been welcome to me.*

grăvis, -e, adj., *heavy, grievous, serious, severe, burdensome.* [βαρύς.]

grăvĭter, adv., *heavily, strongly, forcibly.* [gravis.]

grăvo, -āre, -āvi, -ātum, v. tr., *weigh down, burden.* [gravis.]

gressus, -ūs, m., *step, pace.* [gradior.]

grex, grēgis, m., *flock, herd, litter, company.*

grŭis (older form), or grūs, gruis, f., *crane.* [γέρανος.]

gŭbernātor, -ōris, m., *steersman, pilot.*

gŭla, -ae, f., *gullet, throat.* [gurges.]

gusto, -āre, -āvi, -ātum, v. tr., *taste, sip; eat, drink.* [gustus.]

gȳrus, -i, m., *circle, circuit.* [γῦρος.]

hăbeo, -ēre, -ui, -ĭtum, v. tr., *have, hold, keep, possess; occasion, involve,* i. 12. 15; habent insidias, i. 19. 1, *are fraught with snares;* cura habendi, iii. Prol. 21, *the desire to possess.*

hăbĭtus, -ūs, m., *condition, habit, position, circumstances.* [habeo.]

hac, adv., *in* or *by this way; here.* [hic.]

haereo, -ēre, -si, -sum, v. intr., *stick, cling fast, stick fast, am caught, trapped.*

hāriŏlus, -i, m., *soothsayer, diviner*. [haruspex.]

haud, adv., *not at all, not*.

haustus, -ūs, m., *drinking in, draught ;* ad meos haustus, i. 1. 8, *to the place where I drink*. [haurio.]

Hēbrus, -i, m., river in Thrace, mod. Maritza, rising in Mt. Haemus, and flowing into Aegean Sea, iii. Prol. 59.

helă, interj., *ah! ho! hulloa!*

hercle, vocative form, see under Hercules.

Hercŭlēs, -is, m., famous hero, son of Jupiter and Alcmena, iii. 17. 4 ; iv. 12. 3 ; v. 4. 1. As oath or exclamation, me hercules, iii. 17. 8 ; me hercule, me hercle, i. 1. 12 ; hercules, **hercle**, for me Hercules juvet, *may H. help me*, or me Hercule (or Hercle) juves, *mayst thou, Oh H., help me ; so help me Hercules or by Hercules*.

hēres, -ēdis, m. and f., *heir, heiress*.

heū, interj. expressing grief or pain, *alas! ah!*

heūs, interj. calling a person's attention, *ho, there! ho! harkee! why!*

hĭc, haec, hōc, demonstr. pron., *this ; he, she, it*.

hĭc, adv., *here, in this matter, hereupon, then ;* hic ... illic, *here ... there, in one place ... in another*.

hiemps, hiĕmis, f., lit. *snowy season; winter*. [χεῖμα:χιών.]

hĭlăris, -e, adj., *cheerful, gay*. [ἱλαρός.]

hĭlărĭtas, -ātis, f., *cheerfulness, gaiety, mirth*. [hilaris.]

hinc, adv., *from here, hence, from this*. [hic.]

hircus, -i, m., *he-goat*.

hispĭdus, -a, -um, adj., *rough, shaggy; hairy*.

histŏria, -ae, f., *narrative, history, story, legend*. [ἱστορία, *inquiry*.]

hŏdiē, adv., *to-day, at the present day*. [hoc : die.]

hŏmo, -ĭnis, m., *human being, man ;* often contemptuous, *fellow ;* but *a real man*, iii. 19. 9 ; homo meus, v. 7. 32, '*our friend* '; pl., *mankind*.

hŏnor and **hŏnos**, -ōris, m., *honour, esteem, dignity, position*.

hōra, -ae, f., *hour*, $\frac{1}{12}$ of day or night, reckoned from sunrise to sunset, and so varying in length according to time of year; horae momentum, iii. Prol. 5, *one short hour*, see momentum.

hordĕum, -i, n., *barley*.

horrendus, -a, -um, gerundive of horreo as adj., *terrible, awful*.

horrĭdus, -a, -um, adj., *rough, bristling, harsh, frightful, awful*. [horreo.]

hortor, -āri, -ātus, v. dep. tr., *exhort, encourage*.

hospĭtium, -ii, n., *relation between host and guest, hospitality, lodging ; a re-*

treat, *shelter*, ii. 8. 16.
[hospes.]
hostīlis, -e, adj., *of an enemy,
hostile, of his foe*, i. 21. 8.
[hostis.]
hostis, -is, m. and f., *stranger;
enemy, foe, opponent.*
[hospes.]
hūmānus, -a, -um, adj., *of
man, human.* [hŏmo.]
hūmānĭtas, -ātis, f., *duties of
one human being to another,
kindliness, courtesy.* [hŏmo.]
hŭmĭlis, -e, adj., lit. *on the
ground, low, lowly; humble,
poor, in a humble position.*
hŭmus, -i, f., *the earth,
ground ;* locative, humi, *on
the ground,* as adv. [χαμαί.]
hȳdrus, -i, m., *water-snake.*
[ὕδρος : ὕδωρ.]

ĭbant, see eo.
ĭbī, adv., *there, then.* [locat.
of is.]
ĭco, ēre, ĭci, ictum, v. tr.,
strike; make or *ratify*
treaty by striking and
sacrificing victims, i. 31. 8.
ictus, -ūs, m., *blow.* [ico.]
īdem, eădem, ĭdem, adj.
pron., *the same, very;
he too, yet he.* [is.]
īdeō, adv., *on that account,
therefore;* with neg., *not …
for all that*, ii. 8. 11. [is.]
īgĭtur, adv., *accordingly,
therefore, then.*
ignāvus,-a, -um, adj., *inactive,
lazy, spiritless, cowardly;*
as subst., *a coward.* [in :
gnavus.]

ignis, -is, m., *fire.*
ignōrans, -ntis, part. fr.
ignoro as adj., *ignorant,
ignorant of.*
ignōro, -āre, -āvi, -ātum, v.
tr., *do not know, am ignorant of.* [ignārus.]
ignōtus, -a, -um, adj., *unknown, unfamiliar;* active
sense, ignoto loco, i. 14. 2,
*in a place where he was
unknown;* ignotos fallit,
i. 11. 2 n., *imposes upon
strangers.* [in : gnotus.]
ille, -a, -ud, demonst. pron.,
*that, that famous; he, she,
it.* [is.]
illīc, adv., *in that place, yon-
der, there.* [ille.]
illūc, adv., *to that place, thither.* [ille.]
imber, -bris, m., *rain, rain-
storm, shower.* [ὄμβρος.]
ĭmĭtor, -āri, -ātus, v. dep. tr.,
*imitate, copy; seek to re-
semble, rival.*
immānis, -e, adj., *out of all
measure, enormous, huge.*
[in, *not;* root of metior,
μέτρον.]
immitto, -ĕre, -mīsi, -missum,
v. tr., *send to, send in, let go;*
im. se, *spring in*, iv. 9. 10.
immōdĭcus, -a, -um, adj.,
*beyond measure, immod-
erate, excessive, enormous.*
[modus.]
immōlo, -āre, -āvi, -ātum,
v. tr., lit. *sprinkle sacrificial meal on victim's head;*
hence *sacrifice;* impers.
use, iv. 24. 5. [mola, *meal.*]

impar, -ăris, adj., *unequal, uneven.* [par.]

impĕdio, -īre, -īvi or **-ii, -ītum, v. tr.,** lit. *entangle the feet; entangle, impede, hinder.* [pes.]

impĕdītus, -a, -um, part. fr. impedio as adj., *hindered, entangled.*

impendo, -ĕre, -di, -sum, v. tr., *weigh out; expend, pay; expend* or *devote* care to, iii. Prol. 11.

impensa, -ae, f., *outlay, expense.*

impĕrium, -ii, n., *command, rule, sway.* [impero.]

impĕtro, -āre, -āvi, -ātum, v. tr., *accomplish, obtain by request.* [patro.]

impĕtus, -ūs, m., *onset, assault, onslaught; dash, rush, force; rapid current* of river, iii. Prol. 59; *poetic impulse, inspiration,* iv. 25. 7. [impeto.]

impingo, -ĕre, -pēgi, -pactum, v. tr., *dash into* or *against, throw* stone *to hit,* iii. 5. 2. [pango.]

impleo, -ēre, -ēvi, -ētum, v. tr., *fill in* or *up.*

impōno, -ĕre, -pŏsui, -pŏsĭtum, v. tr., *place upon* or *on.*

importo, -āre, -āvi, -ātum, v. tr., *carry to, bring to; cause to, inflict* grief *on,* i. 28. 6.

imprŏbĭtas, -ātis, f., *badness, dishonesty, self-assertion, rapacity; rapacious creature,* i. 5. 11.

imprŏbus, -a, -um, adj., prop. *out of due proportion* in *excess* or *defect; dishonest, unfair, wicked; bold, shameless, impudent, presumptuous; cruel, relentless; greedy.* [probus.]

imprūdens, -entis, adj., *not forseeing, unsuspecting, not knowing, ignorant, in ignorance, incautious, without forethought.*

imprūdentia, -ae, f., *want of forethought, indiscretion, ignorance.*

impŭdens, -entis, adj., *without shame, shameless.* [pudet.]

impŭdentia, -ae, f., *shamelessness, effrontery.*

impūnĕ, adv., *without punishment, with impunity; without taking vengeance,* iv. 4. 13. [impunio : punio.]

impŭto, -āre, -āvi, -ātum, v. tr., *enter to account of, set down as due to,* i. 22. 8; *attribute to.*

īmus, -a, -um, adj. superl. of inferus, *lowest, deepest, bottom of.*

in, prep. (i.) with acc., *into, to, against; to become, for;* in quaestus, *for gain,* iv. 1. 4; so, in perniciem, *to become the ruin of,* iv. 7. 11; cf. in calamitatem, iii. Prol. 40; in bonas partes, ii. Prol. 11, *in good part;* in commune, v. 6. 3, *shares!* (ii.) with abl., *in, on, among, in the number of, in the case* *of*, v. 5. 31 ; in hoc, iv. Prol. 2, *for this reason ;* in tutela sua, iii. 17. 1, *under their protection.*

ĭnānis, -e, adj., *empty ; useless, worthless ; meaningless.*

incĭdo, -ĕre, -cĭdi, -cāsum, v. intr., *fall into* or *on.* [cădo.]

incĭpĭo, -ĕre, -cēpi, -ceptum, v. tr., *take up, begin.* [capio.]

incĭto, -āre, -āvi, -ātum, v. tr., *set in rapid motion, drive on, urge on.*

incŏla, -ae, m. and f., *inhabitant.*

incŏlŭmis, -e, adj., *unhurt, unharmed, safe.*

incommŏdum, -i, n., *inconvenience, trouble ;* often euphemism for *loss, injury.*

inconveniens, -entis, adj., *not suited, unlike.* [convenio.]

incorruptus, -a, -um, adj., *unspoiled, uncorrupt, upright.*

increpo, -ĕre, -ui, -itum, v. tr. and intr., *make a noise, rattle ; utter aloud : exclaim against* a person, *upbraid, chide.*

incumbo, -ĕre, -cŭbui, -cŭbĭtum, v. intr., *lean on, bend to, devote oneself to.*

incursĭto, -āre, -āvi, -ātum, v. intr., *rush* or *dash upon* or *against*, ii. 7. 8. [freq. of incurro.]

indāgo, -āre, -āvi, -ātum, v. tr., *track out,* iv. Prol. 5.

indĕ, adv., *from there, thence ; from that time, thenceforward, then.* [is.]

indĭco, -āre, -āvi, -ātum, v. tr., *point out, show.* [index.]

indignē, adv., *unworthily ; indignantly ;* indigne fero, see fero.

indignor, -āri, -ātus, v. dep. tr., *deem unworthy ; am indignant, resent.* [dignus.]

indignus, -a, -um, adj., *unworthy, undeserving.* [dignus.]

indūco, -ĕre, -xi, -ctum, v. tr., *lead into* or *to, lead on to. induce.*

industria, -ae, f., *diligence, activity.*

ĭnēdia, -ae, f., *fasting, starvation.* [ĕdo, eat.]

ĭneptus, -a, -um, adj., *unsuitable, foolish, absurd, tasteless.*

ĭnermis, -e, adj., *unarmed, defenceless.* [arma.]

ĭners, -ertis, adj., *without skill ; inactive, sluggish, lazy, spiritless, weak.* [ars.]

infēlix, -īcis, adj., *unfruitful, unhappy, unlucky.*

infērior, -us, adj., comp. of inferus, *lower ; lower down stream,* i. 1. 3.

infĕro, -ferre, -tŭli, inlātum, v. tr., *bring into* or *to ; bring against ; entail, inflict on,* i. 16. 2 ; legal, *bring action against, adduce, allege ;* iurgii causam intulit, i. 1. 4 n., *adduced the grounds for a quarrel.*

infestus, -a, -um, adj., (1) pass., *exposed to, in danger ;*

I

(2) act., *hostile, destructive, dangerous.* [infensus.]

inficio, -ĕre, -fēci, -fectum, v. tr., lit. *put in;* hence *stain, dye.* [facio.]

inflo, -āre, -āvi, -ātum, v. tr., *breathe into, inflate.*

infundo, -ĕre, -fūdi, -fūsum, v. tr., *pour into; spread over, cover,* iii. 13. 9.

ingĕmisco. -ĕre, -gĕmui, no sup., v. intr., *groan over, groan, sigh.*

ingĕnium, -ii, n., *innate qualities; character; ability, wit, genius.* [in : gigno.]

ingrātus, -a, -um, adj., *unpleasant; ungrateful, thankless.*

ingrăvo, -āre, -āvi, -ātum, v. tr., *weigh down, load;* annis ingravantibus, v. 10. 3, *with the* (growing) *weight of years.*

ingrĕdior, -i, -gressus, v. dep. tr. and intr., *go into, enter; advance; step on to stage,* v. 7. 17. [gradior.]

inhospĭtālis, -e, adj., *inhospitable, desolate.* [hospes.]

inĭcio (for iniicio), -ĕre, -iēci, -iectum, v. tr., *throw into; infuse in, inspire,* i. 27. 5. [iacio.]

iniectus, see inicio.

iniūria, -ae, f., *illegal act, outrage, injury, wrong.* [in : ius.]

iniustus, -a, -um, adj., *unjust, unfair.*

inlĭcio, -ĕre, -lexi, -lectum, v. tr., *entice, allure, seduce.* [lacio.]

inlīdo, -ĕre, -si, -sum, v. tr., *dash against* or *upon.*

inlittĕrātus, -a, -um, adj., *unlettered, uneducated;* inlit. plausum, iv. Prol. 20, *the applause of the uneducated.* [littera.]

inlūdo, -ĕre, -si, -sum, v. intr. and tr., *play; make sport of, mock at.*

innŏcens, -ntis, adj., *harmless; innocent, guiltless.* [nocens : noceo.]

innŏtesco, -ĕre, -nōtui, no sup., v. intr. incept., *become known* or *noted, grow famous,* i. 10. 1.

innoxius, -a, -um, adj., *harmless.*

inŏpia, -ae, f., *want of resources, scarcity, want.*

inops, -ŏpis, adj., *without resources, helpless, weak, poor; as* subst., *a poor man,* etc. [ops.]

inquam, -is, -it, v. defect., *say.*

inquĭno, -āre, -āvi, -ātum, v. tr., *defile, pollute.*

inrīdeo, -ere, -si, -sum, v. tr. and intr., *laugh at, mock; laugh.*

inrĭtus, -a, -um, adj., *not settled, invalid; vain, useless.* [ratus.]

inscius, -a, -um, adj., *not knowing, ignorant.* [scio.]

insĕquor, -i, -sĕcūtus, v. dep. tr. and intr., *follow after, follow.*

insĕro, -ĕre, -sĕrui, -sertum, v. tr., *put into, thrust in, insert.*

insĭdiae, -ārum, f. pl., am-
bush, ambuscade; snare,
trap; trick, treachery. [in-
sideo.]
insĭdiōsus, -a, -um, adj., full
of wiles, treacherous. [in-
sidiae.]
insignis,-e, adj.,distinguished,
famous, remarkable. [sig-
num.]
insĭlio, -īre, -ui, no sup., v.
tr. and intr., leap into or
on. [sălio.]
insŏlens, -entis,adj.,unusual;
excessive; arrogant, in-
solent. [soleo.]
insŏlentia, -ae, f., novelty;
excess; arrogance, inso-
lence.
insŏno, -āre, -ui, no sup., v.
intr., make a noise in or on;
strike up a tune, with cogn.
acc., v. 7. 26.
inspĭcio, -ĕre, -spexi, -spec-
tum, v. tr., look into or at,
examine. [specio.]
instans,-ntis, part. from insto
as adj., near at hand, immediate, pressing, urgent,
threatening.
insto, -āre, -stĭti, -stātum,
v. intr., stand upon or over;
attack; press on; impend;
threaten.
insuētus, -a, -um, adj., not
accustomed to, unaccus-
tomed, unfamiliar, strange.
[insuesco.]
insŭla, -ae, f., island.
insulsus, -a, -um, adj., salt-
less, tasteless, insipid, silly,
absurd. [sal.]

insulto, -āre, -āvi, -ātum, v.
intr., leap upon, trample
on, revile, insult. [insilio.]
intĕgrĭtas, -ātis, f., soundness, blamelessness, uprig-
ness, integrity. [integer:
tango.]
intellĕgo, -ĕre, -xi, -ctum, v.
tr., perceive, understand.
intempestīvē, adv., out of
season, unseasonably, in-
opportunely. [tempestas.]
intendo, -ĕre, -tendi, -tentum
and -tensum, v. tr., stretch
out, stretch, direct.
intĕr, prep. with acc.,between,
among, amidst, during, in.
[in.]
intercĭpio,-ĕre,-cēpi,-ceptum,
v. tr., intercept, interrupt,
hinder, preclude. [căpio.]
interdīco, -ĕre, -xi, -ctum, v.
tr. and intr., intervene by
an order, forbid.
interdiū, adv., during the
day, in the day time, by
day. [dies.]
interest, v. impers., it is of
importance, concerns; with
gen. of person or meâ, tuâ,
etc., and inf. or subj. clause.
[intersum.]
interfĭcio, -ĕre, -fēci, -fectum,
v. tr., lit. make away from
among: kill. [facio.]
intĕrior, -us, adj., comp. of
obsolete interus, inner,
interior. [inter.]
intĕro, -ĕre, -trīvi, -trītum,
v. tr., rub into, bruise;
intrito cibo, i. 26. 7, minced
food.

interpōno, -ĕre, -pŏsui, pŏsĭtum, v. tr., put in between,
insert, introduce; inter-
positus, iii. 2. 12, having
intervened, of time.
interrŏgo, -āre, -āvi, -ātum,
v. tr., question, ask.
intervĕnio, -īre, -vēni, -ven-
tum, v. intr., come between,
appear on the scene, intervene, interfere.
intĭmus, -a, -um, superl. adj.,
from obsolete interus,
innermost, deepest; see
interior. [inter.]
intrĭtus, part. of intero.
intro, -āre, -āvi, -ātum, v.
tr., walk into, enter.
intueor, -ēre, -tuĭtus, v. dep.
tr., look at, watch.
inūtĭlis, -e, adj., useless.
[utor.]
invĕnio, -īre, -vēni, -ventum,
v. tr., come upon, find, find
out, discover.
invĭcem, adv., by turns, in
turn; salutatum invicem,
iii. 7 3, to greet one another.
[vicem.]
invictus, -a, -um, adj., un-
conquered, unconquerable.
[vinco.]
invĭdia, -ae, f., envy, hatred,
ill will, jealousy. [invideo,
look askance at.]
invĭdus, -a, -um, adj., envious,
jealous. [see invidia.]
invīsus, -a, -um, part. from
invideo as adj., hated,
hateful.
invīto, -āre, -āvi, -ātum, v. tr.,
invite as guest, entertain.

invītus, -a, -um, adj., against
one's will, unwilling.
involvo, -ĕre, -volvi, -vŏlū-
tum, v. tr., roll in or on;
wrap in, wrap up in; shroud
in. disguise.
ipse, -a, -um, pron., self,
very; himself, etc. [is-pse.]
īra, -ae, f., anger, wrath.
īrācundus, -a, -um, adj., full
of wrath, angry. [ira.]
īrascor, -sci, irātus, v. dep.
intr., grow angry, am
angry. [ira.]
īrātē, adv., angrily, in anger.
[iratus.]
īrātus, -a, -um, part. of
irascor as adj., enraged,
angry, wrathful; dis iratis
natus, iv. 20. 15 note.
īre, see eo.
is, ĕa, ĭd, demonstr. pron.,
that; he, she, it.
iste, -a, -ud, demonstr. pron.,
that near you or of yours;
that. [is.]
ĭtă, adv., thus, so; as follows;
on these conditions. [is.]
ĭtăquĕ, conj., and so, therefore.
ītem, adv., in like manner,
likewise, as well, also, too.
[is.]
ĭter, ĭtĭnĕris, n., way, jour-
ney. [eo: itum.]
ĭtĕro, -āre, -āvi, -ātum, v.
tr., do a second time, repeat. [iterum.]

ĭăceo, -ēre, -ui, -ĭtum, v. intr.,
lie down; lie ill or dead,
i. 24. 10, etc.; lie prostrate

or *ruined*, iv. 7. 13; *lie exposed*, iii. 15. 16. [akin to iacio.]

iăcio, -ĕre, iēci, iactum, v. tr., *throw, cast.* [akin to iacceo.]

iacto, -āre, -āvi, -ātum, v. tr., *throw, cast, toss about, toss, flourish, display, show off, boast of, vaunt.* [freq. of iăcio.]

iam, adv., *by this time, now, already;* iam nunc, iv. 21. 6, *exactly now, this very minute;* iam pridem, *long ago,* v. Prol. 2.

iānua, -ae, f., *door.* [Ianus.]

iŏcor, -āri, -ātus, v. dep. intr. and tr., *joke, jest, say in jest; write in jest or playfully.*

iŏcŭlāris, -e, adj., *done in jest, laughable, droll, entertaining,* iv. 2. 1.

iŏcus, -i, m., pl. -i or -a, *joke, jest, cause of mirth, butt,* i. 21. 2; *merry story,* iii. Prol. 37.

Iovem, see Iuppiter.

iŭbeo, -ĕre, iussi, iussum, v. tr., *bid, order, command.*

iŭcundĭtas, -ātis, f., *pleasantness, delight; delightful sound,* iv. 20. 21.

iŭcundus, -a, -um, adj., *pleasant, delightful.*

iŭdex, -icis, m., *judge, juror, umpire, arbitrator.* [ius: dico.]

iŭdĭcium, -ii, n., *judicial investigation, trial, sentence, opinion, judgment, decision,* iii. Epil. 27; *stant pro iu-*

dicio, v. 5. 2, *stand up for their judgment.* [iudex.]

iŭdĭco, -āre, -āvi, -ātum, v. intr. and tr., *sit in judgment, pass judgment; judge; consider.* [iudex.]

iŭgŭlo, -āre, -āvi, -ātum, v. tr., *cut the throat, kill;* pass., *have the throat cut,* v. 4. 6. [iugulum.]

iŭgum, -i, n., *yoke;* mountain *ridge, height.* [iungo: ζυγόν.]

Iūno, -ōnis, f., *Juno,* queen of heaven, daughter of Saturn, sister and wife of Jupiter, iii. 18. 1.

Iuppiter, Iŏvis, m., *Jupiter* or *Jove,* son of Saturn, King of gods and men, i. 6. 5. etc.

iurgium, -ii, n., *quarrel, strife.*

iūs, iūris, n., *right, justice, law;* iura reddere, iv. 14. 5, *administer law;* simili iure, i. 26. 2, *on the same principle, in the same manner;* ius iurandum, *oath.* [iungo.]

iusiurandum, see under ius.

iussus, see iubeo.

iustē, adv., *justly, rightly;* comp. iustius.

iustus, -a, -um, adj., *just, righteous.* [ius.]

iŭvencus, -i, m., *bullock, steer.* [iuvenis.]

iŭvĕnis, -is, m. and f., *young man or woman.*

iŭvo, -āre, iūvi, iūtum, v. tr., *help, aid; delight, please.* [iucundus.]

lăbo, -āre, -āvi, -ātum, v. intr., *slip, fall ; waver, vacillate*, iv. 14. 6. [lābor.]

lābor, -i, lapsus, v. dep. intr., *slip, glide ; fall away from, fall into error*, v. 5. 1.

lăbor, -ōris, m., *labour, toil, work ;* of poems, ii. Epil. 15.

lăbōro, -āre, -āvi, -ātum, v. tr. and intr., *labour, toil ; labour under ; suffer ; toil at.* [labor.]

lac, lactis, n., *milk* [γάλα.]

lăcĕro, -āre, -āvi, -ātum, v. tr., *tear to pieces, rend, tear, mangle.* [lacer.]

lăcesso, -ĕre, -īvi or -ii, -ītum, v. tr., *provoke, worry.*

Lăcŏn, or Lăcō, -ōnis, m., (1) *A Laconian* or *Spartan,* (2) *A Laconian or Spartan hound,* famed for strength, and used for hunting, v. 10. 7. [Λάκων.]

lăcrĭma, -ae, f., *tear.* [δάκρυ.]

lăcus, -us, m., *tank, pond, lake.*

laedo, -ĕre, -si, -sum, v. tr., *strike, hurt, injure.*

laetor, -āri, -ātus, v. dep. intr., *feel joy, am glad, rejoice.* [laetus.]

laetus, -a, -um, adj., *joyful, glad ; in good condition, luxuriant,* ii. 5. 14.

laevus, -a, -um, adj., *on the left, left ;* of augury, *auspicious,* iii. 18. 12 n.

lăgōna, -ae, f., *large vessel generally of earthenware with neck and handles,*

jug, jar, flagon, i. 26. 8. [λάγηνος.]

lambo, -ĕre, lambi, lambĭtum, v. tr., *lick, lap up.*

languens, -entis, part. from langueo as adj., *faint, feeble.*

langueo, -ēre, -gui, no sup., v. intr., *am faint, weak.*

languĭdus, -a, -um, adj., *faint, weak, weary.* [langueo.]

lānĭger, -ĕra, -ĕrum, adj., *wool-bearing ;* as subst., *a sheep, lamb,* i. 1. 6 n. [lana : gero.]

lănius, -ii, m., *butcher.* [lanio, cut up.]

lăpis, -ĭdis, m., *stone.* [λέπας.]

lăquĕus, -i, m., *noose, springe, snare, halter.* [rt. lac: lacio.]

largē, adv., *abundantly, liberally ;* large divisit, ii. 6. 15, *gave a generous share of.* [largus.]

largus, -a, -um, adj., *abundant, plentiful.*

lasso, -āre, -āvi, -ātum, v. tr., *make weary, tire out.* [lassus.]

lātē, adv., *broadly, far and wide.* [lātus.]

lăteo, -ĕre, -ui, no sup. v. intr., *lie hid, take shelter ; lie safe and sound,* iv. 6. 13 ; *escape notice,* v. 5. 31. [λανθάνω.]

lătĭbŭlum, -i, n., *hiding-place, lair.* [lateo.]

Lătīnus, -a, -um, adj., *Latin, of Latium.*

Lătium, -ii, n., *Latium,* plain of Italy, south of Tiber.

lātro, -ōnis, m., *bandit, robber.*
lātro, -āre, -āvi, -ātum, v.
intr., *bark.*
lātus, -a, -um, adj., *broad,
wide, big;* comp. lātior.
laudābĭlis, -e, adj., *praiseworthy.* [laudo.]
laudandus, -a, -um, gerundive
from laudo, *to be praised,
praiseworthy.*
laudo, -āre, -āvi, -ātum, v.
tr., *praise, extol;* laudatis,
i. 12. 1, *what is praised.*
laurea, -ae, f., *laurel tree,
laurel.* [fem. of laureus,
sc. arbor.]
laus, laudis, f., *praise;* laudis
conscientiam, ii. Epil. 11,
*the consciousness of deserv-
ing praise.*
laxo, āre, -āvi, -ātum, v. tr.,
open out, loosen, relax.
lector, -ōris, m., *reader.*
[lego.]
Lēda, -ae, f., wife of Tyn-
darus, mother of Helen,
Clytemnestra, Castor and
Pollux, iv. 25. 9.
lēgo, -ĕre, lēgi, lectum, v.
tr., *gather, pick up: pluck
out,* ii. 2. 7; *choose: read.*
[λέγω.]
lentus, -a, -um, adj., *pliant,
tough, slow.* [lenis.]
leo, -ōnis, m., *lion.* [λέων.]
lĕpĭdus, -a, -um, adj., *pleasant,
humorous, charming, polite,
gallant,* v. 7. 13. [lepos.]
lĕpus, -ŏris, m., rarely f.,
hare.
lētum, -i, n., *death;* leto
dare, *to kill,* iii. 16. 18.

lĕvis, -e, adj., *light; trifling,
trivial;* of style, iv. 2. 1,
light, playful.
lĕvĭtas, -ātis, f., *lightness,
frivolity, fickleness, levity:
worthlessness, shallowness.*
[lĕvis.]
lĕvo, -āre, -āvi, -ātum, v. tr.,
lift up, raise. [lĕvis.]
lex, lēgis, f., *law; condition,
terms,* iii. 13. 5; *laws of
nature,* iii. 15. 20.
lĭbellus, -i, m., *little book.*
[dim. of liber.]
lĭbenter, adv., *willingly,
gladly.* [libens.]
lĭber, libri, m., *inner bark of
tree; book,* from use of bark
of linden and rind of papyrus for paper. [λέπειν,
peel.]
lĭber, -ĕra, -ĕrum, adj.,
free.
lĭbĕrālis, -e, adj., *befitting a
freeman, honourable, gen-
erous, liberal.* [liber.]
lĭbĕrē, adv., *freely, without
restraint.* [liber.]
lĭbĕri, -ōrum, m. pl., *children.* [the *free members* of
household; liber.]
lĭbĕro, -āre, -āvi, -ātum, v.
tr., *set free, free.* [liber.]
lĭbertas, -ātis, f., *condition
of a freeman, freedom, liberty, independence; license.*
[liber.]
lĭbertus, -i, m., *a freed man.*
[liber.]
lĭbet. -ēre, -uit and libitum
est, v. impers. intr., *it
pleases, is agreeable.*

Lībĭtīna, -ae, f., ancient Italian goddess, originally of gardens and of pleasure, who presided over funerals. In her grove on the Es-quiline were kept all the requisites for funerals ; iv. 20. 25. [libet.]

lĭcentia, -ae, f., *freedom, unrestrained liberty, licence.* [licet.]

lĭcet, -ēre, -uit, -itum est, v. impers., *it is allowed, one may ; it may be that, even if, although,* with subj.

lignĕus, -a, -um, adj., *of wood, wooden.* [lignum.]

lignum, -i, n., *firewood, log ;* in class. Lat. only in pl. ; in sing. i. 2. 20. [lego, *gather.*]

lĭgo, -āre, -āvi, -ātum, v. tr., *bind up, fasten, tie, bandage.*

līma, -ae, f., *file, rasp.*

līmen, -ĭnis, n., *threshold ; door.*

līmus, -i, m., *slime, mud.* [lino.]

lingua, -ae, f., *tongue.*

liuquo, -ĕre, liqui, lictum, v. tr., *leave.*

lintĕum, -i, n., *linen cloth, linen.* [linum, λίνον, *flax.*]

Līnus, -i, m., famous Theban musician, son of Apollo and a Muse ; iii. Prol. 57 note. [Λίνος.]

lĭquĭdus, -a, -um, adj., *flowing liquid.* [liqueo.]

lĭquor, -ōris, m., *liquid ; clear water ; stream,* i. 1. 8.

līs, lītis, f., *strife, quarrel, lawsuit.*

littĕra, -ae, f., *letter* of alphabet ; in pl., *epistle, letter ; letters, literature.* [lino.]

littĕrātus, -a, -um, adj., *marked with letters; lettered; learned.* [littera.]

līvor, -ōris, m., *dull leaden* or *bluish green colour ; envy, jealousy.* Personified, *Envy,* iii. Prol. 60.

lŏcŭplēs, -ētis, adj., *wealthy, rich.*

lŏcus, -i, m. pl. loci and loca ; *place, spot, position, room.*

lŏcūtus, see loquor.

longē, adv., *far off ; far : afar ; by far.* [longus.]

longĭtūdo, -ĭnis, f., *length.*

longus, -a, -um, adj., *long : distant.*

lŏquor, -i, lŏcūtus, v. dep. tr. and intr., *speak, talk, say.* [λάσκω.]

lŭcerna, -ae, f., *oil lamp, lamp.* [luceo.]

lŭcrum, -i, n., *gain, profit.*

luctor, -āri, -ātus, v. dep. intr., *wrestle, struggle.*

luctus, -ūs, m., *grief, mourning.* [lugeo.]

Lŭcullus, -i, m., M. Licinius, see ii. 5. 9 note.

lūdo, -ĕre, -si, -sum, v. intr., *play ; amuse myself, dally,* iv. 2. 2 ; *make sport of.*

lūdus, -i, m., *play, game, sport ;* esp. in pl., *public games, exhibitions.*

lūgeo, -ēre, -xi, -ctum, v. intr. and tr., *mourn, grieve; mourn for.* [luctus: ὀλολύζω: λυγρός.]

lūmen, -ĭnis, n., *light.* [= lucmen : luceo : lux.]

luo, -ĕre, lui, no sup., v. tr., *loose, let go ; pay off ; atone for ;* l. poenas, *pay* or *suffer penalty,* i. 17. l. [λύω.]

lŭpus, -i, m., *wolf.* [λύκος.]

luscĭnius, -ii, m., *nightingale,* iii. 18. 11.

lustro, -āre, -āvi, -ātum, v. tr., *purify by going round and sprinkling ; go round to, traverse; observe, survey.* [lustrum : luo.]

lūsus, -ūs, m., *play, game, sport, recreation.* [ludo.]

lux, lūcis, f., *light, daylight ;* abl., luce adverbially, *by daylight, in the day time.* [luceo : lumen.]

lympha, -ae, f., *water nymph; water,* esp. spring or river water, i. 4. 2. [νύμφη.]

mācĕro, -āre, -āvi, -ātum, v. tr., *make tender; weaken : torment,* iv. 20. 21.

mācies, -ei, f., *leanness.* [macero.]

maerens, -entis, part. of maereo as adj., *grieving, sad.*

maereo, -ēre, no perf. or sup., v. tr. and intr., *mourn, grieve, mourn for.* [maestus.]

maestus, -a, -um, adj., *sad, sorrowful, mournful.* [maereo.]

măgis, comp. adj., *more, rather, the more;* for positive magnopere, *greatly,* is used, for superl. maxime, *most.* [magnus.]

măgistra, -ae, f., *female teacher, instructress.* [magister.]

magnĭtūdo, -ĭnis, f., *greatness, size; rank, dignity.* [magnus.]

magnus, -a, -um, adj., *great : important ;* of sound, *loud :* comp. māior ; maioris, ii. 5. 25, *at a greater price ;* superl. maximus.

māiestas, -ātis, f., *greatness, grandeur, majesty ;* tanti maiestas ducis, ii. 5. 23, *the mighty sovereign's majesty.*

māior, see magnus.

mălĕ, adv., *badly, ill ;* male dimissus, iv. 25. 18, *if he received a bad dismissal,* i. e. *were dismissed in anger ;* male mulcatus, i. 3. 9, *soundly thrashed ;* male dico, with dat., *abuse, slander,* i. 1. 10, 12. [malus.]

mălĕfĭcium, -ii (or -i, i. 17. 1), n., *wickedness, crime, wrongdoing.* [male : facio.]

mălĕfĭcus, -a, -um, adj., *wicked, mischievous ;* as subst., *wrongdoer, criminal.* [male : facio.]

mălignĭtas, -ātis, f., *spite, malice.* [malignus : malus.]

mălĭtia, -ae, f., *spite, malice, roguery.* [malus.]

mālo, malle, mălui, no sup.,
v. tr. and intr., *choose*
rather, *prefer.*   [magis :
volo.]

mălum, -i, n., *evil*, *mischief;*
misfortune, evil *fortune*, i.
2. 30, etc. ; *crime*, *misdeed*,
iv. 10. 4 ; of bone in throat,
illud malum, i. 8. 6, *that*
bane ; injury;   alterius
malo, iv. 9. 2, *at another's*
cost ; est malo, v. 4. 12, *is*
injurious, an evil ; punish-
ment ; malo adficietur, i.
5. 10, *he will suffer for it.*
[mălus.]

mălus, -a, -um, adj., *bad,*
evil, wicked; unskilful, poor
of workman, i. 14. 1 ; as
subst., *a bad man.*

mandātum, -i, n., *order, com-*
mission, command, request,
i. 2. 27.   [mando.]

mando, -āre, -āvi, -ātum, v.
tr., *enjoin, commission, give*
orders.   [manus : do.]

măneo, -ēre, mansi, man-
-sum, v. tr. and intr., *stay,*
remain ; await.

Mānes, -ĭum, m. pl., *deified*
souls of the dead, departed
spirits, M. deos, i. 27. 4 n.

mănĭfestus, -a, -um, adj.,
clear,   plain,   palpable.
[manus fendo, *what one can*
hit with hand.]

mănus, -ūs, f., *hand ; band.*

măre, -is, n., *sea.*

margărīta, -ae, f., *pearl.*
[μαργαρίτης.]

margo, -ĭnis, m. and f., *border,*
edge, margin.

marmor, -ŏris, n., *marble ;*
bright surface of *sea.*

mascŭlus, -a, -um, adj., *male.*
[dim. of mas.]

māter, -tris, f.,   *mother.*
[μήτηρ.]

mātĕria, -ae, and in nom. and
acc. also, mātĕries, -em, f.,
material of which a thing
is composed ; *subject-matter,*
like Greek ὕλη.

mātrōna, -ae, f.,   *married*
woman, matron.   [māter.]

mātūrē, adv., *at the proper*
time ; early ; comp. maturius, iii. 19. 2, *earlier than*
usual.   [maturus.]

mātūrus, -a, -um, adj., *ripe ;*
of proper age, mature.

maxĭmē, superl. of magis,
most.

maxĭmus, superl. of magnus,
very great.

me, acc. of ego, *I ;* me hercules, see under Hercules.

mecum, for cum me, *with me ;*
see ego.

Mēdēa, -ae, f., *celebrated*
sorceress,   daughter   of
Acetes, King of Colchis ; as-
sisted Jason in obtaining
the golden fleece, and fled
with him to Greece, iv. 7.
13 n.

mĕdīcīna, -ae, f., *medical art,*
medicine, surgery ; remedy,
medicinam facere, i. 14. 2,
practise art of medicine ;
but i. 8. 9, *work a cure.*
[medeor.]

mĕdĭcus, -a, -um, adj., *heal-*
ing, medical.   [medeor.]

mědĭcus, -i, m., *medical man, physician, surgeon.*

mědĭus, -a, -um, adj., *in the middle, midst of, mid ;* medio sole, iii. 19. 8, *at mid-day ;* media aetas, ii. 2. 3, *middle age.*

měl, mellis, n., *honey.*

mělĭor, -us, adj., used as comp. of bonus, *better ;* meliores, ii. Epil. 17, *their betters.*

mělĭus, adv., used as comp. of bene, *better.*

mělos, -i, n., *tune, air, song ; poetry,* iv. 22. 2. [μέλος.]

měmĭnī, -isse, v. defect. intr., rarely tr., perf. with pres. force ; *remember, bear in mind.* [mens.]

měmŏrĭa, -ae, f, *memory, recollection, narration ;* dignum memoria, iv. 21. 3, *worth writing ;* tradam memoriae, iv. 25. 3, *I will relate.* [memor.]

Měnander, -dri, m., Greek poet, v. 1. 9 note. [Μένανδρος.]

mendax, -ācis, adj., *lying, false ;* as subst., *a liar.* [mentior.]

mens, mentis, f., *mind, disposition, intellect ; purpose, intention.*

mensa, -ae, f., *table.*

mensis, -is, m., *month.* [measured portion, metior.]

merces, -ēdis, f., *wages, pay, fee, reward ;* sine mercede, iv. 2. 8, *without reward or profit, unprofitably.* [mereo. earn.]

Mercŭrĭus, -ii, m., *Mercury.* son of Jupiter and Maia, messenger of the gods, i. 2. 27.

mergo, -ĕre, -si, -sum, v. tr., *dip in, sink, plunge in.*

měrĭto, adv., *deservedly, justly.* [meritus : mereo.]

měrĭtum, -i, n., *merit, desert ; kindness, good office.* [mereo.]

merx, mercis, f., *goods, merchandise.*

mětuo, -ĕre, -ui, -ūtum, v. tr. and intr., *fear, dread.*

mětus, -ūs, m., *fear, dread.*

měus, -a, -um, poss. pron., *my, mine ; my regular ... ,* i. 15. 10 ; homo meus, v. 7. 32, *'our friend' ;* meā refert, *it concerns me,* see refert.

mi = mihi, iii. 18. 9, see ego, *I.*

mīles, -ĭtis, m. and f., *soldier.*

mīlŭus and milvus, -i, m., *kite, bird of prey.*

mĭnae, -ārum, f. pl., *threats, menaces.* [minor.]

Mĭnerva, -ae, f., Roman goddess, identified with Greek Pallas Athene, daughter of Zeus, goddess of wisdom, arts, poetry, etc. [mens, memini.]

mĭnor, -āri, -ātus, v. dep. tr. and intr., *threaten.* [minae.]

mĭnor, -us, adj. used as comp. of parvus, *less, smaller.* [minuo.]

Mīnos, -ōis, m., mythical King of Crete, iv. 7. 19. [Μίνως.]

minus, adv., comp. adv., *less;*
si or sin minus, *but if
not;* superl. minime.
[minor.]
minutus, -a, -um, part. of
minuo as adj., *little, small,
insignificant,*
miraculum, -i, n., *wonderful
thing, marvel;* of ass's bray,
i. 11. 8. [miror.]
miror, -ari, -atus, v. dep. tr.
and intr., *wonder at, admire, wonder.*
misceo, -ere, miscui, mixtum
or mistum, v. tr., *mix,
mingle, blend; chequer,* iv.
17. 10; *confuse, embroil,* i.
2. 2; se miscuit, i. 3. 7,
join.
Misenensis, -e, adj., *of
Misenum, at Misenum,* ii.
5. 8, promontory, town
and harbour in Campania.
miser, -era, -erum, adj.,
wretched, pitiable.
misereor, -eri, -itus, v. dep.
intr., *feel pity, pity,* with
gen.
miseria, -ae, f., *misery,
wretchedness.*
misericordia, -ae, f., *pity,
compassion.*
misericors, -cordis, adj., *piti-
ful;* as subst., *a compas-
sionate man,* iv. 19. title;
m. contra se, iv. 19. 3,
showing pity to his own hurt.
[misereor : cors.]
mitto, -ere, misi, missum,
v. tr., *send; let go, lower*
curtain, v. 7. 23 n. ; *utter*
sound; *throw, hurl.*

Mnemosyne, -es, f., mother of
Muses, iii. Prol. 18. [Μνη-
μοσύνη = *Remembrance.*]
modestia, -ac, f., *moderation,
modesty.*
modestus, -a, -um, adj., *moderate, forbearing, modest.*
[modus.]
modius, -ii, m., Roman corn
measure, *a peck.*
modo, adv., lit. *with measure;
only, merely;* of time, *just
now, now, a little while ago,
but now.* [modus.]
modus, -i, m., *measure, limit;
method, manner.*
molestia, -ae, f., *trouble, vex-
ation, annoyance.*
molestus, -a, -um, adj., *trou-
blesome, annoying.* [moles.]
molior, -iri, -itus, v. dep. tr.,
*endeavour, labour at, under-
take;* m. fraudem, iv. 9. 7,
lay a trap. [moles.]
mollis, -e, adj., *soft, pliant;
pleasant,* v. 7. 13. [μαλακός.]
momentum, -i, n., *movement,
change; short time, moment;*
m. horae, iii. Prol. 5, *the
short space of an hour, one
short hour.* [moveo.]
moneo, -ere, -ui, -itum, v. tr.,
*remind, advise, instruct,
warn.*
monitum, -i, n., *admonition,
advice.* [moneo.]
mons, montis, m., *moun-
tain.*
monstro, -are, -avi, -atum,
v. tr., *show, point out.*
[moneo.]
mora, -ae, f., *delay.* [moror.]

morbus, -i, m., *sickness, disease.*

mordax, -ācis, adj., *biting;* mordaciorem, iv. 8. 1, *one who bites harder.* [mordeo.]

mordĕo, -ēre, mŏmordi, morsum, v. tr., *bite.*

mŏrĭor, mŏri, mortuus, v. dep. intr., *die.* [mors.]

mŏror, -āri, -ātus, v. dep. intr. and tr., *delay, linger: retard.* [mora.]

mors, mortis, f., *death.* [morior.]

morsus, -ūs, m., *biting, bite.* [mordeo.]

mortālis, -e, adj., *mortal, perishable, human;* as subst., *a mortal.* [mors.]

mortuus, -a, -um, part. of morior as adj., *dead.*

mos, mōris, m., *manner, custom, way, fashion;* pl., *manners, morals, character.*

mōtus, -ūs, m., *movement, motion.* [moveo.]

mŏveo, -ēre, mōvi, mōtum, v. tr., *move, disturb: influence, affect; excite, arouse.*

mox, adv., *soon.*

mūla, -ae, f., *she-mule.*

mulco, -āre, -āvi, -ātum, v. tr., *beat, thrash.*

mūlĭer, -ĕris, f., *woman, wife.*

multo, adv., *by much, by far, far.* [multus.]

multo, -āre, -āvi, -ātum, v. tr., *punish.*

multum, adv., *much, greatly, very.* [multus.]

multus, -a, -um, adj., *much, great, many;* as comp. and

superl. are used plus, plurimus.

mūlus, -i, m., *mule.*

mūnio, -īre, -īvi or -ii, -ītum, v. tr., *defend with a wall, fortify.*

mūnus, -ĕris, n., *service, duty, burden, present, gift;* vestri ornatum muneris, iv. 16. 5, *the adornment which has been given to you.*

mūrus, -i, m., *wall.* [moenia: munio.]

mus, mūris, m. and f., *mouse.*

Mūsa, -ae, f., *a Muse;* nine goddesses of the arts. [μοῦσα.]

musca, -ae, f., *fly.*

muscĭpŭlum, -i, m., *mousetrap,* iv. 2. 17. [mus: capio.]

mūsĭcus, -a, -um, adj., *belonging to music, musical.* [μουσικός.]

mustēla, -ae, f., *weasel.* [mus.]

mūto, -āre, -āvi, -ātum, v. tr. and intr., *change, alter.* Pass. often as middle, *change,* iv. 17. 5, etc.

muttio, -īre, -īvi, -ītum, v. intr., *mutter, speak in low tones.*

mūtus, -a, -um, adj., *dumb, silent, voiceless.*

Mўron, -ōnis, m., famous Athenian sculptor, v. Prol. 7 note.

myrtus, -i and -ūs, f., *myrtle-tree, myrtle.* [μύρτος.]

nam, conj., *for.*

namquĕ, conj., *for indeed, for.*

nanciscor, -sci, nactus and nanctus, v. dep. tr., *get, obtain*.

nāris, -is, f., generally in pl., *nostrils*.

narrātio, -ōnis, f., *narration, narrative, story*. [narro.]

narro, -āre, -āvi, -ātum, v. tr., *tell, relate;* narrandi iocus, ii. Prol. 5, *the jest* or *amusing point of the story;* narratae rei, iv. 25. 31, *of the story;* used absol. i. 6. 2, narrare, *to tell this story*.

nascor, -sci, nātus, v. dep. intr., *am born*.

nāsūtus, -a, -um, adj., *large nosed;* hence *sarcastic, fastidious*, iv. 7. 1. [nāsus, *nose*.]

nāta, -ae, f., *daughter*. [nascor.]

nātālis, -is, adj., *belonging to one's birth*. As subst., natalis, -is, m. (sc. dies), *birthday;* natali, iii. 15. 13, *at my birth*.

nātio, -ōnis, f., *kind, race, nation*. [nascor.]

nāto, -āre, -āvi, -ātum, v. intr., *swim*. [freq. of no, nare.]

nātūra, -ae, f., *nature, quality;* vocem naturae, v. 5. 33 n., *natural voice*. [nascor.]

nātus, -a, -um, part., see nascor.

nātus, -i, m., *son;* pl., *children; young ones,* of fox, etc. [nascor.]

naufrăgus, -i, m., *a shipwrecked man*. [navis: frango.]

nauseo, -āre, -āvi, -ātum, v. intr., *am sick; cause disgust, sicken us*, iv. 7. 25.

nauta, -ae, m., *sailor*. [navis.]

nāvis, -is, f., *ship*. [ναῦς.]

ne, conj. and adv.; final, *to prevent, lest, that not;* after verbs of fearing, *that;* after verbs of entreating, *not to:* in prohibition, *do not;* ut ne, iv. 24. 25.

Něāpŏlis, -is, f., *Naples*.

něc or něquě, adv. and conj., *and not, nor; and not even,* ii. 8. 14, neque enim, *for indeed ... not*.

něcessĭtas, -ātis, f., *necessity, compulsion; connection, relationship; the laws of nature,* iii. 15. 18 n. [necesse.]

něco, -āre, -āvi (and -ui, iv. 19. 4), -ātum, v. tr., *kill by violent means*. [νεκρός.]

něcŏpīnus, -a, -um, adj., *unexpected, unexpectedly*. [opinor.]

nectar, -ăris, n., *nectar,* the drink of the gods.

neglěgenter, adv., *heedlessly, carelessly*. [neglego.]

neglěgo, -ěre, -xi, -ctum, v. tr., *neglect, despise, disregard*. [nec : lego.]

něgo, -āre, -āvi, -ātum, v. tr. and intr., *say no, deny, refuse*.

něgōtium, -ii, n., *business*. [nec : otium.]

němo, -ĭnem; gen. abl. and sometimes dat., from nullus;

no man, no one. [ne : homo.]

nĕmŏrōsus, -a, -um, adj., *full of woods, wooded, woodland.* [nemus.]

nempĕ, conj., *indeed, without doubt, to be sure.*

nĕmŭs, -ŏris, n., *wooded pasture land; wood, grove.* [νέμος, *pasturage.*]

nēnia, -ae, f., *funeral song, dirge;* any song, iii. Prol. 10 n. ; iv. 2. 3. [νηνία.]

nĕquĕ, see nec.

nēquĭtia, -ae, f., *idleness, wickedness, knavery.* [nēquam.]

nēquĭquam, adv., *in vain, to no purpose.* [ne, quiquam, *not in any way.*]

nescio, -īre, -īvi or -ii, -ītum, v. tr., *do not know, am ignorant;* nescio quis, *some one or other.*

[nex], nĕcis, f., *violent death, murder,* not in nom. sing. [neco.]

nīdus, -i, m., *nest; eyrie* of eagle.

nĭger, -gra, -grum, adj., *black, dark.*

nĭhĭl or **nīl,** indecl. n., *nothing:* acc. as adv., *in no way, not at all.*

nĭhĭlum, -i, n., *nothing;* abl. nihilo with comparatives, *by nothing.*

nīl, see nihil.

Nīlus, -i, m., *river Nile* in Egypt. [Νεῖλος.]

nĭmĭus, -a, -um, adj., *beyond measure, excessive, too great.* [nimis.]

nīsĭ, conj., *if not, unless, except.*

nīsus, -ūs, m., *striving, effort.* [nitor.]

nīteo, -ēre, no perf. or sup. v. intr., *shine; am glossy or sleek.*

nĭtor, -ōris, m., *brightness, brilliance.* [niteo.]

nītor, -i, nīsus or nixus, v. dep. intr., *rest upon; press forward; strive.*

nĭvĕus, -a, -um, adj., *snowy, snow-white.* [nix.]

nix, nĭvis, f., *snow;* pl. *frosts.* [νιφάς.]

nōbĭlis, -e, adj., *well known, famous; of noble birth, high-born.* [nosco.]

nŏcens, -entis, part. from nŏceo as adj., *wicked, baneful, culpable.*

nŏceo, -ēre, -cui, -cītum, v. intr., with dat., *am harmful to, harm, injure.* [noxa: pernicies.]

nŏcīvus, -a, -um, adj., *hurtful, injurious.* [nŏceo.]

noctū, adv., *in the night, at night.* [nox.]

noctua, -ae, f., *night owl, owl.* [nox.]

nocturnus, -a, -um, adj., *of the night, nocturnal, at night.* [nox.]

nōlo, nolle, nōlui, v. intr. and tr., irreg., *am unwilling, refuse;* noli or nolite with inf. = imperative, *do not.* [non : volo.]

nōmen, -ĭnis, n., *name.* [nosco : γιγνώσκω.[

nŏmĭno, -āre, -āvi, -ātum, v.
tr., *call by name, name.*
[nomen.]
non, adv., *not.*
nondum, adv., *not yet.*
nos, used as pl. of ego, *we.*
nosco, -ĕre, nōvi, nōtum, v.
tr., *get to know, learn;* in
perf. *I have learnt,* i.e. *I
know,* but in v. 9. 4, *I
learnt, knew;* plup. *I knew.*
[γιγνώσκω.]
nossem, plup. subj. of nosco,
for novissem.
noster, -tra, -trum, poss.
pron., *our, ours.* [nos.]
nŏta, -ae, f., *mark, note,
brand;* often = nota cen-
soria, *censor's brand,* see
i. 3. 11 n.; *distinguishing
feature, trait of character,*
iv. 24. 23.
nŏtesco, -ĕre, nōtui, no sup.
v. intr., *become known.*
nŏto, -āre, -āvi, -ātum, v. tr.,
mark, brand, iii. Prol. 49.
See nota, above.
nŏtus, -a, -um, part of nosco,
as adj., *known, well known;*
active sense, notis, i. 11. 2,
those who know him; comp.
notior, *very well known,* v.
7. 4, properly *better known
than others.*
nŏvācŭla, -ae, f., *razor, dag-
ger; scythe,* v. 8. 1.
novi, see nosco.
nŏvies, num. adv., *nine times.*
[novem.]
nŏvissĭmē, adv., *recently,
lately, at last, lastly, finally.*
[novissimus : novus.]

nŏvĭtas, -ātis, f., *newness,
a novelty,* v. 5. 6 n. [novus.]
nŏvus, -a, -um, adj., *new,
recent, fresh, strange.* [νέος.]
nox, noctis, f., *night.* [νύξ.]
noxius, -a, -um, adj., *harmful; guilty.* [noxa.]
nūdātus, -a, -um, part. of
nudo as adj., *bare, exposed.*
nūdo, -āre, -āvi, -ātum, v. tr.,
make bare, lay bare.
nūdus, -a, -um, adj., *naked,
bare; stripped of everything,*
iv. 22. 17.
nullus, -a, -um, gen. -īus,
adj., *not any, none, no, no
one.* See nemo. [ne :
nullus.]
num, interrog. particle (1) in
direct questions, implying
answer 'no' is expected,
surely...not? (2) in indirect
questions, *if, whether.*
nūmen, -ĭnis, n., lit. *nodding
of head : divine will,* or
power; deity, god. [nuo,
nod.]
nŭmĕro, -āre, -āvi, -ātum, v.
tr., *count, number, reckon.*
nŭmĕrus, -i, m., *number.*
nummus, -i, m., *piece of
money, coin;* pl. *money.*
[νέμω, numerus.]
numquam, adv., *never.* [ne :
umquam.]
nunc, adv., *now, at this time;
under these circumstances,
as it is,* i. 6. 7; i. 22. 6.
[νῦν.]
nūper, adv., *lately, recently.*
nuptiae, -ārum. f. pl., *nup-
tials, marriage.* [nubo.]

nūtrio, -īre, -īvi and -ii, -ītum, v. tr., *nourish, feed.*

nux, nŭcis, f., *nut;* ludere nucibus, iii. 14. 2, of a child's game with nuts.

o, interj., *oh!*

ōbĭcio (for ōbiĭcio), -ĕre, -iēci, -iectum, v. tr., *throw before or in the way of, offer, present, expose;* pass. *meet,* v. 10. 4. [ob : iăcio.]

ōbĭtus, -ūs, m., *downfall; death.* [obeo.]

obiurgo, -āre, -āvi, -ātum, v. tr., *scold, blame.*

oblecto, -āre, -āvi, -ātum, v. tr., *delight, please.*

oblītus, -a, -um, part. of obliviscor as adj., *forgetful of,* with gen.

oblīviscor, -sci, oblītus, v. dep., *forget,* with gen.

obnoxius, -a, -um, adj., *guilty of; liable to, exposed to; submissive, weak,* iii. Prol. 34.

obscūrus, -a, -um, adj., *dark, obscure.* [scutum: σκῦτος.]

obsisto, -ĕre, -stĭti, -stĭtum, v. intr., *place oneself in the way of, withstand, resist.*

obsōnium, -ii, n., *what is eaten with bread as a relish, victuals, meat, fish,* etc. [ὀψώνιον.]

obtĕgo, -ĕre, -xi, -ctum, v. tr., *cover up, conceal.*

obtĕro, -ĕre, -trīvi, -trītum, v. tr., *bruise, trample on;* proculcatas obteret, *trample and tread to death,* i. 30. 10.

obtrecto, -āre, -āvi, -ātum, v. tr. and intr., *disparage, decry.* [tracto.]

obvius, -a, -um, adj., *in the way, meeting.* [ob : viam.]

occāsio, -ōnis, f., *occasion, opportunity, favourable moment.*

occĭdo, -ĕre, -cīdi, -cīsum, v. tr., *strike down, kill.* [caedo.]

occĭdo, -ĕre, -cĭdi, -cāsum, v. intr., *fall down, perish, die.* [cădo.]

occumbo, -ĕre, -cŭbui, -cŭbĭtum, v. intr., *fall dying, die;* occ. neci, iv. 2. 14, *to die.*

occŭpātus, -a, -um, part. of occŭpo as adj., *engaged, busy.*

occŭpo, -āre, -āvi, -ātum, v. tr., *take possession of, seize; attack; do first, anticipate, outstrip,* ii. Epil. 5. [ob : capio, *take hold of.*]

occurro, -ĕre, -curri, rarely -cŭcurri, -cursum, v. intr., *run up to, meet, fall in with.*

ŏcŭlus, -i, m., *eye.* [ὄσσε, *two eyes.*]

ōdi, ōdisse, fut. part. ōsūrus, v. defect. tr., perf. with pres. meaning, *hate.*

ōdiōsus, -a, -um, adj., *hateful.* [odi.]

ŏdor, -ōris, m., *smell, perfume.* [ὄζω: ὀδμή.]

offendo, -ĕre, -di, -sum, v. tr. and intr., *strike against, hit, give offence to, offend.*

offĕro, offerre, obtŭli, ob-
lātum, v. tr., *present, offer.*
offĭcīna, -ae, f., *workshop.*
[ops : opifex.]
offĭcium, -ii, n., *service,
favour, duty.* [opus : facio.]
offundo, -ĕre, -fūdi, -fūsum,
v. tr., *pour out, spread;
inspire with,* ii. 4. 11.
ōlim, adv., *once upon a time,
formerly ; long ago,* iii. 12.
5 ; *at times ; one day, here-
after.* [ollus = ille.]
ŏlīva. -ae, f., *olive, olive tree.*
[ἐλαία.]
ōmen, -ĭnis, n., *sign, omen.*
ōmitto, -ĕre, -mīsi, -missum,
v. tr., *let go, neglect.*
omnīno, adv., *altogether,
entirely.* [omnis.]
omnis, -e, adj., *all, every,
every kind of.*
ŏnĕro, -āre, -āvi, -ātum, v.
tr., *load, burden.* [onus.]
ŏnus, -ĕris, n., *load, burden.*
ŏnustus, -a, -um, adj., *loaded,
laden.* [onus.]
ŏpĕra, -ae, f., *service, work,
pains ;* operā Palladiā. iv.
7. 9, *by the agency or help
of Pallas ;* operam dare, v.
7. 5, *give attention to,
assist ;* pretium est operae,
ii. 5. 6, *it is worth while.*
opes, see [ops].
ŏpīmus, -a, -um, adj., *fat ;
rich, fertile.*
ŏportet, -ēre, -uit, v. impers.,
*it is necessary, proper, one
ought.* [opus.]
oppĕto, -ĕre, -īvi and -ii, -itum,
v. tr., *meet, encounter.*

oppōno, -ĕre, -pŏsui, -pŏsĭtum,
v. tr., *set against, oppose to.*
opportūnus, -a, -um, adj.,
*convenient, suitable ; which
happened to be at hand,*
ii. S. 4.
opprĭmo, -ĕre, -essi, -essum,
v. tr., *press down, crush,
overpower, overwhelm ; come
upon unexpectedly, seize,
catch.* [prĕmo.]
oppugno, -āre, -āvi, -ātum,
v. tr., *attack.* [pugno.]
[ops], opis, f., defect., nom.
and dat. sing. not found ;
power, strength, help ; pl.,
resources, wealth. [opu-
lentus.]
optĭmus, -a, -um, adj., used
as superl. of bonus ; *best.*
opto, -āre, -āvi, -ātum, v. tr.,
choose, wish for, desire.
[*look out for,* cf. ὄψομαι.]
ŏpus, -ĕris, n., *work, labour ;
work of art,* v. Prol. 5 ;
poem, book ; opus est, *it is
needful, there is need ;* iii.
13. 9, *your work,* i.e.
honey.
ordo, -ĭnis, m., *order, arrangement ; order, class, rank ;*
ordo equester, v. 7. 30, *the
Order of Knights ;* ordo narratae rei, iv. 25. 31, *complete version of the story.*
ŏrior, -īri, ortus, v. dep.
intr., *arise, rise.* [ὄρνυμι.]
ornātus. -ūs, m., *dress, attire,
ornament, decoration.* [orno.]
orno, -āre, -āvi, -ātum, v. tr.,
*furnish, equip, adorn ;
praise, honour.* [os.]

ōro, -āre, -āvi, -ātum, v. tr.
and intr., *plead, pray, be-
seech, supplicate.* [os, oris.]
Orpheus, -ei, m., famous
Thracian bard, son of the
Muse Calliope, husband of
Eurydice; iii. Prol. 57 note.
ōs, ōris, n., *mouth.*
ŏs, ossis, n., *bone.* [ὀστέον.]
oscŭlor, -āri, -ātus, v. dep.
tr., *kiss.* [osculum.]
oscŭlum, -i, n., lit. *little
mouth ; kiss.* [dim. of os:
oris.]
ostendo, -ĕre, -di, -sum and
-tum, v. tr., *exhibit, show,
display, declare, make
known.*
ōtiōsus, -a, -um, adj., *idle,
unoccupied, at leisure.*
[otium.]
ōtium, -ii. n., *leisure, case;*
otio, i. 25. 6, *at your leisure;*
occupata in otio, ii. 5. 2,
very busy doing nothing.
ŏvis, -is, f., *sheep.* [ὄϊς.]

pactum, -i, n., *agreement;* in
abl., pacto, *way, manner;*
ullo pacto, ii. 6. 6, *anyhow;*
so quovis pacto, iv. Prol. 5.
[paciscor.]
pactus, -a, -um, part. from
obsolete pacisco as adj.,
*settled, agreed upon, stipu-
lated;* pactam fidem, iii.
13. 17, *promise.* [paciscor.]
paenĕ, adv., *nearly, almost.*
paenĭtentia, -ae, f., *repentance, penitence.* [paeniteo.]
paenĭteo, -ĕre, -ui, no sup.,
v. intr., *repent, generally*

impersonal ; ad paeniten-
dum, *to repentance,* v. 5. 3.
paenŭla, -ae, f., *cloak, worn
esp. on journeys,* v. 2. 5.
pălam, adv., *openly, publicly.*
Pallădius, -a, -um, adj., *of
Pallas.*
Pallas, -ădis and -ădos, f.,
name of Greek goddess
Athēnē, identified with
Roman Minerva.
pallium, -ii, n., *Greek cloak*
or *mantle.*
pălor, -āri, -ātus, v. dep.
intr., *wander about, stray,
roam.*
pălūs, -ūdis, f., *swamp,
marsh.* [πηλός.]
pānis, -is, m., *bread, loaf* or
piece of bread.
panthēra, -ae, f., *panther.*
[πάνθηρ.]
pār, păris, adj., *equal, of the
same age.*
părātus, -a, -um, part. fr.
paro as adj., *prepared,
ready.*
parcē, adv., *sparingly, mode-
rately.* [parcus.]
parco, -ĕre, pĕperci, rarely
parsi, parsum, v. intr.,
spare, forbear, desist.
[parcus.]
părens, -ntis, m. and f.,
parent, father or *mother.*
păreo, -ēre, -ui, -ĭtum, v.
intr., *appear, obey.*
părio, -ĕre, pĕpĕri, partum,
v. tr., *bring forth, produce,
give birth to, create, procure.*
părĭter, adv., *equally, in like
manner.* [par.]

păro, -āre, -āvi, -ātum, v. tr., prepare, provide. [πόρος.]

pars, partis, f., part, portion, share; pl., parties at law, iii. 13. 5; partibus factis, i. 5. 6, when it had been divided into shares; in plur., often part or character on stage, duty, function, iii. 18. 10 n.; factionum partibus, i. 2. 4, the parties or sides of the factions, i.e. the different factions; bonas in partes ... accipias, ii. Prol. 11, receive in good part.

Partĭcŭlo, -ōnis, m., iv. Prol. 10 note; iv. Epil. 5.

partio, -īre, -īvi or -ii, -ītum, v. tr., and partior, -īri, -ītus, v. dep. tr., share, divide, distribute. [pars.]

partŭrio, -īre, -īvi or -ii, no sup., v. tr. and intr., desire to bring forth, am in labour, am about to bring forth, i. 19. 3. [desid. of pario.]

părum, indecl. subst. and adv., too little. [parvus.]

parvŭlus, -a, -um, adj., small, little. [dim. of parvus.]

parvus, -a, -um, adj., small, insignificant, little; comp. mĭnor; superl. mĭnĭmus.

pasco, -ĕre, pāvi, pastum, v. tr. and intr., drive to pasture, feed; pass. as mid., pasci, iv. 24. 18, feed on; pastum exire, ii. 4 14, go out to feed. [pabulum.]

passer, -ĕris, m., sparrow.

passim, adv., in different directions, hither and thither. [passus.]

pastor, -ōris, m., herdsman, shepherd. [pasco.]

pastum, supine of pasco.

pătĕfăcio, -ĕre, -fēci, -factum, v. tr., throw open, open up; lie open to all, ii. Epil. 3. [pateo.]

păteo, -ĕre, -ui, no sup., v. intr., lie open or ready.

păter, -tris, m., father; The Father (of Jupiter), iv. 12. 6. [πατήρ.]

pătiens, -entis, part. of pătior as adj., bearing, patient, with gen., i. 5. 3.

pătientia, -ae, f., patience, endurance. [patior.]

pătĭna, -ae, f., flat broad dish, i. 26. 4. [pateo.]

pătior, păti, passus, v. dep. tr., bear, endure, suffer, put up with, am content with, i. 3. 14. [πάθος : ἔπαθον.]

pătria, -ae, f., fatherland, native land. [pater.]

pătrĭmōnium, -ii., n., estate inherited from one's father, inheritance, patrimony [pater.]

paucus, -a, -um, adj., rare in sing., few. [παῦρος: paullus.]

paullo, adv., by a little, a little. [paullus.]

pauper, -ĕris, adj., of small means, poor but not destitute; pl., the lower classes, i. 15. 2.

paupertas, -ātis, f., small means, poverty but not indigence.

păvens, part. fr. paveo, *in a panic*, i. 11. 9.

păveo, -ēre, pāvi, no sup., v. tr. and intr., *tremble, am afraid, dread.*

păvĭdus, -a, -um, adj., *trembling, fearful, timid.* [paveo.]

pāvo, -ōnis, m., *peacock*, sacred to Juno, see iii. 18. [ταώς.]

păvor, -ōris, m., *trembling, fear, panic.*

pecco, -āre, -āvi, -ātum, v. intr., *sin, err.*

pecten, -ĭnis, m.. *comb* for hair.

pectus, -ŏris, n., *breast; heart, feelings.*

pĕcūnia, -ae, f., *property, riches; money.* [pecus, because wealth in ancient times consisted in *cattle.*]

pĕcus, -ŏris, n., *cattle, herd, flock.*

pegma, -ătis, n., wooden *platform* used in theatres on which performers were raised or lowered, v. 7. 7. [πῆγμα.]

pĕlăgius, -a, -um, adj., *of the sea; over the sea*, iv. 22. 7. [pelagus.]

Pĕlĭădes, -um, f. pl., *daughters of Pelias*, who killed their father through Medea's guiles, iv. 7. 16 note.

Pĕlias, -ae, m., King of Thessaly, iv. 7. 13.

Pĕlius, -a, -um, adj., *of Pelion*, mountain in Thessaly, iv. 7. 6.

pellis, -is, f., *skin, hide.* [πέλλα.]

pello, -ĕre, pĕpŭli, pulsum, v. tr., *push, drive, drive away.* [πάλλω.]

Pēlūsius, -a, -um, adj., *of Pelusium*, town at mouth of Nile, ii. 5. 12 note.

pendeo, -ēre, pĕpendi, no sup., v. intr.. *hang, am suspended, hang up for sale*, iii. 4. 1; pendens in, v. 8. 1, *resting on.*

pendo, -ĕre, pĕpendi, pensum, v. tr., *weigh, weigh out:* hence, as in early times payments were made by weighing out metals, *pay*, iii. 17. 7; *suffer* or *pay penalty*, i. 27. 6.

pĕnĭtus, adv., *inwardly, deeply, entirely.* [penetro: Penates.]

pepererat, plup. of pario.

pĕr, prep. with acc., *through, during, by means of, over* the plain, i. 12. 8: per te, *by yourself*, ii. 1. 3. [παρά.]

pēra, -ae, f., *bag, wallet.* [πήρα.]

pĕrăgo, -ĕre, -ēgi, -actum, v. tr., *pass through, traverse, carry through, accomplish.*

pĕrambŭlo, -āre, -āvi, -ātum. v. tr., *roam through, traverse*, poet. and in post-Augustan prose.

perdo, -ĕre, -dĭdi, -dĭtum, v. tr., *destroy, lose.*

perdŏmo, -āre, -ui, -ĭtum, v. tr., *tame* or *subdue thoroughly.*

perdūco, -ĕre, -xi, -ctum, v. tr., *lead, guide* to.

pĕrĕgrīnus, -a, -um, adj.,
foreign, strange. [per :
ager.]

pĕreo, -īre, -ii, -ĭtum, v. intr.,
pass away, perish, am lost :
nequiquam perit, ii. 5. 24,
is spent in vain. [per : eo.]

perfĕro, -ferre, -tŭli, -lātum,
v. tr., *bear through, carry
through ; endure to the end.*

perfĭcio, -ĕre, -fēci, -fectum,
v. tr., *achieve, perform :
finish, perfect.* [facio.]

pĕrīclĭtor, -āri, -ātus, v. dep.
tr. and intr., *make trial of,
put in danger ; attempt,
am in danger.* [periclum.]

pĕrīclum or pĕrīcŭlum, -i, n.,
danger, peril.

pĕrīcŭlōsus, -a, -um, adj.,
dangerous, perilous. [peri-
culum.]

pĕrītus, -a, -um, adj., *experienced ;* peritis, i. 23. 2,
men of experience. [ex-
perior.]

periūrium, -ii, n., *false oath,
perjury.* [per : iuro.]

perlĕgo, -ĕre, -lēgi, -lectum,
v. tr., *read through.*

perlustro, -āre, -āvi, -ātum,
v. tr., *wander through.*

permŏveo, -ēre, -mōvi. -mō-
tum, v. tr., *thoroughly
move, arouse.*

pernĭcies, -ēi, f., *destruction,
ruin.* [per : nĕco.]

pernĭcĭtas, -ātis, f., *nimble-
ness, swiftness.* [pernix.]

pĕrōro, -āre, -āvi, -ātum, v.
tr., *plead throughout, wind
up one's speech,* i. 10. 7.

perpastus, -a, -um, adj., *well-
fed.* [pasco.]

persălūto, -āre, -āvi, -ātum,
v. tr., *salute one after the
other.*

persĕquor, -sĕqui, -sĕcūtus, v.
dep. tr., *follow after, pursue.*

persolvo, -ĕre, -solvi, -sŏlū-
tum, v. tr., *pay in full :* p.
poenas, *pay* or *suffer
penalty in full.*

persōna, -ae, f., *mask,* esp.
used by actors ; hence *character,* and Eug. *person.*
[persono or πρόσωπον.]

persuādeo, -ēre, -si, -sum, v.
intr., *convince, persuade,*
with dat. ; but persuasa
est, pass. used personally,
i. 8. 7, and perf. part. pass.
iii. 5. 8 n.

pertĭneo, -ēre, -ui, no sup.,
v. intr., *reach to ;* p. ad,
*relate to, concern, affect, am
applicable to :* hoc quo p.,
iii. 1. 7, *the application of
this.* [teneo.]

perturbātus, -a, -um, part. of
perturbo as adj., *disturbed,
uneasy,* iv. 25. 27.

perturbo, -āre, -āvi, -ātum, v.
tr., *throw into confusion,
disturb greatly.*

pervello, -ĕre, -velli, no sup..
v. tr., *pull, twitch* or *pinch
hard.*

pervĕnio, -īre, -vēni, -ventum,
v. intr., *come to, reach.*

pēs, pĕdis, m., *foot ;* referre
pedem, ii. 1. 6, *retire, retreat.* [πούς.]

pessĭmus, -a, -um, adj., used as superl. of **mălus**, *worst, very bad.*

pĕto, -ĕre, -īvi and -ii, -ītum, v. tr., *attack, seek, make for, ask, claim, aim* a blow, etc., *at.* [πέτομαι: impetus.]

pĕtŭlans, -antis, adj., *forward, impudent, saucy.* [part. fr. obsolete petulo, cf. peto.]

Phaedrus, -i, m., author of these fables, iii. Prol. 1. See Introd.

Phălērĕus, -ēi, m., *from Phalerum*, harbour of Athens ; iii. Prol. 1.

Phĭlētus, -i, m., see v. 10. 10, note.

Phoebus, -i, m., name of Apollo, as god of *light.* [Φοῖβος, *the radiant one.*]

Phryx, Phrȳgis, m., a *Phrygian, of Phrygia* in Asia Minor.

pĭācŭlum, -i, n., *propitiatory* or *sin offering; sin, crime.*

pictus, see pingo.

Pĭĕrĭus, -a, -um, adj., (1) *Pierian*, or sacred to the Muses, who were called Pierides ; (2) *Thessalian*, from Mt. Pierus in Thessaly ; iii. Prol. 17.

pĭĕtas, -ātis, f., *dutifulness* to gods or men, *piety* ; = *the pious*, iv. 11. 10. [pius.]

pĭgnus, -ŏris and -ĕris, n., *pledge; wager*, iv. 21. 5 ; *token, proof*, v. 5. 37 ; *pledges of love, children*, iv. 25. 9. [pango: paciscor.]

pĭlus, -i, m., *hair.*

pingo, -ĕre, pinxi, pictum, v. tr., *paint, embroider.*

pinna, -ae, f., *feather;* pl., *wing.* [πέτομαι.]

pīnus, -ūs and -i, f., *pine tree, pine, fir.*

Pīsistrătus, -i, m., tyrant of Athens, i. 2. 5, note.

plăceo, -ēre, -cui, -cĭtum, v. intr., *please, am pleasing to, find favour with;* impers. placet, *it pleases me*, etc.

plăcĭdus, -a, -um, adj., *gentle, quiet, calm.* [placeo: placo.]

plăco, -āre, -āvi, -ātum, v. tr., *soothe, calm, reconcile.* [placeo: placidus.]

plāga, -ae, f., *blow, stroke.* [πληγή.]

plānē, adv., *distinctly, completely, quite, certainly, to be sure.* [plānus.]

plānus, -a, -um, adj., *level, flat ; clear, plain ;* in plano, ii. 4. 10, *on the level ground.*

plaudo, -ĕre, -si, -sum, v. tr. and intr., *beat ; clap the hands, applaud.*

plausus, -ūs, m., *clapping sound, applause.* [plaudo.]

plēbēĭus (or plēbēĭus, trisyl.), -a, -um, adj., *of the common people, plebeian, vulgar :* as subst., *a plebeian*, iii. Epil. 34.

plēbs or **plēbes**, plēbis, f., *the commons, lower orders, plebeians.* [rt. ple =*fill*, cf. πίμπλημι.]

plector, -i, no perf., only in pass. in class. Latin, *am beaten, punished, suffer.* [πλήττω.]

plēnus, -a, -um, adj., *full, filled.* [rt. ple, cf. πίμπλημι.]

plērumquĕ, adv., *for the most part, commonly.* [plerusque.]

plūrĭmus, -a, -um, adj., used as superl. of multus, *most, very many.* plurimum, acc. neut. as adv., *most;* videre plurimum, ii. 8. 28, *is most keen sighted,* or *sees most.*

plus, plūris, adj., used as comp. of multus; *more;* pluris, iv. 24. 3, *of more value;* plus valeo, i. 5. 9, *I am stronger.*

Plūtus, -i, m., god of riches, iv. 12. 5. [Πλοῦτος.]

pōcŭlum, -i, n., *drinking cup, goblet.* [πίνω, potus.]

poena, -ae, f., *compensation, penalty, punishment.* [ποινή: punio.]

pŏēta, -ae, m., *poet.* [ποιητής.]

pŏlĭo, -īre, -īvi and -ii, -ītum, v. tr., *smooth, polish.*

pollĭceor, -ēri, -ĭtus, v. dep. tr. and intr., *offer, promise.*

pondus, -ĕris, n., *weight.*

pōno, -ĕre, pŏsui, pŏsĭtum, v. tr., *place, set, erect, build,* iii. 9. 6; *set up* statue, ii. Epil. 1; *place before, set before,* i. 26. 5, v. 4. 3; *offer* as reward, i. 14. 9; *propose* a subject for discussion, or *set* a problem, iii. 14. 5. 8; *lay aside,* i.

2. 19; ut positum fuit, iii. 8. 4, *as it lay.*

pontus, -i, m., *the sea.* [πόντος.]

pŏpŭlus, -i, m., *the people; the common people,* iii. 9. 5. [plenus: plebs, rt. ple.]

pōpŭlus, -i, f., *poplar tree.*

porcellus, -i, m., *little pig.* [dim. of porcus.]

porro, adv., *forward, onward; in turn, next,* iii. Prol. 38; *further, besides,* iii. 15. 11. [πόρρω : pro.]

porta, -ae, f., *gate, door.* [περάω.]

porto, -āre, -āvi, -ātum, v. tr., *bear, carry.*

posco, -ĕre, pŏposci, no sup., v. tr., *ask, claim, demand, call for.*

possum, posse, pŏtui, v. intr. irreg., *am able, can.*

post, prep. with acc. and adv., *behind, after.*

postĕrus, -a, -um, adj., *coming after;* pl., m., postĕri, -ōrum, *posterity, future generations.* [post.]

postquam, conj., *after that, after.*

postrīdĭē, adv., *on the next day, on the morrow.* [posterus: dies.]

postŭlo, -āre, -āvi, -ātum, v. tr., *ask for, demand.* [posco.]

pŏtens, -entis, pres. part. fr. possum as adj., *able, powerful;* as subst., *a powerful man;* pl., *the powerful.*

pŏtestas, -ātis, f., *ability, power.*

pŏtior, -ius, adj., comp. of potis, *more able, better, preferable; dearer* or *has a stronger claim on you,* iii. 15. 9.

pŏtius, adv., *rather, by preference.* [potior : potis.]

pōto, -āre, -āvi, -ātum, v. tr. and intr., *drink.* [πίνω, πέπωκα : poculum.]

praebeo, -ēre, -ui, -itum, v. tr., *hold out, offer, afford, furnish, supply.* [prae : habeo.]

praeceptum, -i, n., *maxim, rule, command, injunction.* [praecipio : capio.]

praeclūdo, -ēre, -si, -sum, v. tr., *shut a thing to anyone ; hinder, impede, stop* mouth of dog, i. 23. 5. [claudo.]

praecurro, -ēre, -cŭcurri and -curri, -cursum, v. tr. and intr., *run in front, on in advance ; precede.*

praeda, -ae, f., *booty, plunder, prey ; piece of stolen meal,* i. 4. 4 ; the '*find,*' v. 6. 4. [prehendo.]

praedātor, -ōris, m., *plunderer; hunter,* ii. 1. 2. [praeda : praedor.]

praedo, -ōnis, m., *plunderer, robber.* [praeda.]

praefulgeo, -ēre, -si, no sup., v. intr., *shine in front, shine forth* or *brightly.*

praegusto, -āre, -āvi, -ātum, v. tr., *taste beforehand.*

praelūceo, -ēre, -xi, no sup., v. intr., *shine before or forth, shine forth on,* iv. 11. 9.

praemětuo, -ěre, no perf. or sup., v. tr. and intr., *fear beforehand.*

praemium, -ii, n., *profit, reward.* [prae : emo.]

praepōno, -ěre, -pŏsui, -pŏsitum, v. tr., *put first, set before, prefer.*

praesens, -entis, part. fr. praesum as adj., *present.*

praesentia, -ae, f., *presence.* [praesens.]

praesēpě, -is, n., *stall, stable.*

praesĭdium, -ii, n., *defence, protection, guard.*

praesto, -āre, -iti, -ātum and -itum, v. tr. and intr., *stand before, excel; surpass; fulfil, discharge, perform ; furnish, supply : warrant,* iii. 4. 4 ; *render,* i. 31. 9.

praeter, prep. with acc., *except, beyond.*

praetereo, -ire, -ivi and -ii, -itum, v. tr. and intr., *go past* or *by, pass by, omit.*

praevăleo, -ēre, -ui, no sup., v. intr., *have greater power, prevail over,* with abl. of comparison, i. 13. 14.

prātum, -i, n., *meadow.* [πλατύς.]

prăvus, -a. -um, adj., *misshapen, bad, vicious.*

Praxĭtěles, -is, m., celebrated Greek sculptor, v. Prol. 6.

prece, see [prex].

prěmo, -ěre, pressi, pressum, v. tr., *press, press hard upon ; pursue, assail* with insult, iii. Epil. 31 ; *check, stop,* i. 11, 12.

prendo or prĕhendo, -ĕre, -di, -sum, v. tr., *lay hold of, seize, grasp.*

prensus, see prendo.

prĕtiōsus, -a, -um, adj., *valuable, precious.* [prĕtium.]

prĕtium, -ii, n., *price, value, reward, fee,* i. 8. 1, iv. 25. 6; p. est operae, ii. 5. 6, *it is worth while.* [πιπράσκω.]

[prex,] prece, f., defect. in sing., only in abl. and rarely acc., *prayer.* [precor.]

prīdem, adv., *long ago, long since.* [prior.]

prīmo, adv., *at first, firstly.* [primus.]

prīmum, adv., *at first, first.* [primus.]

prīmus, -a, -um, superl. adj., *first, foremost;* sella p., iii. 6. 5, *front seat* of waggon. [prae : prior.]

princeps, -ĭpis, m., *chief person, leader;* principes, v. 1. 4, *the chief men;* = the Emperor, v. 7. 27.

Princeps, -ĭpis, m., name of flute player, v. 7. 4, etc.

princĭpātus, -ūs, m., *first place, command, lordship* of herd, i. 30. 5; *government,* i. 15. 1. [princeps.]

prior, -us, comp. adj., *former, first, superior;* priores, iv. 20. 16, *forefathers, those who have lived before you.* [prae : primus.]

pristĭnus, -a, -um, adj., *former, original.* [prius.]

prius, adv., *before, first;* prius quam, *before that.*

prīvātus, -a, -um, part. of privo as adj., *of an individual, private.*

prō, prep. with abl., *before, in front of ; for, in favour of, on behalf of ; in defence of ; instead of ; in return for.* [πρό : prac.]

prŏbo, -āre, -āvi, -ātum, v. tr., *test, approve, prove ;* probandus, *to be approved of,* iv. 13. 2. [probus.]

prŏcax, -ācis, adj., *bold, impudent, insolent.*

procēdo, -ĕre, -cessi, -cessum, v. intr., *go forth or forward, proceed.*

prōclīvis, -e, adj., *sloping downhill ; inclined to, ready, willing,* iii. Epil. 21. [clivus.]

prŏcŭl, adv., *afar off, from afar.*

prŏculco, -āre, -āvi, -ātum, v. tr., *tread down, trample upon.* [calco.]

prōdeo, -īre, -ii, -ĭtum, v. intr., *go forth or out, step forth, come forward.* [eo.]

prōdesse, see prosum.

prōdo, -ĕre, -dĭdi, -dĭtum, v. tr., *give forth, make known, hand down to posterity.*

proelium, -ii, n., *battle.*

profecto, adv., *actually, indeed, in truth.*

prōfĕro, -ferre, -tŭli, -lātum, v. tr., *bring forth, bring forward, produce ; pro-*

nounce sentence, iii. 13. 13 ;
stretch forth, put out, i. 2. 17.
prŏfessus, -a, -um, part. from
profiteor as adj., *manifest,
known*, iv. 7. 8.
prŏfĭcio, -ĕre, -fēci, -fectum,
v. tr. and intr., *advance,
profit, accomplish.* [făcio.]
prŏfĭteor, -ēri, -fessus, v. tr.
and intr., *declare publicly,
confess, profess, promise ;*
professae mortis, iv. 7. 8,
see professus.
prŏfŭgio, -ĕre, -fūgi, no sup.,
v. tr. and intr., *flee before or
from, flee, flee away.*
prŏgēnies, -ēi, f., *descent ;
descendants, posterity, offspring.* [pro : gigno.]
prŏgrĕdĭor, -i, -gressus, v. intr.,
*come or go forth, advance,
more forward.* [gradior.]
prolātus, see profěro.
prōles, -is, f., *offspring, young.*
[pro : rt. ol, cf. adolescens.]
prōlŏgus, -i, m., *preface, prologue.* [πρόλογος.]
prōlŏquor, -qui, -cūtus, v.
dep. tr. and intr., *speak
out, utter, declare.*
prŏmitto, -ĕre, -mīsi, -missum,
v. tr., *promise ; promise to
come, engage to dine* with
anyone, iv. 25. 15.
prŏmōrat for promoverat, see
promoveo, iv. 25. 28.
prŏmŏveo, -ĕre, -mōvi, -mō-
tum, v. tr., *more forward,
advance.*
prŏpĕ, prep. with acc. and
adv., *near, nearly.* [pro.]
prŏpĕro, -āre, -āvi, -ātum, v.

tr. and intr., *hasten, do
with haste.*
prŏpior, -us, comp. adj.,
nearer ; superl. **proximus**,
see below. [prope.]
prŏpōno, -ĕre, -pŏsni, -pŏsi-
tum, v. tr., *put forth ; set
forth, relate ; offer, propose.*
prŏpŏsĭtum, -i, n., *plan,
purpose ; preliminary asser-
tion ; proposition*, i. 5. 2 ;
*main point, subject, theme ;
set task*, iv. 21. 9.
prŏprium, -ii, n., *property,
possession.* [proprius.]
prŏprius, -a, -um, adj., *one's
own, special, personal,
characteristic.*
propter, prep. with acc. and
adv., *near, hard by ; on
account of.* [prope.]
prorsus, adv., *by all means,
certainly, utterly.* [pro :
versus.]
prōsĕquor, -qui, -sēcūtus, v.
dep. tr., *accompany, follow
after ; honour, bestow upon ;
pursue, proceed with*, iii. 5. 4.
prospecto, -āre, -āvi, -ātum,
v. tr. and intr., *look forth
or upon, have a distant view
of*, ii. 5. 10.
prospĭcio, -ĕre, -exi, -ectum,
v. tr. and intr., *look forwards, look out, descry,
keep a look-out*, ii. 4. 20.
prosterno, -ĕre, -strāvi, -strā-
tum, v. tr., *throw to the
ground, prostrate.*
prōsum, prŏdesse, prōfui, v.
intr., *am useful, benefit,
profit, aid.*

prŏtĭnus, adv., *straight for- wards; forthwith, immedi- ately.*

prŏtrŭdo, -ĕre, -si, -sum, v. tr., *thrust forwards* or *forth.*

prŏvŏco, -āre, -āvi, -ātum, v. tr., *call forth.*

prŏvŏlo, -āre, -āvi, -ātum, v. intr., *hasten* or *rush forth. fly forth.*

proxĭmus,-a,-um,adj.,superl. of propior, *nearest, next:* culpae p., i. 10. 5 n., *guilty.*

prūdens, -entis, adj., *fore- seeing, experienced, sensible.* [providens.]

prūdentia, -ae, f., *knowledge of, skill in.*

publĭcum, -i, n., *public pro- perty,* etc.; *public place;* pub. ingredi, v. 7. 17, *appear in public.*

pŭdet, -ēre, -uit or puditum est, v. impers., rarely pers., *one feels ashamed, it makes one feel ashamed,* with acc. of person.

pŭdor, -ōris, m., *shame, modesty.*

puella, -ae, f., *girl, maiden, young woman,* ii. 2. 10. [puer.]

puer, -ĕri, m., *boy, child.* [pubes.]

puĕrīlĭter, adv., *like a child, foolishly.* [puer.]

pugna, -ae, f., *fight, battle.* [pugil : πύξ.]

pulcher, -chra, -chrum, adj., *beautiful.*

pulchrē, adv., *beautifully, ex- cellently; clearly, well,* iv. 20. 6 etc.: *gracefully, skil- fully,* i. 10. 10; *carefully;* superl. pulcherrime, iii. 13. 4, *very thoroughly.*

pullus, -i, m., *young animal; young bird,* i. 28. 4; p. gallinaceus, iii. 12. 1, *chicken, pullet.*

pulmentārium, -ii, n., *any- thing eaten with bread* as a *relish, sauce, fruit,* etc., iii. 7. 27. [pulpā.]

pulpĭtum, -i, n., *stage, plat- form.*

pulsus, see pello.

pulvis, -ĕris, m., *dust.*

punctum, -i, n., *small hole, puncture; sting, bite,* v. 3. 3. [pungo.]

pūnio, -īre, -īvi or -ii, -ītum, v. tr., *punish;* punitorum, *men punished,* v. 4. 11.

purgo, -āre, -āvi, -ātum, v. tr., *purify, cleanse.* [purus.]

pŭtĕus, -i, m., *well.* [purus : purgo.]

pŭto, -āre, -āvi, -ātum, v. tr., *trim, prune; clear up, reckon* accounts, etc.; *value as; think.* [purus: purgo.]

pycta or **pyctes**, -ae, m., *boxer, pugilist.* [πύκτης.]

quā, adv., *by which road, where.* [abl. f. of qui.]

quădrans, -antis, m., *a fourth: fourth of an as, farthing.* [quattuor.]

quaero, -ĕre, -sīvi or -sii, situm, v. tr., *seek, seek or search for ; ask, desire.*

quaeso, -ĕre, -ivi or -ii, no sup., v. tr. and intr., *beg, pray :* often parenthetically in 1st sing., *pray !* [old form of quaero.]

quaestio, -ōnis, f., *inquiry, question, subject* for discussion, *problem,* iii. 14. 8. [quaero.]

quaestus, -ūs, m., *gain, profit.* [quaero.]

quālis, -e, pron. adj., interrog. and rel., *of what* or *which sort* or *kind ; such as, as.* [quis.]

quam, adv., *in what way, how ; as,* correl. of tam ; quam...non, v. 2. 13, *how little :* in comparisons, *than.* [qui.]

quamlibet, adv., *as it pleases, as much as you please.*

quamvis, adv. and conj., *as much as you will, ever so, however much, although.* [volo.]

quando, adv. and conj., interrog. and rel., *when, since;* indef., *at any time, ever.*

quanto, adv., *by how much* or *as much :* with comparatives, tanto...quanto, *the more...the more,* iv. Epil. 9.

quantum, adv., *as much as, so much as ; how much ;* q. valet, i. 13. 13, *the value* or *power of.*

quantus, -a, -um, adj., *how great* or *much :* correl. of tantus, *as, such as ;* quan-

tum est laboris, ii. 8. 24, *how much labour does it require ?* [quam : quis.]

quāpropter, adv., rel. and interrog., *why, wherefore.*

quāre, adv., interrog. and rel., *by which means, wherefore, why.* [qui : res.]

quartus, -a, -um, num. adj., *fourth ;* quartam, i. 5. 10. *fourth share.* [quattuor.]

quāsī, adv., *as if, as though, just as ;* quasi inventuri, iii. 2. 8, *thinking they would find,* like Gr. ὡς with fut. participle. [quam : si.]

-quĕ, conj., enclitic, *and ;* que...que or et, *both...and.*

quercus, -ūs, f., *oak, oak-tree.*

quĕrēla, -ae, f., *complaint ; ground for complaint,* ii. Epil. 14. [queror.]

quĕror, -i, questus, v. dep. tr. and intr., *complain, complain of.*

questus, -ūs, m., *complaining, complaint, lament.* [queror.]

qui, quae, quod, rel. pron., *who, which, what ; and he,* etc. With subj. (1) final, *in order that he, to,* etc., i. 2. 12 ; (2) causal, *because he,* etc., i. 8. 12, etc. ; (3) consecutive, *so that he, such as to.*

qui, quae (qua), quod, indef. adj., *any.*

qui, quae, quod, interrog. adj., *who? which? what? how great,* i. 13. 6.

qui, adv., *in what manner, how.* [abl. of qui.]

quĭă, conj., *because.*

quicquam, see quisquam.

quīcumquĕ, quaecumque, quodcumque, rel. pron., *whoever, whatever, whosoever.*

quĭd, interrog. adv., *how, why;* quid multa, ii. 4. 23, sc. dicam, *why say much? what need of many words?* [quis.]

quĭdam, quaedam, quoddam and quiddam (subst.) indef. pron., *a certain one, some one, a.*

quĭdem, adv., *indeed.*

quĭesco, -ĕre, -ēvi, -ētum, v. intr., *rest, remain quiet.* [quies.]

quĭētus, -a, -um, pass. part. formed fr. intrans. quiesco, as adj., *at rest, quiet, steady, silent.*

quīlĭbet, quaelĭbet, quodlĭbet and quidlĭbet (subst.), indef. pron., *any you will.*

quīn, conj., *that not, but that,* with subj. ; *indeed, truly; nay even, moreover,* with or without etiam, v. 1. 7. [qui : ne.]

quīntus, -a, -um, num. adj., *fifth.* [quinque.]

quippĕ, adv. and conj., *certainly, to be sure:* with participles and adjectives causal, *since;* q. tuta, i. 28. 7, *since she was safe,* so iii. 2. 5 n.; iii. 8. 8 n.; with relatives, *since.*

quis, quid, interrog. pron., *who? what? which?* quid

tibi videtur, iv. 7. 17, *what think you?*

quis, quă, quid, indef. pron., *any one, any, some one;* nescio quis, *some one or other.*

quisnam, quaenam, quidnam, interrog. pron., *who pray? which pray? what pray? whoever?* quidnam voluisti tibi, ii. 8. 5, *whatever did you mean?* [enclitic -nam, like Gr. ποτέ and our *ever.*]

quisquam, quaequam, quicquam or quidquam, indef. pron. in neg. sentences, *any one at all, any;* acc. quicquam as adv., *in any way.*

quisquĕ, quaeque, quodque and (subst.) quicque or quidque, indef. pron., *each, every.*

quisquĭs, quicquid or quidquid and (adj.) quodquod, rel. pron. *whoever, whatever.*

quīvis, quaevis, quodvis and (subst.) quidvis, indef. pron., *any you please.* [volo.]

quŏ, adv., *to which place, whither, to what end or purpose, wherefore,* iii. 18. 9 ; hoc quo pertinet, iii. 1. 7, *the application of this;* final, *to the end that, in order that,* esp. with comparatives; iii. Epil. 12, *in proportion as, as;* indef., *in any direction, any whither,* iii. 7. 25.

quod, conj., *in that, because;
that, the fact that;* quod si,
but if. [qui.]

quondam, adv., *at one time,
once, once upon a time,
formerly; at times, some-
times; some day.*

quŏnĭam, adv., *since, seeing
that, because.*

quŏquĕ, adv., *also, too.*

quŏt, indecl. adj., *how many;*
correl. of tot, *as many,
as.*

răbŭla, -ac, m., *wrangling
advocate, pettifogger,* ii.
Epil. 15.

rāmōsus, -a, -um, adj., *full
of branches, branching.*
[ramus.]

rāmus, -i, m., *branch, bough.*
[radix: radius.]

rāna, -ae, f., *frog.*

răpīna, ac, f., *robbery, plunder, pillage.* [rapio.]

răpĭo, -ĕre, răpui, raptum,
v. tr., *carry off, seize upon,
snatch, steal, plunder;* r.
ad se, iii. Prol. 46, *appropriate to himself;* pegma
rapitur, v. 7. 7, *is raised
hurriedly.*

raptor, -ōris, m., *robber,
plunderer.* [răpio.]

rārus, -a, -um, adj., *scattered,
scanty, few, rare;* rara
mens, iv. 2. 6 note.

rătio, -ōnis, f., *reckoning, cal-
culation, method; cause,
motive, reason.*

rătis, -is, f., *raft, bark, boat.*
[ἐρέτης: remus.]

rēcĭdo, -ĕre, reccĭdi, rĕcāsum,
v. intr., *fall back; relapse
into, am reduced to,* iii. 18.
15. [cădo.]

rēcĭpio, -ĕre, -cēpi, -ceptum,
v. tr., *take back, receive
back, receive, get back, re-
cover;* ad se rec., iv. 22,
23, *welcome, entertain;*
pass., in middle sense, *win
one's way back, retreat,* iv.
6. 4. [căpio.]

rectā, adv., *straight forwards,
right on, directly, straight.*
[rectus.]

rectē, adv., *straightly, rightly:*
r. loqui, iv. 13. 1, *speak
accurately,* i.e., *the truth.*
[rectus.]

rĕcumbo, -ĕre, -cŭbui, no
sup., v. intr., *lie down
again; recline* at table, iv.
25. 19.

rĕcūso, -āre, -āvi, -ātum, v.
tr. and intr., *decline, refuse;
refuse to suffer,* iii. 2. 16.

reddo, -ĕre, -dĭdi, -ditum, v.
tr., *give back, restore, repay,
pay* or *give as due,* iv. 25.
13, etc. ; iii. Epil. 8 ; red.
tempora, iii. Prol. 12, *give
time to,* i.e. *spend time
with;* ius red., *administer
justice,* iv. 14. 5; red. iudicium, iii. Prol. 63, *grant a
trial.* [re: do.]

rĕdeo, -īre, -ii, -ĭtum, v. intr.,
come or *go back, return;*
eunt et redeunt, ii. 8. 12,
come and go; red. in gratiam, v. 3. 6, *become reconciled, forgive.* [re: eo.]

rĕdūco, -ĕre, -xi, -ctum, v. tr., *lead* or *bring back.*

rĕfello, -ĕre, -felli, no sup., v. tr., *disprove, refute.*

rĕfĕro, -ferre, rettŭli or rē-tŭli, rĕlātum, v. tr., *carry back, repeat, report, relate,* i. 2. 9 ; ref. gratiam, *return thanks, show gratitude ;* par referri gratia, iii. 2. 1, *fit for tat ;* ad animum rettulit, iii. 19. 10, *took to heart ;* ref. pedem, ii. 1. 6, *retire, withdraw ;* absol. use, de quo rettuli, iv. 25. 4, *of whom I have spoken.*

rĕfert, -ferre, -tŭlit, v. im-pers., *it is for one's interest* or *advantage, it matters, concerns,* with gen. of per-son or thing, or meâ, tuâ, etc., i. 15. 9. [for rei, fert, *it contributes to one's ad-vantage.*]

rĕfĭcio, -ĕre, -fēci, -fectum, v. tr., *re-make, restore, re-cruit* strength ; refectus, iv. 19. 4 ; *restored, revived.* [facio.]

rĕgālis, -e, adj., *kingly, royal.* [rex.]

regno, -āre, -āvi, -ātum, v. intr., *am king, reign.* [reg-num.]

regnum, -i, n., *royal authority, lordship, rule, kingdom.* [rex.]

rĕĭcio (for rĕiĭcio), -ĕre, -iēci, -iectum, v. tr., *throw back, reject, refuse* request of, ii. 1. 4. [re : iacio.]

rĕiectus, see reicio.

rĕlaxo, -āre, -āvi, -ātum, v. tr., *stretch out, unloose, relax.*

rĕlĭcŭus or **rĕlīquŭs**, -a, -um, adj., *remaining ; other, rest of,* iii. 4. 2 ; rĕlĭcŭam, iv. 25. 12, sc. partem, *re-mainder.* [relinquo.]

rĕlĭgio, -ōnis, f., *reverence for gods, religious scruple* or *awe ; obligation* of oath, *scrupulousness, conscien-tiousness,* iii. 13. 8, iii. Epil. 26 ; personified Religio, i. 27. 6 n. ; iv. 11. 4, *the Oracle.*

rĕlinquo, -ĕre, -līqui, -lictum, v. tr., *leave behind, leave.*

rĕlĭquĭae, -ārum, f., pl., *re-mains, relics, fragments* of food, i. 22. 6.

rĕlĭquus, see relicuus.

rĕmĕdium, -ii, n., *remedy, medicine, relief.* [medeor.]

rĕpello, -ĕre, reppŭli, rĕpul-sum, v. tr., *thrust* or *drive back, reject, spurn.*

rĕpendo, -ĕre, -di, -sum, v. tr., *weigh back, repay,* ii. Prol. 12.

rĕpentē, adv., *suddenly, un-expectedly.* [rĕpens.]

rĕpĕrio, -īre, reppĕri, rĕper-tum, v. tr., *find, discover.* [lit. *procure again,* pārio.]

rĕpĕto, -ĕre, -īvi or -ii, -ītum, v. tr., *attack again ; seek again ; renew, repeat.*

rĕpleo, -ēre, -ēvi, -ētum, v. tr., *refill, fill up ;* repletum, iv. 10. 2, *full.*

rĕpo, -ĕre, -psi, -ptum, v. intr., *creep, crawl ; come*

grovelling up, v. 1. 4.
[serpo : ἕρπω.]

rĕposco, -ĕre, no perf. or sup.,
v. tr., *demand back, ask to
give back or up.*

reppĕri, perf. of rĕpĕrio.

rĕprĕhendo, -ĕre, -di, -sum,
v. tr., *hold back, seize or
catch again*, v. 8. 4.

rĕpulsa, -ae, f., *rejection,
defeat.* [repello.]

repulsus, see repello.

rĕquīro, -ĕre, -sīvi or -sii,
-sĭtum, v. tr., *seek for, look
for, ask after, inquire.*
[quaero.]

rēs, rēi, f., *thing, matter,
fact, affair, business, property, possessions; story,
fable*, i. 27. 1; *his design*,
ii. 5. 19; res domestica,
iii. Prol. 11, *house-keeping;*
rem expedire, i. 16. 2,
settle the business; hac re,
iv. 10. 4, *on this account,
for this reason.*

rĕsĕs, -idis, adj., lit. *staying
behind; inactive, idle.*
[resideo.]

rĕsĭdeo, -ēre, -sēdi, no sup.,
v. intr., *remain behind,
sit, perch on*, i. 13. 4.
[sĕdeo.]

rĕsĭdŭus, -a, -um, adj., *left
behind, remaining.* [rĕ-
sĭdeo.]

rĕsisto, -ĕre, -stĭti, no sup., v.
intr., *stand still, stop, stand
firm.*

rĕsŏno, -āre, -āvi, no sup., v.
tr. and intr., *resound, resound with.*

respectus, -ūs, m., *looking
back; respect, consideration.*
[respicio.]

respĭcio, -ĕre, -spexi, -spec-
tum, v. tr. and intr., *look
back or behind, look back
at; have a view behind
one*, ii. 5. 10. [obsolete
specio : specto : σκέπτομαι.]

respondeo, -ēre, -di, -sum, v.
tr. and intr., *answer, reply.*

responsum, -i, n., *reply.*
[respondeo.]

restĭtit, see resisto.

restĭtuo, -ĕre, -ui, -ūtum, v.
tr., *set up again, restore.*
[stătuo.]

retendo, -ĕre, -di, -tum and
-sum,v.tr., *unbend, slacken;*
retensus (of bow), *loosened,
unstrung*, iii. 14. 5.

rĕtĭneo, -ēre, -ui, -tentum, v.
tr., *hold back, detain, check.*
[teneo.]

rĕtorrĭdus, -a, -um, adj.,
*parched or dried up,
wizened, wrinkled;* hence
experienced, cunning, iv. 2.
16. [torreo.]

rĕtro, adv., *backwards, back.*
[re : cf. intro, ultro.]

rettŭdi, see retundo.

rettŭli, see refero.

rĕtundo, -ĕre, rettŭdi, -tūsum,
v. tr., *beat back, check.*

rĕus, -i, m., *one who is accused,
defendant, culprit.* [res :
party to an action.]

rĕverto, -ĕre, -verti, no sup.,
v. intr., and revertor, -i,
-versus, v. dep. intr.. *turn
back, return* (in pres. tenses

the act. form is rare in classical writers).

rĕvŏco, -āre, -āvi, -ātum, v. tr., *call back; invite to one's house in return,* i. 26. 7.

rex, rēgis, m., *ruler, king.* [rego.]

rīdeo, -ēre, -si, -sum, v. tr. and intr., *laugh, laugh at.*

rīdĭcŭlē, adv., *laughably, humorously.* [ridiculus : rideo.]

rĭgens, -entis, part. of rigeo as adj., *stiff, frozen.*

rĭgeo, -ēre, no perf. or sup., v. intr., *am stiff* or *numb.*

rīsus, -ūs, m., *laugh, laughter.* [rideo.]

rīvus, -i, m., *brook, stream.*

rōdo, -ēre, -si, -sum, v. tr., *gnaw.* [rostrum : rado.]

rŏgo, -āre, -āvi, -ātum, v. tr., *ask, ask for, question, beg, entreat.*

Rōma, -ae, f., *Rome.*

rostrum, -i, n., *bill, beak.* [rodo.]

rŭdis, -e, adj., *unformed, rough,inexperienced;* mulier non r., ii. 2. 3, *not inexperienced in the ways of the world, a 'woman of the world.'*

rūgōsus, -a, -um, adj., *wrinkled.* [rūga, *wrinkle.*]

ruīna, -ae, f., *a falling down, downfall, fall; the fall of the tree,* ii. 4. 21. [ruo.]

rūmor, -ōris, m., *report, rumour.*

rumpo, -ĕre, rūpi, ruptum, v. tr., *burst, break asunder.*

ruo, -ĕre, rui, rūtum, f. part. ruĭturus, v. tr. and intr., *rush down, rush, fall, hasten; cast down.*

rursus, adv., *backwards, again.* [reversus : reverto.]

rustĭcus, -a, -um, adj., *of the country, rural, rustic;* as subst., rustĭcus, -i, m., and rustica, -ae, f., *rustic, peasant.* [rus.]

saccus, -i, m., *bag, sack.* [σάκκος.]

săcrĭlĕgium, -ii, n., *sacrilege; sacrilegious plunder,* iv. 11. 3. [sacer : lego.]

săcrum, -i, n., *a sacred thing, sacrifice,* iv. 11. 13. [sacer.]

saecŭlum, -i, n., *generation, age; century.*

saepĕ, adv., *often;* comp., saepius, *more often, as a rule,* i. 15. 1.

saevio, -īre, -ii, -ītum, v. iutr., *rage, rave.* [saevus.]

saevus, -a, -um, adj., *raging, cruel, fierce.*

sal, sălis, m., *salt; shrewdness, wit,* v. 5. 8. [ἅλs.]

sălio, -īre, -ui, saltum, v. intr., *leap, jump.* [ἅλλομαι.]

saltem, adv., *at least, at all events.*

salto, -āre, -āvi, -ātum, v. tr. and intr., *dance; represent by dancing.* As subst., saltans, -antis, *a dancer,* v. 7. 15.

saltus, -ūs, m., *forest pasture, woodland glade.*

saltus, -ūs, m., *leap, spring.* [sălio.]

sălūs, -ūtis, f., *safety, health.* [salvus.]

sălūto, -āre, -āvi, -ātum, v. tr., *greet, wish health to.* [salus : salvus.]

salvus, -a, -um, adj., *safe, sound, well.* [salus : ὅλος.]

sanctus, -a, -um, part. from sancio as adj., *sacred, holy, venerable, just, pure, inviolable.*

sānē, adv., *sensibly; indeed, truly; in truth, certainly,* in concessive sense. [sānus.]

sanguis, -ĭnis, m., *blood; race, stock; offspring,* i. 28. 10.

sānĭtas, -ātis, f., *soundness of body, health.*

săpiens, -entis, part. from sapio as adj., *wise, discreet.* As subst., sapiens, -entis, m., *a wise man, sage.*

săpientia, -ae, f., *good sense; wisdom.*

săpio, -ĕre, -ūi or -ii, no sup., v. tr., *have a taste or flavour;* quidnam saperet, iii. 4. 3, *how it tasted;* v. intr., *am sensible, wise.*

săpor, -ōris, m., *taste, flavour; refinement, wit;* iii. 4. 4 n., play on words.

sarcĭna, -ae, f., *bundle, load, burden.* [sarcio.]

sătio, -āre, -āvi, -ātum, v. tr., *fill, satisfy, satiate.* [satis.]

sătis, adv. *sufficient, sufficiently, sufficiently well, well,* v. 7. 6; fecisset ... satis, v. 10. 2, tmesis, see satisfacio.

sătisfăcio, -ĕre, -fēci, -factum, v. intr. with dat., *give satisfaction to, satisfy;* by tmesis, fecisse ... satis, v. 10. 2.

sător, -ōris, m., *sower, planter; father, creator;* title of Jupiter, iii. 17. 10. [sero : satus.]

saxum, -i, n., *rock.*

scaena, -ae, f., *stage, scene* of theatre, v. 5. 13; v. 7. 5. [σκηνή.]

scando, -ĕre, no perf. or sup., v. tr. and intr., *climb, mount, ascend.*

scĕlestus, -a, -um, adj., *wicked, villainous;* as subst. *a scoundrel.* [scĕlus.]

scĕlus, -ĕris, n., *crime, wickedness.*

schŏlă, -ae, f., *disputation, lecture; place of learning, school,* iii. Prol. 20, of Greece. [σχολή, *spare time.*]

sciens, -entis, part. of scio, as adj., *knowingly, purposely.*

scīlicet, adv., *you must know, of course, certainly.* [scīrelicet.]

scio, scīre, -īvi, -ītum, v. tr., *know, understand.* [rt, sci, cf. scindo.]

scŏpŭlus, -i, m., *rock, cliff,* [σκόπελος.]

scrībo, -ĕre, -psi, -ptum, v. tr., *write.* [γράφω : Germ. schreiben.]

scriptor, -ōris, m., *writer, author.* [scribo.]

scriptum, -i, n., *anything written, writing, book.* [scribo.]

scrŭtor, -āri, -ātus, v. dep. tr., *search thoroughly, examine carefully.*

scurra, -ae, m., *buffoon, jester.*

scỹphus, -i, m., *goblet, cup.* [σκύφος.]

Scỹtha and Scỹthes, -ae, m., *a Scythian.*

se, sui, reflex. pron. of 3rd pers., *himself, herself, itself, themselves.*

sēcrētum, -i, n., *secrecy; solitude; place of retirement, retreat.* [secretus : secerno.]

sēcrētus, -a, -um, part. of secerno, as adj., *separate, lonely, hidden, secret.*

sĕcundō, adv., *secondly, in the second place.*

sĕcundus, -a, -um, adj., lit. *following; second; favourable, fair* of wind, etc.; secundae res, v. 2. 15, *prosperity.* [sequor.]

sēcūrus, -a, -um, adj., *free from care, careless, untroubled, unconcerned;* in *fancied security,* i. 9. 9. [sc = sine, cūra.]

sĕd, conj., *but, yet.*

sĕdeo, -ēre, sēdi, sessum, v. intr., *set;* of magistrate, *take my seat on the bench, sit in court,* i. 10. 6. [sēdes : ἕζομαι.]

sēdes, -is, f., *seat; abode, home.* [sedeo.]

sēdo, -āre, -āvi, -ātum, v. tr., *allay, settle, calm, assuage.* [sĕdeo.]

segnis, -e, adj., *slow, lazy.*

sēgrĕgo, -āre, -āvi, -ātum, v. tr., *set apart, separate.* [grex.]

Sēiānus, -i, m., L. Aelius Seianus, iii. Prol. 41 note.

sella, -ae, f., *seat, chair.* [dim. of sedes.]

sĕmĕl, adv., *once, once for all.* [sui : gulus.]

sēmiănĭmus, -a, -um, adj., *half alive, half dead.*

sēmĭta, -ae, f., *path, lane.*

sempĕr, adv., *always, ever.*

sēnārius, -ii, m., *verse of six feet,* esp. *aniambic,* i. Prol. 2.

sĕnecta, -ae, f., *old age.* [senex : senectus.]

sĕnex, sĕnis, adj., *old, aged;* as subst., m. or f., *old man* or *woman;* of Aesop, ii. Prol. 9 ; iii. 14. 4.

sĕnium, -ii, n., *old age, decay.* [senex.]

sensim, adv., *gently, gradually, in moderation,* iv. 17. 9. [sentio, lit. *visibly.*]

sensus, -ūs, m., *feeling, sensation, sense;* pl., *the senses;* s. communis, i. 7. 4 note, *common sense.*

sententia, -ae, f., *opinion; legal decision, sentence,* i. 10. 8; iii. 13. 13; *vote; aphorism, maxim,* iii. Epil. 33, iv. 13. 2; *meaning, purport,* v. 7. 26. [sentio.]

sentio, -īre, sensi, sensum, v. tr., *feel, hear, see, perceive, think.*

sēpărātus, -a, -um, part. from sēpăro as adj., *separate, distinct, apart, different.*

sĕquor, -qui, -cūtus, v. dep. tr. and intr., *follow;* sequentes otium, v. l. 7, *the followers of ease ;* me sequetur, i. 5. 9, *shall fall to my share.* [ἕκομαι.]

sĕrēnus, -a, -um, adj., *clear, bright ; tranquil, serene.*

sermo, -ōnis, n., *talk, conversation, mode of expression,* iv. 22. 22. [*what is strung together,* sĕro.]

serpens, -entis, f., *snake, serpent.* [serpo.]

sērus, -a, -um, adj., *late, too late.*

servio, -īri, -īvi or -ii, -ītum, v. intr., *am a servant or slave to, serve.* [servus.]

servītūs, -ūtis, f., *slavery, servitude ;* = servus, *slave,* iii. Prol. 34. [servus.]

servo, -āre, -āvi, -ātum, v. tr., *save, preserve, keep.* [ὅλος : salvus : sălus.]

servŭlus, -i, m., *young slave.* [dim. of servus.]

servus, -i, m., *slave, servant.*

sētōsus, -a, -um, adj., *bristly.* [seta or sacta, *bristle.*]

sĕvērĭtas, -ātis, f., *severity, strictness.* [sĕvērus.]

sex, num. adj., indecl., *six.* [ἕξ, German sechs.]

si, conj., *if; to see if,* iv. 8. 4 note. [εἰ.]

sĭbi, see se.

sīc, adv., *in this manner, so, thus ; to such an extent.*

sīcŭbi, adv., *if anywhere, wheresoever.*

Sīcŭlus, -a, -um, adj., *Sicilian, of Sicily,* island to S. W. of Italy ; S. mare, ii. 5. 10, sea to East of Sicily.

sīdus, -ĕris, n., *star, constellation.*

signĭfĭco, -āre, -āvi, -ātum, v. tr., *show, intimate, signify.* [signum : făcio.]

signum, -i, n., *mark, sign ; signal ; standard,* iv. 6. 7.

sĭlentium, -ii, n., *silence.*

sĭleo, -ĕre, -ui, no sup., v. tr. and intr., *am still or silent.*

silva, -ae, f., *wood, forest.* [ὕλη.]

sĭmĭlis, -e, adj., *like, similar.*

sĭmĭlĭtĕr, adv., *in like manner.* comp., similius, *more like.* [similis.]

sīmius, -ii, m., *ape.*

Sīmōnĭdes, -is, m., lyric poet, iv. 22. 2 note.

simplĭcĭter, adv., *plainly, frankly.* [simplex.]

sĭmŭl, adv., *at once, together, at the same time ;* simul or simul ac, *as soon as.* [ἅμα : semel.]

sĭmŭlăcrum, -i, n., *image, statue ; reflection,* i. 4. 3.

sĭmŭlo, -āre, -āvi, -ātum, v. tr., *make like, imitate, feign, pretend.* [similis.]

sīn, conj., *if however, but if;* sin minus, *but if not,* iii. Prol. 31. [si-ne.]

sincērĭtas, -ātis, f., *purity, honesty.* [sincerus.]

sincērus, -a, -um, adj., *pure, genuine, real.* [sim-plex : sem-el.]

sĭnĕ, prep. with abl., *without.*

singŭli, -ae, -a, num. distrib. adj., *one to each, separate, individual, one by one, one after the other,* i. 2. 25 ; often as subst., *in horas singulas,* iii. 15. 14, *from hour to hour.* [simul : simplex.]

sĭnister, -tra, -trum, adj., *left, on the left ; wrong, perverse, unlucky.*

sĭno, -ĕre, sīvi, sĭtum, v. tr., *allow, permit.*

Sĭnon, -ōnis, m., *a Greek through whose guile the Trojans were induced to admit the wooden horse into Troy,* iii. Prol. 27.

sĭnus, -ūs, m., *curve, fold ; fold of toga over breast forming pocket ; lap, bosom ; hollow ; bay.*

sĭtiens, -entis, part. of sitio as adj., *thirsting, thirsty.*

sĭtio, -īre, -īvi or -ii, no sup., v. tr. and intr., *am thirsty ; thirst for.*

sĭtis, -is, f., *thirst.*

sīvĕ or seu, conj., *or if ; sive ... sive, whether ... or if.* [si.]

smăragdus, -i, m. and f., *emerald.*

sŏcĭĕtas, -ātis, f., *fellowship, alliance, companionship.* [sŏcius.]

sŏcius, -ii, m., *partner in business, etc., comrade, ally, companion.* [rt. sec., cf. sequor.]

Sŏcrătes, -is, m., famous Greek philosopher ; put to death by Athenians in 399 B.C.

sol, sōlis, m., *sun ; medio sole,* iii. 19. 8, *at mid-day.* [ἥλιος : σέλας.]

sōlācĭum, -ii, n., *comfort, consolation ; mortis s.,* i. 9. 8, *what reconciles me to dying.* [solor.]

sŏleo, -ēre, -ĭtus sum, v. dep. intr., *am wont, accustomed.*

sŏlĭdus, -a, -um, adj., *firm, solid, real, genuine.* [ὅλος.]

sŏlĭtus, -a, -um, part. fr. soleo, as adj., *customary, usual.*

sollemnis, -e, adj., *established, appointed ; solemn ; wonted, usual.* [sollus=totus, annus; prop., *yearly, annual.*]

sollertia, -ae, f., *shrewdness, ingenuity, cunning.* [sollers.]

sollĭcĭtus, -a, -um, adj., *violently moved, disturbed ; troubled, agitated.* [sollus = totus, cieo ; = *thoroughly moved.*]

sōlus, -a, -um, gen. solius, adj., *alone ; only.*

sŏlūtus, -a, -um, part. fr. solvo as adj., *free, free from care, at leisure, disengaged.*

solvo, -ĕre, solvi, sōlūtum, v. tr., *loosen, untie, relax ; pay.* [se-luo, *unbind.*]

somnus, -i, m., *sleep.* [ὕπνος.]

sŏnĭpēs, -pĕdis, adj., *with*

sounding hoof; as subst., *a horse, charger,* iv. 4. 3. [sonus.]

sŏno, -āre, -ui, -ĭtum, v. tr. and intr., *sound, resound, make to sound;* sonare citharam, iii. 16. 12 n., *ring with the sound of* .... [sonus.]

sŏnus, -i, m., *noise, sound.* [sono.]

sŏphus, -i, m., *a wise man, philosopher, sage,* i. 14. 9 n. [σοφός.]

sorbĭtio, -ōnis, f., *drink, broth, mess,* i. 26. 5. [sorbeo.]

sordĭdus, -a, -um, adj., *dirty, squalid, mean, despicable.* [sordes.]

sŏror, -ōris, f., *sister.* [Germ., Schwester.]

spargo, -ĕre, sparsi, sparsum, v. tr., *scatter, sprinkle, spread.* [σπείρω.]

spātĭum, -ii, n., *space, room; space of time; racecourse, course.*

spēcies, -ēi, f., *appearance, form, look, beauty.* [obsolete specio, cf. aspicio, etc., σκέπτομαι.]

spectācŭlum, -i, n., *show, spectacle.* [specto.]

spectātor, -ōris, m., *observer, spectator.* [specto.]

specto, -āre, -āvi, -ātum, v. tr. and intr., *look at, watch.* [see species.]

spēcŭlum, -i, n., *looking-glass, mirror.* [obsol. specio, see species.]

spēcus, -ūs, m. and f., *cave, cavern.* [σπέος.]

spēlunca, -ae, f., *cave, cavern, den.*

spēs, spĕi, f., *hope.*

spīrĭtus, -ūs, m., *breeze, breath, breath of life, life; spirit, soul; high spirit, energy.* [spiro.]

splendeo, -ēre, no perf. or sup,, v. intr., *shine, glitter.*

splendor, -ōris, m., *brightness, magnificence.* [splendeo.]

spŏlio, -āre, -āvi, -ātum, v. tr., *strip, spoil, plunder.* [spolium.]

spondeo, -ēre, spŏpondi, sponsum, v. tr. and intr., *promise, pledge; become surety or bail* for a person; supine, sponsum vocat, i. 16. 1 n., *asks them to become his security.*

sponsor, -ōris, m., *surety, voucher,* i. 16. 4. [spondeo.]

spontĕ, f., abl. of obsolete spons, generally with meâ, tuâ, etc., *of one's own free-will or accord.* [spondeo.]

spŭmo, -āre, -āvi, -ātum, v. intr., *foam, froth.* [spuma.]

stagnum, -i, n., *pool, pond, swamp.* [τέναγος.]

stătim, adv., *forthwith, immediately.* [sto.]

stătio, -ōnis, f., *abode, home, place where they live,* i. 30. 7; *post, station.* [sto.]

stătua, -ae, f., *image, statue.* [statuo.]

stătuo, -ĕre, -ui, -ūtum, v. tr., *set up, station, place, set.*

stătus, -ūs, m., *position, place, situation.* [sto.]

stercŭlīnum, -ii, n., *dung pit or heap.* [stercus.]

stercus, -ŏris, n., *dung, filth.* [σκώρ.]

stĕrĭlis, -e, adj., *unfruitful, barren.*

stĭlus, -i, m., *a style,* pointed metal instrument used for writing on wax tablets ; hence *mode of composition, style.* [= stiglus ; cf. στίζω, στίγμα.]

sto, stāre, stĕti, stătum, v. intr., *stand ;* stant pro iudicio, v. 5. 2 n., *stand up for their judgment.*

strāmentum, -i, n., *straw, litter.* [sterno.]

stringo, -ĕre, -inxi, -ictum, v. tr., *draw tight ; draw out* sword.

strŏpha, -ae, f., *trick, artifice ;* see i. 14. 4 n. [στροφή.]

stŭdeo, -ēre, -ui, no sup., v. tr. and intr., *am eager, strive after, desire.* [studium.]

stŭdĭōsē, adv., *eagerly, carefully.* [studiosus.]

stŭdium, -ii, n., *eagerness, desire, zeal, devotion to learning, study ; fruits of study, works,* ii. Epil. 12. [studeo.]

stultē, adv., *foolishly, sillily.* [stultus.]

stultĭtia, -ae, f., *folly, silliness.* [stultus.]

stultus, -a, -um, adj., *foolish, silly.*

stŭpor, -ŏris, m., *astonishment, amazement ; dullness,*

stupidity ; corvi stupor, i. 13. 12, *the stupid raven.*

suādeo, -ēre, -si, -sum, v. tr. and intr., *advise, persuade, urge.* [suavis.]

suāvis, -e, adj., *sweet, pleasant.* [suadeo.]

sŭb, prep. with acc. and abl., *under, beneath, up to.* [ὑπό.]

subdŏlus, -a, -um, adj., *somewhat cunning* or *sly ;* verbis subd., i. 13. 1, *crafty compliments.*

subesse, see subsum.

sūbĭcio (for sūbiĭcio), -ĕre, -iēci, -iectum, v. tr., *throw* or *place under* or *near ;* versus subiecti, i. 19. 2, *the lines given below.* [iăcio.]

sūbiectus, see subicio.

subindĕ, adv., *immediately after, from time to time, repeatedly,* ii. 8. 12.

sŭbĭtō, adv., *suddenly, unexpectedly.* [subitus.]

sŭbĭtus, -a, -um, part. from subeo as adj., *sudden, unexpected.*

sublātus, see tollo.

sublīmis, -e, adj., *high, lofty ; exalted, eminent,* i. 28. 1. ; in sublime, ii. 6. 4, *aloft ;* in sublimi quercu, ii. 4. 1, *on the top of an oak.*

submŏveo, -ēre, -mōvi, -mōtum, v. tr., *move away* from below, *remove, banish.*

subrĭpio, -ĕre, -rĭpui, -reptum, v. tr., *snatch away secretly, stealthily carry off, steal, plunder.* [rapio.]

subsĭdium, -ii, n., *reserves,
help, support.*

subsum, -esse, no perf., v.
intr., *am under* or *beneath.*

successus, -ūs, m., *approach ;
good result, success.* [suc-
cēdo.]

succlāmo, -āre, -āvi, -ātum,
v. intr., *cry out, shout.*

succumbo, -ĕre, -cŭbui, -cŭbĭ-
tum, v. intr., *fall down ;
yield, give in, give up* problem, iii. 14. 9.

succurro, -ĕre, -curri, -cur-
sum, v. intr., *run up to
help, succour, aid.*

sūdor, -ōris, m., *sweat, perspiration.*

sum, esse, fui, v. intr. irreg.,
am, exist ; quodcumque
fuerit, iii. Prol. 27, *whatever happens.*

summus, -a, -um, adj., superl.
of superus, *highest, top of,
utmost,* iv. 3. 2 ; summo
monte, *on the top of the hill.*

sūmo, -ĕre, sumpsi, sumptum,
v. tr., *take up, take, choose.*
[sub : emo.]

sŭper, adv. and prep. with
acc. and abl., *above, upon,
over, moreover, in addition.*
[ὑπέρ.]

sŭperbia, -ae, f., *haughtiness,
pride, arrogance.* [super-
bus.]

sŭperbio, -īre, no perf. or
sup., v. intr., *am haughty*
or *proud, take pride in.*

sŭperbus, -a, -um, adj.,
haughty, proud, arrogant.
[super.]

sŭperior and sŭpĕrius, see
under superus.

sŭpersum, -esse, -fui, v. intr.,
am over, remain over.

sŭpĕrus, -a, -um, adj., *that
is above, upper, higher ;*
plur., superi, *the gods above,*
i. 17. 9, etc. ; comp.,
sŭpĕrior, *higher ; higher
up stream,* i. 1. 2 ; adv.,
sŭpĕrius, *higher, above,* iv.
25. 2 ; superl., sŭprēmus
or summus, see summus.

supplex, -ĭcis, adj., *begging,
entreating ;* as subst. m.,
a suppliant. [sub : plico,
bending knees.]

supplĭcium, -ii, n., *punishment, torture.*

sŭprā, prep. with acc. and
adv., *above.* [super.]

sūs, suis, m. and f., *pig,
boar, sow.* [ὑς.]

suscĭto, -āre, -āvi, -ātum, v.
tr., *raise ; stir up, arouse,
excite.*

suspendo, -ĕre, -di, -sum, v.
tr., *hang up, suspend ; hold
up, lift up.*

suspensus, -a, -um, part. from
suspendo as adj., *raised,
suspended ; touching lightly :*
suspenso pede, ii. 4. 18, *on
tiptoe, softly.*

suspĭtio, -ōnis, f., *mistrust,
suspicion ;* suspitione suā,
iii. Prol. 45, *almost evil
conscience.* [suspicio.]

sustĭneo, -ēre, -tĭnui, -tentum,
v. tr., *hold up, support,
sustain, restrain, hold up
against, endure, bear, put*

up with; tristem sustinuit notam, i. 3. 11, *was obliged to endure* .... [sub: tenco.]

sustŭli, see tollo.

sūtor, -ōris, m., *shoemaker, cobbler.* [suo, *stitch.*]

suus, -a, -um, poss. pron. reflexive, *his own, her own, its own, their own, one's own;* sui, *one's friends, people,* etc., *her young,* i. 28. 11 ; *their young ones,* ii. 4. 23 ; *its kind,* i. 3. 6. [sui.]

tăberna, -ae, f., *hut; stall; shop; tavern.* [rt. ta, cf. tabula.]

tăbŭla, -ae, f., *board; writing tablet; painting, picture,* iv. 22. 24 ; v. Prol. 7. [see taberna.]

tăceo, -ēre, -ui, -ĭtum, v. tr. and intr., *am silent, pass over in silence.*

tăcĭtē, adv., *silently, secretly.* [tacitus.]

tăcĭtus, -a, -um, part. of taceo as adj., *not spoken of; silent, secret;* tacito corde, iv. Prol. 3, *in the secrecy of my heart.*

tālis, -e, adj., *of such a kind, such; so famous,* iii. 9. 6. [τηλίκος.]

tam, adv., *so, thus.*

tămen, conj., *nevertheless, however, yet, in spite of that;* si tamen possum, ii. 5. 5, *if at least I can.* [tam.]

tandem, adv., *at length, at last.*

tango, -ĕre, tĕtĭgi, tactum, v. tr., *touch, reach; affect,*

move with envy, i. 24. 3. [rt. tag, cf. θιγγάνω.]

tanto, adv., *by so much;* with comparatives, *so much the more.* [tantus.]

tantum, adv., *so much; only.*

tantummŏdŏ, adv., *only, merely.*

tantus, -a, -um, adj., *so great, so mighty, such;* tanti, gen. of price, *of such value;* tanti ... est, iii. Prol. 4, *it is worth so much.*

tardus, -a, -um, adj., *slow.*

tartărĕus, -a, -um, adj., *of the infernal regions, Tartarean, hellish.*

taurus, -i, m., *bull, bullock, ox, steer.* [ταῦρος.]

tectum, -i, n., *roof; house, dwelling.* [tĕgo.]

tĕgo, -ĕre, -xi, -ctum, v. tr., *cover, hide, conceal, protect.* [τέγος : στέγω.]

tēlum, -i, n., *missile, dart, spear, javelin.*

tĕmĕrĭtas, -ātis, f., *rashness, heedlessness.* [temere.]

tēmo, -ōnis, m., *pole of cart or plough.*

tempĕrātus, -a, -um, part. fr. tempero as adj., *moderate, temperate.*

tempĕro, -āre, -āvi, -ātum, v. tr. and intr., *regulate, rule, manage, restrain myself.* [tempus.]

tempestas, -ātis, f., *season; weather; storm, tempest.* [tempus.]

templum, -i, n., originally *space marked out* in sky by augur for observation; *sanctuary, temple.* [rt. tem., cf. tempus: τέμνω: τέμενος.]

tempto, -āre, -āvi, -ātum, v. tr., *handle, touch, attack, attempt, try.* [freq. of tendo.]

tempus, -ŏris, n., *portion of time, time; temples* of head; adverso tempore, iii. 8. 16, *in adversity;* tempore, adv., *at the right time, in time;* Tempus, personified, v. 8. 8.

tendo, -ĕre, tĕtendi, tentum and tensum, v. tr., *stretch, extend;* as hunting term, *set* snares; t. dolos, i. 23. 2, *spreads his guiles.* [τείνω: teneo.]

tĕnĕbrae, -ārum, f., pl., *darkness.*

tĕneo, -ĕre, -ui, tentum, v. tr., *hold, keep, hold fast, hold back, restrain, stay; hold in one's power,* ii. 2. 4; *possess, engross,* v. 5. 25.

tĕner, -ĕra, -ĕrum, adj., *soft, tender.*

tensus, see tendo.

tĕnŭis, -e, adj., *thin, slender, trifling, meagre.* [lit. *stretched out,* cf. tendo, τείνω.]

tĕnŭĭtas, -ātis, f., *slenderness, smallness, insignificance, humble condition;* hominum t., ii. 7. 13, = tenues, *the humble.* [tenuis.]

tergum, -i, n., *back.*

tergus, -ŏris, n., *back; carcase, the meat,* ii. 1. 9 n.

termĭnus, i, m., *limit, boundary, end.* [τέρμα.]

tĕro, -ĕre, trīvi, trītum, v. tr., *rub, bruise;* trito argento, v. Prol. 7, *burnished silver.* [rt. ter., cf. τείρω, τρίβω, teres.]

terra, -ae, f., *earth, soil, land;* pl., terrae, *the world;* in terris, *on earth,* iv. 23. 2.

terreo, -ēre, -ui, -ītum, v. tr., *frighten, terrify.* [τρέω.]

terror, -ōris, m., *fear, dread, terror.* [terreo.]

tertius, -a, -um, ord. adj., *third.* [tres.]

testa, -ae, f., *earth pot* or *tile, jug, jar.* [torreo, bake.]

testĭmōnium, -ii, n., *evidence, testimony.* [testis.]

testis, -is, m. and f., *witness.*

testor, -āri, -ātus, v. dep. tr., *bear witness to, attest, prove.* [testis.]

testūdo, -ĭnis, f., *tortoise, tortoise shell; lyre* of shell. [testa.]

thĕātrum, -i, n., *theatre.* [θέατρον.]

thēsaurus, -i, m., *treasure, treasury.* [θησαυρός.]

Thessălus, -a, -um, adj., *Thessalian, of Thessaly* in N. Greece.

Threīssa, -ae, f., adj., *Thracian* woman, etc.

Tĭbĕrius, -ii, m., Roman praenomen, esp. the second Emperor, successor of Augustus, i. 2. 5, 7.

tībia, -ae, f., *shin bone ; pipe,
flute,* orig. made of bone,
v. 7. 8, iv. 20. 21.

tībīcen, -ĭnis, m., *flute player.*
[tibia : cano.]

tĭgillum, -i, n., *small beam,
log.* [dim. of tignum.]

tĭmeo, -ēre, -ui, no sup., v. tr.
and intr., *fear ;* with dat.,
*fear for one's safety or one-
self,* iii. 2. 15 ; timens, i. 1.
6, *in dread.*

tĭmĭdus, -a, -um, adj., *timid,
cowardly.* [timeo.]

tĭmor, -ōris, m., *fear, dread.*

tinctus, see tinguo.

tinguo or tingo, -ĕre, -nxi,
-nctum, v. tr., *wet, bathe,
drench, dye.* [τέγγω.]

tintinnābŭlum, -i, n., *bell.*

tĭtŭlus, -i, m., *inscription,
title ; repute, renown,* iv.
Prol. 4.

tollo, -ĕre, sustŭli, sublātum,
v. tr., *lift up, pick up, raise,
take away, remove, carry
off, raise* cry, etc. [tolero :
τλάω.]

Tŏnans, -antis, m., name of
Jupiter, "*The Thunderer.*"
[tono.]

tŏnĭtrus, -ūs, m., *thunder.*

tŏno, -āre, -ui, no sup., v.
intr., *thunder.*

torqueo, -ēre, torsi, tortum,
v. tr., *turn, bend, twist,
torment, torture ;* se t.,
puzzle or *worry* over problem, iii. 14, 7. [τρέπω.]

tōtus, -a, -um, gen. tōtius,
adj., *all, the whole, the
whole of.*

toxĭcum, -i, n., *poison.*
[τοξικόν.]

trādo, -ĕre, -dĭdi, -dĭtum, v.
tr., *hand over, surrender,
deliver to, transmit, hand
down to tradition, relate,
recount.* [trans : do.]

trăgĭcus, -a, -um, adj., *of
tragedy, tragic.* [τραγικός.]

trăho, -ĕre, -xi, -ctum, v. tr.,
*draw, drag, draw in, drink
in ; drag out, prolong, spend*
life, etc., iii. 7. 12.

transeo, -īre, -īvi or -ii, -ĭtum,
v. tr. and intr., *go over,
cross, pass, go across.*

transfĕro, -ferre, -tŭli, -lātum,
v. tr., *carry across, transfer,
copy, transcribe.*

translātĭcius, -a, -um, adj.,
*transmitted, customary, con-
ventional,* v. 7. 24. [trans-
latus from transfero.]

trĕpĭdans, -ntis, part. from
trepido as adj., *bustling,
agitated, trembling.*

trĕpĭdē, adv., *hastily, in alarm.*

trĕpĭdo, -āre, -āvi, -ātum, v.
intr., *bustle about ; am
alarmed, in confusion* or
agitation.

trĭbuo, -ĕre, -ui, -ūtum, v.
tr., *assign, allot, give, grant.*
[tribus.]

trīclīnium, -ii, n., *couch* which
runs round three sides of
dining table ; *dining room,*
iv. 25. 28. [τρικλίνιον.]

trīcor, -āri, -ātus, v. dep.
intr., *shuffle, play tricks,
trifle,* iii. 6. 9. [tricae,
trifles.]

tristis, -e, adj., *sad, sorrow-ful; gloomy, stern, harsh.*

trītĭcum, -i, n., *wheat.* [tritus fr. tero.]

trītus, see tero.

trĭvium, -ii, n., *place where three roads meet, cross roads.* [ter : via.]

trŭcīdo, -āre, -āvi, -ātum, v. tr., *slaughter, butcher, massacre.* [trux : trucu-lentus.]

trūdo, -ĕre, -si, -sum, v. tr., *thrust, push.*

tu, tui, pers. pron. of 2nd pers.; pl., vos, etc.; *thou, you.*

tueor, -ēri, tuĭtus, v. dep. tr., *look at, watch, guard, protect.* [tueor.]

tŭgŭrium, -ii, n., *hut; kennel,* i. 19. 4. [tĕgo.]

tŭli, see fĕro.

tum, adv., *at this* or *that time, then.*

tŭmens, -entis, part. of tumeo as adj., *swelling.*

tŭmeo, -ēre, no perf. or sup., v. intr., *swell, am puffed out, puffed up* with pride. [tuber : tumulus.]

tunc, adv., *then.* [tum and suffix -ce.]

tŭnĭca, -ae, f., *tunic,* under-garment of Romans. [tĕgo.]

turba, -ae, f., *uproar, dis-turbance; crowd, throng, band, company; litter,* i. 19. 9. [τύρβη : turma.]

turbo, -āre, -āvi, -ātum, v. tr., *distrust, throw into con-fusion, agitate; make thick*

or *turbid,* of water, etc. [turba.]

turbŭlentus, -a, -um, adj., *agitated, disturbed;* of water, *muddy, turbid.* [turbo.]

turpis, -e, adj., *ugly, foul, disgraceful, base, dishonour-able.*

turpĭter, adv., *basely, dis-gracefully.* [turpis.]

tūs, tūris, n., *incense, frank, incense.* [θύος.]

Tuscus, -a, -um, adj., *Tuscan, Etrurian; of Etruria,* dis-trict on N. of Tiber; T. mare, ii. 5. 10, the part of Mediterranean off coast of Etruria and W. Italy.

tūtēla, -ae, f., *defence, pro-tection; charge, care.* [tueor: tutor.]

tūtor, -āri, -ātus, v. dep. tr., *watch, guard, protect, de-fend;* se committit tutan-dum, i. 31. 1, *entrusts him-self to the protection of.* [tueor.]

tūtus, -a, -um, adj., obsolete past part. of tueor as adj., *safe, secure.*

tŭus, -a, -um, poss. pron., *thy, thine, your.* [tu.]

tympănum, -i, n., *timbrel, tambourine, drum.* [τύμ-πανον.]

tўrannus,-i, m.,*despot,tyrant.* [τύραννος.]

ūber, -ĕris, n., *udder, breast.* [οὖθαρ.]

ŭbĭ, adv., *in which* or *what place, where; when.*

ulcĭscor, -sci, ultus, v. dep. tr., *avenge myself on.*

ullus, -a, -um, gen. ullius; adj., *any* in neg. sentences.

ultĭmus, -a, -um, superl. adj., *furthest, last;* comp., ulterior. [ultra.]

ultro, adv., *to the further side; beyond* what is natural or could be expected, *of one's own accord, actually, even, voluntarily, without any trouble to me,* iii. 7. 21.

ŭmĕrus, -i, m., *shoulder.* [ὦμος.]

umquam, adv., *at any time, ever;* gen. in neg. clauses.

ūnā, adv., *in the same place, at the same time, together, in company.* [unus.]

undĕ, adv., *from which place, whence; from whom.*

unguentum, -i, n., *ointment, perfume.* [unguo.]

unguis, -is, m., *nail, talon.*

ūnĭversus, -a, -um, adj., *all together, one and all.* [unus : verto.]

ūnus, -a, -um, gen. unĭus, num. adj., *one, one alone, alone, only.*

urbānus, -a, -um, adj., *of a city* or *town;* as opp. to a rustic, *polished, refined, witty, humorous,* v. 5. 8. [urbs.]

urbs, urbis, f., *city.*

ūsurpo, -āre, -āvi, -ātum, v. tr., *use, enjoy, practise;*

acquire, *appropriate,* iv. 16. 5. [usus.]

ūsus, -ūs, m., *use, employment; enjoyment,* iv. 11. 21. [utor.]

ŭt, conj. and adv., (1) with indic., *how, in what manner, as, when;* (2) with subj., final, *in order that, to;* consec., *so that, that;* on condition that, iii. 7. 27; after verbs of asking, *to, that;* after verbs of advising, *to.*

utcumquĕ, adv., *howsoever, in any way whatever, any how.*

ŭterquĕ, -trăquĕ, -trumquĕ, pron., *both* or *each of two.* [uter.]

ūtĭlis, -e, adj., *useful, serviceable;* comp. utilior. [utor.]

ūtĭlĭtās, -ātis, f., *usefulness; advantage, profit,* i. 22. 11. [utilis.]

ŭtĭnam, adv., *oh that! would that!* in wishes. [ut.]

ūtor, ūti, ūsus, v. dep. intr., with abl., *make use of, use, employ.*

ūva, -ae, f., *grape, bunch of grapes,* iv. 3. 2.

uxor, -ōris, f., *wife.*

vacca, -ae, f., *cow.*

văco, -āre, -āvi, -ātum, v. intr., *am empty, am free from, at leisure;* with dat., *have leisure for, devote myself to,* iii. Prol. 12; impers. vacat, *there is leisure,* iv. Prol. 14.

văcuus, -a, -um, adj., *empty.*

vădum, -i, n., *shallow, ford ; stream ; sea ; water.*

văgor, -āri, -ātus, v. dep. intr., *wander about, roam.* [văgus.]

văleo, -ēre, -ui, -ĭtum, v. intr., *am strong, healthy, power-ful ;* plus v., *I am stronger,* i. 5. 9 ; with inf., *am strong enough to,* iv. 2. 11 ; quantum valent, iv. 25. 1, *how great is the power of ;* vale or valeas, *farewell,* iv. 2. 19 n. [validus.]

vălĭdē, adv., *strongly ; earnestly, vehemently, loudly,* etc. ; comp. validius, superl. validissime. [validus : valeo.]

vānus, -a, -um, adj., *empty, idle, worthless, useless ; vainglorious, conceited,* v. 7. 1. [vacuus.]

vărĭĕtas, -ātis, f., *difference, variety ;* multam rerum v., iii. Epil. 3, *much business of different sorts.* [varius.]

vărius, -a, -um, adj., *different, varying, various.*

vasto, -āre, -āvi, -ātum, v. tr., *make empty, lay waste.* [vastus.]

vastus, -a, -um, adj., *empty, waste, devastated ; vast, immense.* [vanus : văcuus.]

vātes, -is, m. and f., *prophet, bard, poet.*

vector, -ōris, m., *rider, traveller, passenger.* [vĕho.]

vĕhĕmens, -entis, adj., *violent, furious, savage* bite, ii. 3. 1.

vel, conj. and adv., *either, or, even;* vel … vel, *either … or.* [volo, *choose.*]

velle, see volo, *wish.*

vēlox, -ōcis, adj., *swift.* [volare, *fly.*]

venantes, see venor.

vēnātor, -ōris, m., *hunter, huntsman.* [venor.]

vendĭto, -āre, -āvi, -ātum, v. tr., *offer for sale.* [freq. of vendo.]

vēneo, -īre, -īvi or -ii, -ĭtum, v. intr., *am sold.* [venum : eo.]

vēnĭa, -ae, f., *indulgence, favour, pardon.* [veneror.]

vēnĭo, -īre, vēni, ventum, v. intr., *come ;* v. in dubium, iii. 13. 7, *be a matter of doubt.* [βαίνω.]

vēnor, -āri, -ātus, v. dep. tr. and intr., *hunt ;* venantes, i. 12. 7, *hunters.*

venter, -tris, m., *belly.*

Vĕnus, -ēris, f., *goddess of love,* iii. 17. 3.

verbōsus, -a, -um, adj. *full of words, wordy.* [verbum.]

verbum, -i, n., *word ;* pl., *conversation, talk.* [ἐρῶ : ῥῆμα.]

vērē, adv., *truly, in fact,* [verus.]

vĕreor, -ēri, -ĭtus, v. dep. tr. and intr., *revere, respect, fear ;* verendus, *to be reverenced, revered.*

vērĭtas, -ātis, f., *truth, truthfulness.* [verus.]

vĕrō, adv., *in truth;* adversative, *but in fact, however, indeed.* [verus.]

verres, -is, m., *boar-pig.*

versus, -ūs, m., *line, row, verse;* pl., *poem.* [verto.]

verto, -ĕre, verti, -sum, v. tr. and intr., *turn, change;* pass., *am engaged in, am in a place or condition;* vita vertetur in periclo, ii. 8. 19, *your life will be in danger.*

vĕrum, -i, n., *truth, reality, fact.* [verus.]

vĕrum, adv., *truly;* adversative, *but in truth, but.* [verus.]

vĕrus, -a, -um, adj., *true, real.*

vescor, -sci, no perf., v. dep. tr. and intr., *take food, feed on;* generally with abl., ii. 6. 13; rarely acc., as i. 31. 11.

vespa, -ae, f., *wasp.* [σφήξ.]

vester, -tra, -trum, poss. pron., *your.* [vos.]

vestīmentum, -i, n., *clothing.* [vestis.]

vestis, -is, f., *clothes, clothing, garment.*

vestītus, -ūs, m., *clothing, dress.*

vĕto, -āre, -ui, -ĭtum, v. tr., *forbid.*

vĕtus, -ĕris, adj., *old, ancient.* [ἔτος.]

vĕtustas, -ātis, f., *old age, age.* [vetus.]

vĕtustus, -a, -um, adj., *aged, old.* [vetus.]

vexo, -āre, -āvi, -ātum, v. tr., *agitate, trouble, harass.* [freq. of veho.]

via, -ae, f., *way, road.* [veho.]

viātor, -ōris, m., *wayfarer, traveller.* [via.]

vīcīnus, -a, -um, adj., *neighbouring, near.* [vicus, *street, village.*]

vĭcis genitive, vicem, vice; pl., vices and vicibus, f., defect., *change, interchange, turn;* adsuetam v., iii. Prol. 14, *accustomed duty.*

victor, -ōris, m., *conqueror, victor;* in apposition as adj., *victorious.* [vinco.]

victus, -ūs, m., *sustenance, food.* [vivo.]

vĭdeo, -ēre, vīdi, vīsum, v. tr., *see;* vide ne, *take care lest,* iii. 6. 3; pass. videor, *seem, appear; am thought to be,* iii. 7. 18; *seem to myself,* i. 21. 12; as legal phrase in giving judgment, i. 10. 9 n.; videtur, *it seems right, good, it pleases;* qua visum est, sc. mihi, iii. 7. 20, *where I please.*

vĭgĭlia, -ae, f., *watchfulness, vigilance; watch, guard.* [vigil.]

vĭgĭlo, -āre, -āvi, -ātum, v. intr., *keep awake, watch.* [vigil.]

vĭgor, -ōris, m., *activity, rigour.* [vigeo.]

vīlĭcus, -i, m., *farm-bailiff* or *steward.* [villa.]

vīlis, -e, adj., *cheap, common, worthless.*

villa, -ae, f., *country house, farm, villa.* [for vicula, dim. of vicus.]

vinco, -ĕre, vīci, victum, v. tr. and intr., *conquer, overcome, surpass, excel.*

vindĭco, -āre, -āvi, -ātum, v. tr., *claim legally, assert; avenge, punish.* [vim: dico, assert authority.]

vindicta, -ae, f., *protection; vengeance, revenge, punishment.* [vindico.]

vīnea, -ae, f., *vineyard; vine tree,* iv. 3. 1 n. [vinum.]

vĭŏlo, -āre, -āvi, -ātum, v. tr., *injure, violate, profane.* [vis.]

vīpĕra, -ae, f., *adder, snake.* [= vivipera, *bringing forth live young ones,* fr. vivus, pario.]

vĭr, vĭri, m., *man, husband; hero.*

vĭrĭdis, -e, adj., *green;* n. pl., viridia, -ium, *green plants or trees,* ii. 5. 14. [vireo.]

virtūs, -ūtis, f., *manliness, courage, virtue, worth, valour;* iii. 6. 11, *the power to act or carry out their threats.* [vir.]

vis, 2nd sing., fr. volo, *wish.*

vīs, vim, vi; pl., vīres, vīrium, vīrĭbus, f. defect., *strength;* in sing. often *violence;* in pl. generally, but sing. sometimes, *power, force.* [ἴς, ἴφι.]

visum, see video.

vīta, -ae, f., *life, way of life,* iv. 20. 7. [vivo.]

vĭtium, -ii, n., *fault, vice, blemish.*

vīto, -āre, -āvi, -ātum, v. tr., *shun, avoid, evade.*

vĭtŭlus, -i, m., *calf.* [ἰταλός.]

vĭtŭpĕro, -āre, -āvi, -ātum, v. tr., *blame, censure.*

vīvo, -ĕre, vixi, victum, v. intr., *live.*

vīvus, -a, -um, adj., *living, alive.* [vivo.]

vix, adv., *scarcely, with difficulty.*

vŏco, -āre, -āvi, -ātum, v. tr., *call, summon;* vocat sponsum, i. 16. 1, *asks them to become his security.* [vox: ἔπος = Ϝέπος.]

vŏlo, velle, vŏlui, no sup., v. irreg. tr. and intr., *will, am willing, wish;* quidnam voluisti tibi, ii. 8. 5, *whatever did you mean;* in threats, non vis progredi, iii. 6. 2, *won't you go on!* velim, ii. Prol. 11, *I could or should wish.* [βούλομαι.]

vŏlo, -āre, -āvi, -ātum, v. intr., *fly.* [velox: volucer.]

vŏlŭcer, -cris, -cre, adj., *flying, winged, swift.* [volo, fly.]

vŏlŭcris, -is, f., *bird; insect,* v. 3. 3. [volucer.]

vŏluntas, -ātis, f., *will, wish, desire, goodwill, favour.* [volo, wish.]

vŏluptās, -ātis, f., *pleasure, delight.* [volo, wish.]

vŏlūto, -āre, -āvi, -ātum, v. tr., *roll, twist;* se. v., *roll about, wallow,* iv. 4. 2. [freq. of volvo.]

M

vos, pl. of **tu**, *you.*

vōtum, -i, n., *vow.* [vŏveo.]

vox, vōcis, f., *voice, sound ; words, speech ;* pl., *cries* of hunters, i. 12. 7 ; vocis fidem, iii. Epil. 9, *the fulfilment of your promise.* [voco.]

vulgāris, -e, adj., *usual, ordinary, common.* [vulgus.]

vulgo, -āre, -āvi, -ātum, v. tr., *make general or common, publish, spread abroad.* [vulgus.]

vulgus, -i, n., rarely m., *the common people, public, common herd.*

vulnus, -ĕris, n., *wound.*

vulpēcŭla, -ae, f., *a little fox.* [dim. of vulpes.]

vulpes, -is, f., *fox.* [ἀλώπηξ.]

vulpīnus, -a, -um, adj., *of a fox.* [vulpes.]

vultŭrius, -ii, m., *vulture.*

vultus, -ūs, m., *countenance, expression.*

xystus, -i, m., *flower-bed* in front of a portico, ii. 5. 18 n. [ξυστός.]

Zeuxis, -is or -ĭdis (acc. -idem, v. Prol. 7), m., *famous Greek painter*, v. Prol. 7 note.

zōna, -ae, f., *belt, girdle ; money belt, purse.* [ζώνη.]

GLASGOW: PRINTED AT THE UNIVERSITY PRESS BY ROBERT MACLEHOSE AND CO.

MACMILLAN'S ELEMENTARY CLASSICS.

Pott 8vo, Eighteenpence each.

The following contain Introductions, Notes, and **Vocabularies**, and in some cases **Exercises** :—

ACCIDENCE, LATIN, AND EXERCISES ARRANGED FOR BEGINNERS. By W. WELCH, M.A., and C. G. DUFFIELD, M.A.

Aeschylus.—PROMETHEUS VINCTUS. By Rev. H. M. STEPHENSON, M.A.

Arrian.—Selections. With Exercises By Rev. JOHN BOND, M.A., and Rev. A. S. WALPOLE, M.A.

Aulus Gellius, Stories from. Adapted for Beginners. With Exercises. By Rev. G. H. NALL, M.A., Assistant Master at Westminster.

Caesar.—THE HELVETIAN WAR. Selections from Book I., adapted for Beginners. With Exercises. By W. WELCH, M.A., and C. G. DUFFIELD, M.A.

THE INVASION OF BRITAIN. Selections from Books IV. and V., adapted for Beginners. With Exercises. By the same.

SCENES FROM BOOKS V. AND VI. By C. COLBECK, M.A.

TALES OF THE CIVIL WAR. By C. H. KEENE, M.A.

THE GALLIC WAR. BOOK I. By Rev. A. S. WALPOLE, M.A.

Books II. and III. By the Rev. W. G. RUTHERFORD, M.A., LL.D.

BOOK IV. By CLEMENT BRYANS, M.A.

BOOK V. By C. COLBECK, M.A., Assistant Master at Harrow.

BOOK VI. By C. COLBECK, M.A.

BOOK VII. By Rev. J. BOND, M.A., and Rev. A. S. WALPOLE, M.A.

THE CIVIL WAR. BOOK I. By M. MONTGOMERY, M.A.

Cicero.—DE SENECTUTE. By E. S. SHUCKBURGH, M.A.

DE AMICITIA. By the same.

STORIES OF ROMAN HISTORY. Adapted for Beginners. With Exercises. By Rev. G. E. JEANS, M.A., and A. V. JONES, M.A.

Curtius (Quintus).—SELECTIONS.—Adapted for Beginners. With Notes, Vocabulary, and Exercises. By F. COVERLEY SMITH.

Euripides.—ALCESTIS. By Rev. M. A. BAYFIELD, M.A.

MEDEA. By Rev. M. A. BAYFIELD, M.A.

HECUBA. By Rev. J. BOND, M.A., and Rev. A. S. WALPOLE, M.A.

Eutropius.—Adapted for Beginners. With Exercises. By W. WELCH, M.A. and C. G. DUFFIELD, M.A.

Books I. and II. By the same.

Exercises in Unseen Translation in Latin. By W. WELCH, M.A., and C. G. DUFFIELD, M.A.

Herodotus, Tales from. Atticised. By G. S. FARNELL, M.A.

Homer.—ILIAD. BOOK I. By Rev. J. BOND, M.A., and Rev. A. S. WALPOLE, M.A.

BOOK VI. By WALTER LEAF, Litt.D., and Rev. M. A. BAYFIELD, M.A.

BOOK XVIII. By S. R. JAMES, M.A., Assistant Master at Eton.

BOOK XXIV. By W. LEAF, Litt.D., and Rev. M. A. BAYFIELD, M.A.

ODYSSEY. BOOK I. By Rev. J. BOND, M.A., and Rev. A. S. WALPOLE, M.A.

Horace.—ODES. Books I., II., III. and IV. separately. By T. E. PAGE, M.A., Assistant Master at the Charterhouse. Each 1s. 6d.

Livy.—BOOK I. By H. M. STEPHENSON, M.A.

BOOK V. By M. ALFORD.

BOOK XXI. Adapted from Mr. CAPES's Edition. By J. E. MELHUISH, M.A.

BOOK XXII. Adapted from Mr. CAPES's Edition. By J. E. MELHUISH, M.A.

SELECTIONS FROM BOOKS V. and VI. By W. CECIL LAMING, M.A.

THE HANNIBALIAN WAR. BOOKS XXI. and XXII. Adapted by G. C. MACAULAY, M.A.

BOOKS XXIII. and XXIV. Adapted by the same. [In preparation.

THE SIEGE OF SYRACUSE. Being part of Books XXIV. and XXV. Adapted for Beginners. With Exercises. By G. RICHARDS, M.A., and Rev. A. S. WALPOLE, M.A.

LEGENDS OF ANCIENT ROME. Adapted for Beginners. With Exercises. By H. WILKINSON, M.A.

Lucian.—EXTRACTS FROM LUCIAN. With Exercises. By Rev. J. BOND, M.A., and Rev. A. S. WALPOLE, M.A.

MACMILLAN AND CO., LONDON.

Nepos.—SELECTIONS ILLUSTRATIVE OF GREEK AND ROMAN HISTORY. With Exercises. By G. S. FARNELL, M.A.

Ovid.—SELECTIONS. By E. S. SHUCKBURGH, M.A.

EASY SELECTIONS FROM OVID IN ELEGIAC VERSE. With Exercises. By H. WILKINSON, M.A.

STORIES FROM THE METAMORPHOSES. With Exercises. By Rev. J. BOND, M.A., and Rev. A. S. WALPOLE, M.A.

TRISTIA. BOOK I. By E. S. SHUCKBURGH, M.A.   [*In Preparation.*

BOOK III. By E. S. SHUCKBURGH, M.A.   [*In Preparation.*

Phaedrus.—THE FABLES OF PHAEDRUS. By Rev. G. H. NALL, M.A.

SELECT FABLES. Adapted for Beginners. By Rev. A. S. WALPOLE, M.A.

Sallust.—JUGURTHINE WAR. By E. P. COLERIDGE, B.A.

Thucydides.—THE RISE OF THE ATHENIAN EMPIRE. BOOK I. Chs. 89-117 and 228-238. With Exercises. By F. H. COLSON, M.A.

THE FALL OF PLATAEA, AND THE PLAGUE AT ATHENS From Books II. and III. By W. T. SUTTHERY, M.A., and A. S. GRAVES, B.A.

Virgil.—SELECTIONS. By E. S. SHUCKBURGH, M.A.

BUCOLICS. By T. E. PAGE, M.A.

GEORGICS. BOOK I. By T. E. PAGE, M.A.

BOOK II. By Rev. J. H. SKRINE, M.A.

Books III. and IV. separately. By T. E. PAGE, M.A.   [*In preparation.*

AENEID. BOOK I. By Rev. A. S. WALPOLE, M.A.

BOOK I. By T. E. PAGE, M.A.

BOOK II. By T. E. PAGE, M.A.

BOOK III. By T. E. PAGE, M.A.

BOOK IV. By Rev. H. M. STEPHENSON, M.A.

BOOK V. By Rev. A. CALVERT, M.A.

BOOK VI. By T. E. PAGE, M.A.

BOOK VII. By Rev. A. CALVERT, M.A.

BOOK VIII. By Rev. A. CALVERT, M.A.

BOOK IX. By Rev. H. M. STEPHENSON, M.A.

BOOK X. By S. G. OWEN, M.A.

Xenophon.—ANABASIS. Selections, adapted for Beginners. With Exercises. By W. WELCH, M.A., and C. G. DUFFIELD, M.A.

BOOK I. With Exercises. By E. A. WELLS, M.A.

BOOK I. By Rev. A. S. WALPOLE, M.A.

BOOK II. By Rev. A. S. WALPOLE, M.A.

BOOK III. By Rev. G. H. NALL, M.A.

BOOK IV. By Rev. E. D. STONE, M.A.

BOOK V. By Rev. G. H. NALL, M.A.

BOOK VI. By Rev. G. H. NALL, M.A.

SELECTIONS FROM BK. IV. With Exercises. By Rev. E. D. STONE, M.A.

SELECTIONS FROM THE CYROPAEDIA. With Exercises. By A. H. COOKE, M.A.

TALES FROM THE CYROPAEDIA. With Exercises. By C. H. KEENE, M.A.

SELECTIONS ILLUSTRATIVE OF GREEK LIFE. By C. H. KEENE M.A.

SELECTIONS ILLUSTRATIVE OF ROMAN LIFE FROM THE LETTERS OF PLINY.   [*In the Press.*

The following contain Introductions and Notes, **but no Vocabulary :—**

Cicero.—SELECT LETTERS. By Rev. G. E. JEANS, M.A.

Herodotus.—SELECTIONS FROM BOOKS VII. AND VIII. THE EXPEDITION OF XERXES. By A. COOKE. M.A.

Horace.—SELECTIONS FROM THE SATIRES AND EPISTLES. By Rev. W. J. V. BAKER, M.A.

SELECT EPODES AND ARS POETICA. By H. A. DALTON, M.A.

Plato.—EUTHYPHRO AND MENEXENUS. By C. E. GRAVES, M.A.

Terence.—SCENES FROM THE ANDRIA. By F. W. CORNISH, M.A.

The Greek Elegiac Poets.—FROM CALLINUS TO CALLIMACHUS. Selected by Rev. HERBERT KYNASTON, D.D.

Thucydides.—BOOK IV. Chs. 1-41. THE CAPTURE OF SPHACTERIA. By C. E. GRAVES, M.A.

MACMILLAN AND CO., LONDON.

www.ingramcontent.com/pod-product-compliance
Lightning Source LLC
Chambersburg PA
CBHW030542040726
47497CB00008B/2560